IN THE NEUTRAL ZONE with My Best Friend

DINEEN MILLER

VINCI BOOKS

Vinci Books

vinci-books.com

Published by Vinci Books Ltd in 2026

1

A CIP catalogue record for this book is available from the British Library.
Paperback ISBN: 9781036716424
The EU GPSR authorised representative is Logos Europe, 9 rue Nicolas Poussion, 17000 La Rochelle, France
contact@logoseurope.eu

By Dineen Miller

Romancing the Sun Kings

In the Defensive Zone with My Enemy

In the Offensive Zone with My Fake Bride

In the Neutral Zone with My Best Friend

Messy Love on Mango Lane

Bloomed to Be Messy

Rescued to Be Messy

Tamed to Be Messy

A Very Messy Christmas

The Holiday Arrangement

Seashells and Sunsets

The Desperate Deal

The Friendly Disaster

To my beautiful grandson, Everett.
May all your dreams come true, my sweet boy.

Wade's Song for Bree
Perfect by Ed Sheeran

Chapter One

WADE

Ever have one of those moments where life takes a left turn when you were about to make a right? Life is great. Seamless. Moving along as expected. Then, something happens that changes everything.

Like a text from your friend, saying they got the PR job you recommended them for. Seems innocent enough. Except this is Aubrey Sutton—my best friend.

Or used to be anyway.

I've known Bree since I was ten years old, but over the last year, we hardly talked or texted. At all.

Which is odd, considering we once talked and texted regularly. But I get it. Life happens. However, for Bree to go radio silent and not even reply to my texts? For a year? That's not our norm.

Still, she was the first person who sprang to mind when the paparazzi showed up at the arena after a news leak revealed that Payton Maxwell, our star center, is connected to British royalty. I'm still wrapping my head around that bit of trivia. I figured the Pay-man hailed from an uppity

English family—how could he not when his full name is Payton Gerard Maxwell the 3rd, and he sounds like he came from a polo match?

We needed someone equipped to handle press like that, and I happened to know someone who fit the bill to a branded T.

I glance at Bree's text again.

> Bree: Wade, they hired me! I got the job!
> Thank you so much for the recommendation.
> You're a lifesaver!

See? It's a win-win situation—she needed a job, and we needed a publicist to help navigate our growing popularity. Among other things, like a rookie doing something stupid. Don't even get me started on that one.

I put my phone down and tug the towel hanging around my neck over my head to dry my hair. The rest of the guys straggle in from the showers to finish getting dressed.

Coach worked us hard today, on and off the ice. Plus, I had an extended training session with my goalie coach. The Sun Kings are on a winning streak, and we aim to keep it.

Right winger Mathéo Barbier, aka Barbie-man, lifts his chin at me in acknowledgment as he walks by, followed by Elias Brunner, who plays defense. Those two stick as close to each other off the ice as on. Maybe it's because they're both transplants from different countries—Canada and Switzerland—so they have a lot in common.

Plus, Elias is the only other team member who can speak some French with Mathéo, despite claiming Elias's French is a Swiss dialect of his mother tongue. But you didn't hear that from me.

Payton strolls in, hashing out the last play during practice with Ethan McKennen, who's paired on defense with Elias, aka the E-team.

"Coach said play up the center. When I passed the puck, you were supposed to feed it to Brunner," Ethan says, pointing to his partner, "so he could backhand it to Barbier."

Pay-man nods but then shakes his head. "Yes, if I were blocked. I wasn't, so I made the shot."

Ethan pops him on the shoulder. "This was practice, bro. Save the goals for the actual game and get with the program."

"Bloody hell." Payton stops, clutching his towel at his waist with one hand while gesturing with the other. "Give a man credit where credit's due, at least. I passed the biscuit to Barbie-man on the first go."

Our team captain, Luke "Jammer" Jameson, grunts and shakes his head. "Whatever you need to show up ready, Pay."

Payton snorts but grins with mischief. "What a lot you are."

After pulling on his jeans, Elias stands next to Ethan. "You're both right."

Ethan scowls at him. "We're not in Switzerland, Brunner. Pick a side."

I tug on my joggers and face them. "Fellas, take a rest. We need the E-team at their best tomorrow. Just do your job."

They look at each other, then relent and nod. They're mostly blowing off steam over our game tomorrow night against Savannah, the team we love to hate largely because one of their players seems to have it out for Payton. Probably because he's one of the best snipers in the league.

Thankfully, Luke is a great captain. He knows how to

handle the guys on the ice, and he keeps his cool with the refs. But I'm the peacemaker in this bunch. Not sure how I wound up with that job, but I don't mind. As goalie, I can't be captain, but I can contribute some of what I learned in keeping the peace with my two sisters, one of whom—Piper—plays in the Professional Women's Hockey League and is a spitfire, to boot.

I knew my younger sister was destined for hockey the day she slammed me in the gut at age nine with my own hockey stick. The girl packed a punch, and she still does, whereas Ellie, my youngest sister, recently started college to become a lawyer, which suits her argumentative side.

A chirp from my phone pulls me back to the bench, and I'm not at all prepared for what I see there.

Bree: They want me to start right away. Any chance I can stay with you until I find a place?

I stare at my screen, as if I misread her message. Or am I hoping she'll send another text, telling me she's joking?

But she doesn't.

This, I did not see coming.

Do I want to see Bree? Hell, yeah. Do I want her living with me? Not sure. After a year of near silence, I honestly don't know what to expect. Between Bree's PR work with the Texas Stars and a boyfriend I'm not even sure exists, I don't have a clue about anything going on in her life.

When she stopped answering my texts, I resorted to keeping up with her on social media. Funny thing is, I never saw any pictures of her with him. Just group shots with her friends on her personal private feed, and nothing but business on her professional profile. All of which I found somewhat strange.

What if she's changed? I know I have to some degree. A year is a long time not to see or really talk to each other…

Wade: I thought they'd get a room for you at the Sandpiper Inn.

Bree: No room at the Inn (smiley face, Christmas tree)

Finally, the expected joke, but I'm not laughing. I'm still baffled as to why she ghosted me. We've never not communicated for that long. What if things are awkward or weird between us?

Even if they are, she'll likely spend most of her time stuck in an office somewhere in the arena while I'm on the ice, practicing. And during games, I'll be in the crease, focused on the game and doing my job. With my travel schedule, we won't see much of each other.

And when we are together, we'll pick up where we left off, like always.

Maybe…

I sit on the bench and plant my forehead on my fists, staring at the floor as I try to figure out what to say to her. We're about a quarter of the way through the first half of the season, and so far, we're ranking near the top. Focus will be key in carrying our winning streak through the rest of this half and into the second. A distracted goalie means shots on goal turn into points for the other team. Not good.

A pair of feet walks past me, then backtracks. "What's up, Cowboy? Bad news?"

Water drips from his hair, landing on his shoulders, as Luke stares down at me with a puzzled expression.

Do I look messed up? She's not even here yet, and I'm already losing my game face. "Nothing serious."

His brows drop. "You sure? If you need help—"

"I can handle it." I force a smile, trying to convince myself and my team captain that this will work out *just fine,* as my nana would say. Suddenly, I'm missing her homemade chocolate chip cookies and the ranch with a fierce ache.

Maybe a touch of homesickness? I haven't visited in over a year and, well, home and Bree are pretty synonymous in my mind. Like I said, she and I go way back. The Suttons used to own the property next to my family's homestead in Texas. We grew up together, went to the same schools, and ran in the same friend circles. My younger sisters treated Bree like a big sister because she was almost the same age as me.

When I discovered my love for hockey and realized I could be good at it, some things changed, but that didn't mean we didn't stay close. Kind of like one big happy blended family, and I was the big brother.

Maybe seeing her again will be like a homecoming without horses. Or cookies. I can show her around Sarabella and help her get settled. Shouldn't be too difficult.

I pick up my phone and tap out a reply.

Wade: Mi casa es su casa. When are you arriving? I'll pick you up from the airport.

Bree: Thank you! I knew you'd have my back.

Wade: Always. Just send me your itinerary.

Bree: Is today too soon?

I think my eyebrows merged into my hairline. Bree

always did have an impulsive side and still does, apparently. I scrub a hand down my face, mentally tallying what I need to do to get my one-bedroom apartment ready for her. I can take the couch, but I should change the sheets and clean up my room so she'll feel comfortable.

Wade: Not a problem. Just tell me when to pick you up.

Bree: No need. I'm parked in the lot.

Wade: Haha, very funny. Seriously, when will you be here?

Bree: Not kidding. Walk outside.

I take a beat to assess my situation, like when I see an opponent flying my way with the puck, and I have a split second to decide to go right or left, up or down. My hair's still wet from my shower, and I'm partially dressed. A bunch of half-naked hockey players surround me, and my best friend has suddenly shown up on my doorstep after a year of silence.

What's my move?

After tugging on a clean T-shirt, I push my feet into my slides and take off toward the door. That same feeling I get when I'm in the crease, moving as fast as I can to block shot after shot, attempts to overwhelm me. It's like I'm watching myself in slow motion, frustrated that I can't move faster.

Like a madman, I rush out of the locker room, heart pounding and head swimming. I'm in so deep, I barely register Jammer's booming voice shouting after me or the smack of multiple feet sounding down the hallway behind me.

All I can think about is holding her in my arms when she hugs me. Because Bree, as they say, is a hugger.

And she has never, in all the years I've known her, felt like a sister to me. Far from it.

And then it dawns on me. One thing definitely hasn't changed.

I'm still in love with Aubrey Sutton.

Chapter Two

BREE

I know I'm impulsive. Always have been and clearly, still am. I mean, who loads up their car and a small U-Haul with everything they own—or will fit—and drives from Texas to Florida without having a plan?

Apparently, I do.

I'm not making excuses. Just pointing out that extenuating circumstances are at play here—ones I'd rather not think about at the moment. Let's just say I ran out of options, needed to get out of Cedar Park fast, and going home would have meant admitting defeat. Not that I really have a home since my parents sold our ranch right after I started college, and now live in a small craftsman-style house in Austin. They don't even have a dog.

When Wade texted me about a PR position with the Florida Sun Kings, I jumped on it. After months of agonizing over what I was going to do, the universe finally cut me some slack.

Not only did I have a new job, but I could leave behind the dumpster fire my life had turned into and start fresh.

Did it matter that I hadn't thought things through, like where I would live? Not really.

As long as I stayed in Texas, my ex would constantly try to run my career or ruin it if I didn't comply with his ever-growing list of demands in managing his social media presence.

How did I let a pretty face from my past manipulate me like that?

I know—because I believe in the innate goodness that exists in everyone. I really do. But I guess my Spidey sense didn't work when it came to Chase Langston. I knew he and Wade were rivals when they were coming up through junior league together. I attended Wade's games back then and interacted with Chase occasionally. He came across as a decent guy, and despite their intense rivalry on the ice, he and Wade acted like they were okay with each other once the skates came off.

So when our paths crossed again while I was doing PR for the Texas Stars, it seemed almost providential. As Nana Pierce often says, "Pay attention to the ones who cross your path more than once."

Did I mention I think of Wade's grandmother as mine? Or I should say, she always made me feel that way. She pretty much claimed me as one of her own the minute she found out I didn't have grandparents. And that woman… She makes the best chocolate chip cookies on the planet.

But back to Chase—I really thought he was 'The One' in the beginning. Until it became clear he wasn't. That he'd only used me and my PR skills to catch more attention from their affiliate team, the Dallas Stars. The NHL was always his end game, and I was simply a tool to get him there.

I lean against my old 4Runner—aka Big Blue—as the back of my neck heats from both the blinding Florida sun and the swirl of thoughts in my head. The cloudless azure sky almost matches her faded paint.

After checking if Wade replied to my last text, which he hasn't, I tug the band off my wrist and pull my hair up into a messy bun. Maybe this was a bad idea. I should have called him before I left, or at least from the road.

And then, I see him—Wade—flying through the arena door. He jogs toward me, his expression stern at first, but when he sees me, that lopsided grin I know so well splits his face.

A flood of memories hits me as I launch off my car and take a step forward.

Racing our horses across open pastures to the old knurled oak at one end and then sitting in the shade of the branches to munch on the snacks we stole from the pantry and stowed in Wade's tattered saddlebag. Then we'd race home, the winner getting to watch the loser remove tack and groom the horses while they sipped iced tea and gobbled down one—or two—of Nana's famous chocolate chip cookies.

Or the smell of her freshly baked bread, cooling on the kitchen counter. One loaf always wound up sliced and buttered while still warm, but she always had an extra, packaged and ready for me to take home to my parents.

Trampling through the woods with Piper and Ellie on a fairy tale mission to find the prince and save him from the evil dragon—Wade inevitably played both roles, alternating back and forth until all three of us girls toppled over in a fit of giggles.

And then, my favorite… lying on a blanket in the middle of his backyard, watching for shooting stars. Just Wade and me. That was our thing. We'd take turns making wishes, sharing dreams. His, of course, was to one day play professional hockey.

And mine? Secretly, I wanted to stay on my family's ranch and turn it into a venue for weddings and family reunions. I imagined families coming on the weekends to enjoy a petting zoo or apple picking, then visiting a small shop with homemade jams and jellies crafted from our orchards, along with other specialty items sourced locally.

A rush of emotion overwhelms me, making me acutely aware for the first time in months of how lost I've felt. That's what propels me forward into a jog toward the one person who always made me feel safe and protected. By the time I launch myself at Wade, wrapping myself around him like a kitten clinging to a tree—the man's as tall as one—tears I haven't let myself shed since my life started to crumble stream down my cheeks.

His clean scent—a mix of soap and something spicy—fills my nose. The ends of his wet auburn hair tickle my forearm as I clutch him tighter, and his T-shirt feels damp, as if he pulled it on in a rush before he finished drying off from a shower.

I know I should let go, but I don't want to. I'd forgotten how grounded Wade always made me feel, that everything would be okay, no matter what. And right now, I'm desperate for a dose of that—a ray of hope, a safe place to land.

Wade's arms hold me like a vise, and his warm chuckle rumbles through me, shaking loose the lingering tension left over from driving for hours. "Wow, you're that happy to see me?"

A wave of embarrassment surges through me. Wade knows nothing about what happened over the last year or why I stopped communicating. I want to tell him, but I can't. What if he doesn't understand? What if he thinks I'm stupid for being so gullible? Which I was. A complete idiot to be so trusting…

I let go of Wade and drop my feet so fast that I stumble back. He catches me, one hand on my back, the other around my upper arm. His hold on me is comforting, yet solid and uncompromising. For a moment, I allow myself to languish in this place. It's been a long time since I felt safe—protected.

When I notice the mix of confusion and concern in his expression, I wipe my cheeks and force a laugh. "Just glad you're not still sweaty from practice."

Wade's smirk returns, and a gleam of mischief sparks in his hazel-green eyes. Laughter trickles from behind him. That's when I realize we're not alone. Several guys, who I assume are his teammates, stand about twenty feet away, their expressions filled with curiosity.

I'm sure my face is redder than apples at harvest time, but it's Florida. Maybe they'll just think I'm sunburned. Or better yet, heatstroke. That would be a convenient explanation for my emotional reaction to seeing him, right?

Wade, ever the gentleman, takes my arm and tugs me closer to him as he faces his teammates. "Fellas, this is my best friend, Aubrey Sutton. She's going to be our new PR specialist."

Half a dozen sets of eyes stare at me with varying levels of curiosity as they express various welcomes and greetings.

I attempt a bubbly wave, which probably makes me appear like a flabbergasted teenager. "Hi, just call me Bree."

One by one, the guys come forward and introduce themselves. I'd pictured this scene with me dressed in my favorite flared pants with a bodysuit and oversized jacket to make my first impression. Not a pair of tattered jean shorts, my old Lone Creek Coyotes T-shirt that I wore to every one of Wade's junior league games, and my hair pulled up in a messy bun to hide how much I need to wash it.

But this is what I get for being impulsive, right?

Wade stares at me with a funny expression on his face.

Then it dawns on me that I've barged into his life with no warning and interrupted him in the middle of his workday. I forget that sometimes. That hockey isn't just something Wade does for fun; it's his *job*.

Moving closer to him, I lower my voice. "I'm sorry, I should have called sooner. Or just waited at your apartment until you got home."

His eyes widen ever so slightly. "It's okay. We're done for the day. Perfect timing."

I point at my old SUV and the small U-Haul that holds my entire life. Or rather, what's left of it. "I can wait in Big Blue."

Wade's expression turns nostalgic when his gaze lights on my rundown vehicle. "Still running, huh?"

With a shrug, I hold out my hands. "If you don't mind the occasional backfire and an AC system with commitment issues."

He chuckles as he tips his head toward the arena. "You could come inside and look around."

The other players watch us, their expressions remaining curious. He's right. This place will become my new work home in a couple of days. Enough time to get settled and figure out my next steps. Also on my to-do list? Give Wade an explanation for my silence…and an apology.

"Sure. Give me the tour." I flash him a smile I hope convinces him I have my act together.

But my best friend knows me, probably better than anyone. And judging by the look he's giving me, he's not buying it.

Chapter Three

WADE

I think I'm still in shock. The way Bree wrapped herself around me—she's never done that before. Was she crying? Were those tears on her cheeks?

When she stumbled, my only thought was to make sure she didn't get hurt, so I did what anyone would do—I caught her. But when I had a chance to really look at her, she had a smile plastered on her face again that didn't reach her cornflower blue eyes.

But I could tell. Bree's been through something. I want to ask her what's wrong, but now's not the time. Not with all the other knuckleheads around. I'll have to wait until we get back to my place, or they'll shove their noses into it faster than a dog sniffing out a bone.

Payton motions Bree over. "Let us give you the tour. And I suppose I need to fill you in on the drama we've had recently."

"You're British." Surprise coats her words.

He chuckles. "What gave me away?"

His voice fades as he leads Bree into the arena. I lurch

forward, intent on following and keeping an eye on her, but Luke blocks me.

His brows take a nosedive. "Is she your best friend or the woman you're in love with?"

After a sharp exhale, I stare him straight in the face. "Both?"

He hooks a thumb over his shoulder. "Is she the one you never told—"

I nod, cutting him off before he can finish that statement. I've never told Bree how I feel about her because, one, I didn't want to risk ruining our friendship. Two, our relationship wasn't the only one on the line. If you knew my sisters, Ellie and Piper, you'd understand. The only other female who scares me as much as they do is a fresh cow with her calf. They'd have my hide if I did anything to wreck my friendship with Bree.

Obviously, the last year has done nothing to change how I feel about her. I'm still so far gone for this woman that I can't think straight. Or keep my feelings hidden. I held on to her entirely too long after I stopped her from falling.

Did she notice?

I'll have to work on that, especially while she's living with me.

Her honeysuckle scent lingers, teasing my senses and reminding me of the past, home, and everything I love about Bree.

I harden my gaze, so Luke knows I mean business. "Not a word."

He rears his head back. "Of course not."

Leaning in, I lower my voice. "Not even to Sophie."

He studies me for a moment, then nods. "You know she'll figure it out, though."

My eyes drift to the door again. "I just need some time to figure things out."

Luke nods again but says nothing. Not even his usual grunt.

I brush past him and jog into the arena. The boys took Bree down the tunnel to the rink. Always the showman, Ethan's voice filters over the sounds of my slides smacking the floor as I rush toward them.

"And this is where the magic happens," he says with dramatic effect. The man could headline a stage production the second he hangs up his skates.

They're standing on the ice by the half door. Bree covers her mouth, laughing, while she holds her phone up with her other hand, recording the entire thing.

Elias joins him. "There's no magic. Just blood and sweat."

The two of them high-five and say, "We're the E-team!" at the same time.

So hokey, these idiots. But whatever.

Bree taps her screen. "That was great. Content like that will go a long way."

I join them, hooking my arm around Bree's waist so she doesn't slip on the ice. It's still rough from practice, so not as slippery, but I don't want her to take a fall and get hurt. That's the reason I'm telling myself, at least.

This has nothing to do with the ache in my chest, which makes me realize how much I've missed her. "She just got here, fellas, and you're already putting her to work?"

They stare at each other before falling all over themselves with apologies.

Bree shoots me a questioning glance as I lift her off the ice. When I set her down onto the rubber mats, I catch a glimpse of the freckles running across her nose and cheeks. Specifically, the freckle sitting on the right side of her bottom lip—the one I'd like nothing more than to kiss.

That impulse definitely didn't change over the last year.

I drop my gaze to her feet, ensuring she's off the ice, then let go of her before I'm tempted to act on it. "Don't want you to fall and get hurt."

She pats my chest. "I'm fine, Wade."

But she's not. However, the faint wobble in her voice is all it takes for me to let the argument go. Whatever's going on, she'll tell me when she's ready. "I'll grab my stuff, and we can head home."

"Can I see the locker rooms first?" She shoots a hopeful glance my way.

The rest of the boys are likely done and gone by now. "Sure. Come with me."

Luke walks ahead of us with Payton, while Ethan and Elias keep the rear. I want to talk to Bree, just not with the team acting like they bought front-row seats.

When the guys offer to help unload her U-Haul, I tell them I've got it. They don't ask where she's staying, and I don't tell them.

Not yet. Like I told Luke, I need to figure things out.

Because right now, I'm not sure of anything.

I pull into a space on the other side of the parking area near my apartment, leaving the spot in front for Bree. Before she parks, I jump out and jog up to Old Blue as she rolls down her window. I honestly can't believe this thing is still running.

"Get out so I can back you in." I rest my arms on the

door, noting the haphazardly packed boxes filling the back seat.

She shakes her head, making the blonde knot on top bob back and forth. “I can do it.”

I glance at the empty spaces next to the sidewalk edged with grass and palm trees. Beyond that sits the teal door to my apartment, surrounded by tan stucco. The splash of orange blooms dotting the hibiscus bushes completes the tropical picture.

“You sure? Because I remember how well you used to back up Daisy into her stall.”

She rolls her eyes at me. “That was a cranky cow. This is a U-Haul.”

I crack a grin. “What’s the difference?”

She snorts but laughs. “I can handle this, Wade.”

And she does. For the most part. Good thing she had two parking spaces to her advantage.

We unload the trailer first, stacking boxes in the corner of the living room. Then we unpack the rest of her SUV. Bree rolls one of her suitcases over the threshold of the front door.

A cringe contorts her delicate features. “Sorry for making your place look like a war zone.”

Those questions clamor again in my head as I add another box to the stack. What about her boyfriend? Is he still in the picture? Are they doing the long-distance thing? “It’s temporary. Don’t worry about it.”

She leans to the right, looking toward the doors leading to my bedroom and the half bath. “Where’s your guest room?”

I take the suitcase from her and roll it toward my room. “Just give me a minute to get it ready for you.”

She follows me to the doorway, swinging her gaze across the room. "Wade, no. This is your bedroom."

"It's the only one in the place." I tug the lightweight comforter off the bed, intending to strip the sheets off.

"Then I'll take the couch." She turns around, pulling her suitcase behind her.

I snatch it out of her hand. Our fingers brush as I do, amping up that ache in my chest again. How can it be even stronger after not hearing from her for a year?

"No, I will. I have to get up early for practice, so this will be better. I won't have to worry about waking you up."

"I have to get up early, too. I'll be fine out there." She reaches for her suitcase, but I'm quick to heft it out of her reach and place it by the oak dresser on the left side of the room.

I finish stripping the bed so that I can change the sheets. Thinking of her sleeping in my bed does funny things to my head, but I push those feelings down, just like I always have. "Nana would have my hide if she found out I let you sleep on the couch."

She narrows her eyes at me. "I won't tell her if you don't."

"I will if you keep being stubborn about it." I give her a challenging stare.

The way her shoulders slant tells me she's about to relent. Nana may be my grandmother, but she claimed Bree as her own the first day she walked into our house and introduced herself with the caveat that she didn't have grandparents.

I think Nana fell in love with ten-year-old Bree at that moment, and I may have a little, too.

Bree crosses her arms. "Fine, but I'll find something as

soon as possible so you can have your bed back. And your living room."

"I'm not worried about it, Bree. Like I said, my home is yours for however long you need it." I toss the dirty sheets by the door.

We still have to share the closet and the dresser, but I'm certain we can make it work. It's not like we never stayed together before. Our families used to camp together every summer, so I'm sure we'll find a rhythm, just like we did then.

I grab my basic toiletries out of the bathroom. "I'll put these in the half bath and use yours to shower."

She gives me a bewildered look as I walk past her. "But—"

"It's fine. As you said, you'll find a place. Until then, I'm glad you're here."

I swear I see tears in her eyes when she nods, but as she looks down, her blonde hair falls forward, shielding her face.

Before I can talk myself out of it, I dump the stuff I'm holding onto the carpet at my feet and pull her into a hug. She tucks her hands between us with the side of her face pressed against my chest. If she notices how fast my heart is racing, she says nothing. But if she did, I'd blame it on stripping the bed—a lame excuse for a hockey player who works out four to six hours a day.

Her messy bun tickles my chin and fills my nose with her sweet honeysuckle scent again. I can't help wondering what it would feel like to brush my lips over her temple and then kiss—

Nope, shutting that down right now. "Want to talk about it?"

Shock waves rip through me when she buries her face against me. My shirt muffles her voice. "Not really."

I run my hand down her back, enjoying her closeness more than I should. "Okay, but I'm here when you're ready."

"I'm fine. Really. Just tired from the road trip."

She's lying. Bree only tacks on the word 'really' when she's trying to hide the truth. But I won't push because she'll just clam up more if I do. Bending over, I scoop up my toiletries. "I'll grab some clean sheets."

What made me think this would be easy? Oh, *right.* I thought a year of no communication would nix my feelings for her.

Guess that saying about absence making the heart grow fonder has some merit.

After I arrange my shaving and soap paraphernalia in the corner by the sink in the half-bath, I grab a set of fresh linens from the closet. When I return to the bedroom, Bree's curled up on her side on the bed, my pillow clutched against her, and sound asleep. I place the sheets at the end of the mattress and tug the comforter over her legs.

She looks so peaceful except for a crease between her brows, as if she's worrying in her sleep. My fingers twitch with the desire to smooth away whatever's causing it.

Obviously, she wasn't lying about being tired, but I know Bree, and this version of her is just a shadow of the confident and vivacious woman I know…and love.

A simmering anger burns deep inside me as I imagine what could have happened to her over this last year. Was it her job? Or the boyfriend she never talked about?

One way or another, I intend to find out.

Chapter Four

BREE

I snuggle into the pillow and inhale. Wade's clean, soapy scent, mixed with something spicy, fills my nose. Then reminds me of where I am. I snap my eyes open and push up on the bare mattress. A neatly folded stack of pale blue sheets sits at the foot. Three dresser drawers hang ajar, as if waiting to be filled, and the nightstand surface is cleared off.

Soft dusk light filters through the window blinds, dousing the room in a rosy blush. I toss off the lightweight navy comforter draped over my legs and feet—Wade must have thought I was cold. He's always done things like that—looking out for his sisters and me. I knew he would be a safe place to land until I could figure out how to deal with my past.

Am I nuts to think—hope—Florida is far enough away from Texas that I won't have to worry about my ex crashing into my life here? I'm sure he'll find some other gullible woman to fill my shoes. That thought brings a fresh wave of guilt and shame. I shouldn't wish that on any woman. If I could expose him for what he is without tanking my career, I'd do it in a heartbeat.

For now, a new job in a different state will have to do the trick.

I make quick work of putting the clean sheets on the bed, hesitating a moment before I strip the pillowcase, but notice the other pillow is missing. Wade must have grabbed it for the couch, but he left the comforter. Another wave of guilt washes over me for taking over his room. The man even emptied half his dresser for me, and a glance into the closet confirms what I suspect—he moved his stuff over, leaving me the larger side, which includes a shoe rack.

Does he think I hoard shoes or something? I pretty much live in boots or slip-on trainers for easy shedding because I'm a hands-on kind of girl when it comes to my profession. If a video clip would look better shot while hanging upside down, that's what I'll do—and have done in the past. When you're building a sports brand, physicality is a big part of it, just like it is for the players.

I'm a firm believer in doing whatever it takes to get the job done. Although that might be why I wound up in the predicament I'm in. Chase certainly took advantage of my work ethic.

Once I divide the clothes in my suitcase between the drawers and the closet, I pick out my favorite pajama shorts and top to change into after a shower. I drove straight through from Texas and feel like I'm wearing half of the road I traveled.

Since I'm almost positive my hair dryer is in one of the many boxes in the living room, I pull the wet strands into a messy bun, then grab my phone and laptop before walking out of the bedroom.

Wade's running on a treadmill positioned in front of a

glass sliding door that faces a lake in the center of the apartment complex. His earbuds must have masked my sounds because he's clueless that I'm watching him.

I lean against the doorjamb, admiring his physique as he keeps a steady rhythm. Well-developed biceps swing back and forth with his strides. Muscled thighs and calves pump up and down as he jogs. My perusal lands on his shoulders, which seem broader than I remember.

The last time I saw Wade in person was about three years ago at Christmas. He'd just signed with the Sun Kings and hadn't filled out yet. But now…now I understand why he's referred to often as one of the top goalies in the ECHL, if not the best. He's honed his body and done the work to earn that reputation.

When his strides slow, I push off the doorway and head to the dining room table to set up my laptop. The owner, Rebecca Piedmont, gave me the go-ahead to set up multiple social media accounts when she confirmed I had the position. I want to get those in place and optimized so I don't waste any time on my first day. Even though I already have the brief video clip with Ethan and Elias, I'd like to create some branding graphics to run by Rebecca and Zach, her general manager, so we're on the same page.

I sit at the table with one leg folded under me as Wade steps off the treadmill. He still hasn't noticed me watching him. Sweat drips down the side of his face and neck. He lifts the front of his shirt, pulling it over his head and then using it to wipe himself down.

Wade Pierce has a six-pack? What happened to the lanky guy I used to hang out and ride horses with? He was always the tallest one in the school, but the rest of his body hadn't caught up yet. Well, it certainly has now.

He startles when he finally notices me. "Hey, you're awake."

I'm careful to keep my eyes on his face, even though I'd rather study those abs of his. But he's my best friend. Friends don't check each other out, do they?

"Yeah, sorry about that. Guess driving straight through caught up with me."

Caught up with me? That's the understatement of the century. I still feel embarrassed about wrapping myself around him and crying like a scared kitten.

The analogy fits well, though. I did kind of climb him like a tree. "Look, about earlier…"

His brows furrow as he watches me, but he says nothing.

"I didn't mean to get so…"

"Clingy?"

I cover my face with my hands, then drop them to my lap with a groan. "Yes, whatever. I was exhausted and…"

"Happy to see me?" His grin tilts, and that mischievous spark I remember from our childhood appears in his eyes.

This would be way more humorous if he weren't standing there, shirtless, looking more like a sports model than my best friend. "Don't get a colossal head about it, okay?"

He slings his shirt over his shoulder. "No promises." His expression turns serious as he approaches the table. "What happened, Bree?"

I'm not sure exactly what he's asking me. So much *happened* that I don't know where to start. I'm still trying to make sense of what was real and what I misread. What if I tell him all the sordid details, and he winds up thinking I'm the biggest idiot in existence for allowing someone to use me that way? I know I do.

I blow out a breath and shrug. I'm not ready to tell him

everything, but I don't want to lie either. "Oh, you know—the usual. I left the Stars to start my own business, and it didn't work out. Your text couldn't have come at a better time."

It's all true. I did try to start my own PR firm, more like a one-woman show, to get away from my ex. But that didn't deter him from trying to manipulate me into making him my biggest client. The jerk didn't even pay me. Unless you call takeout from Whataburger fair payment—his idea of buying me dinner to say thank you.

Wade's lips purse together as he studies me. "Okay, let me know when you're ready to talk about it."

Holding my hands up, I attempt a bubbly tone. "There's not much to it. Really."

Shaking his head, he grabs a bottle of water from the fridge and gives me one last pointed stare. "I'm going to take a shower. Then I'll make us some dinner. Maybe you'll feel more like talking then."

With that, he disappears into his—my—bedroom, but he doesn't shut the door. I open my laptop, intending to lose myself in tweaking my presentation, which doesn't require more fine-tuning; it's ready. But I need to make sure I am.

I catch glimpses of Wade in my peripheral vision as he grabs clothing from his side of the dresser and the closet before disappearing into the bathroom. He closes the door, and somehow, it feels personal, as if he's closing himself off from me.

We've never put up walls between us before. Not really.

And I know Wade. He wouldn't do that. I shake my head at myself for reading more into a simple need for privacy. With Chase, that became my way to survive—to read the room and anticipate his unpredictable moods.

But with Wade, I know I'm safe. He's always looked out

for me, even when he didn't have to. And what did I do? I quit returning his texts and calls because I was afraid—knew deep down—he wouldn't approve of me dating Chase Langston.

The thing is, if I'd known then what I know now, I would have agreed with him.

Like I said, I'm an idiot for allowing myself to believe Chase wanted me for me, not what I could do for him.

I just wish I'd figured that out much sooner than I did.

Chapter Five

WADE

Bree used to tell me everything—sometimes too much. Like word vomit on steroids.

The worst one was in middle school when she got her first period, and she decided to talk to *me* about it. My sisters hadn't reached that milestone yet, so I understood why she wanted to tell her best friend about a major event in her life. Despite my discomfort when she shared her in-depth study of pads and tampons, I put on my game face and tried not to show how squeamish the whole thing made me feel.

As much as I didn't want to know the details, part of me felt honored that she wanted to confide something so personal in me. That's what best friends do for each other, right?

But this time?

She's hiding something. Piper or Ellie might know more about it...maybe. I could call one of them, or both, if Bree doesn't open up. Unless she starts talking to me, there's not much I can do to help her. It's killing me that I can't figure this out and fix it for her.

I finish getting dressed, careful to leave the bathroom in decent shape before I return to the main living area. Bree's sitting in front of her laptop at the dining room table with one leg folded underneath her. She's wearing a cream shorts set dotted with pink roses. The fabric looks soft, touchable, like her skin. The glow of the screen reflects off her glasses, which I've never seen her wear before. That and the concentration on her face make her look intellectual and sexy all at once.

Closing my eyes, I pinch the bridge of my nose. Those kinds of thoughts will only make this arrangement impossible. Good thing she didn't notice me studying her with entirely too much interest, or else I'd have to scramble for some lame excuse that borders on a lie.

After a quick mental shake, I pause between the table and the kitchen island. "Hungry?"

She pushes her glasses up on top of her head, which only makes me want to gawk at her again. Who knew I had a thing for the hot librarian look?

"Famished. Did you learn to cook?" She eyes me with a hefty dose of skepticism.

"I've always known how to cook." I point to the glasses. "Those new?"

She looks confused at first, then touches her head. "Oh, those. They're for doing work on my computer. Helps with eyestrain."

A streak of mischief hits me. "Reminds me of Nana."

With a harrumph, she grabs the pepper shaker off the table and tosses it at me.

Of course, I catch it with ease—I'm a goalie. I get paid to snatch small, hurtling objects out of the air. "Nice try."

She rolls her eyes. "I should have known better."

I set the shaker down, then open the fridge. "Do you like salmon? I can grill it and add a fresh salad."

She hums as if she's thinking. "Or we could order a pizza."

Not ready to give in to her obsession with cheese and meat on bread, I glance over my shoulder. "Would you prefer chicken with the salad?"

"If it's on the pizza, sure." She grins as if to punctuate her point.

I shut the fridge and face her, leaning my arms on the counter. "Still not a salad eater?"

She scrunches her nose. "Nope."

After a noisy sigh of resignation, I lean over and grab my phone. "Fine. We'll do pizza tonight, but after that, you either eat what I'm making or fend for yourself. Deal?"

Without looking away from her screen, she gives me a thumbs-up.

Once I place the order for a half pepperoni, half veggie pizza, I sit down at the table near Bree. "So, are you ready to talk about it yet?"

She continues to stare at her screen, making me wonder if she even heard me. Then she closes her laptop, takes off her glasses, and sighs. "Things didn't work out the way I'd hoped."

That's it? That's all she's going to tell me? Fine. I'll annoy her with more questions. "Freelancing wasn't working?"

She shrugs. "Not really. The income wasn't stable."

I lean back in the chair, crossing my arms as I stretch my legs out in front of me. "Why'd you leave the gig at the Texas Stars?"

Her eyes dart to me before dropping to her hands as she

pulls them into her lap. "It wasn't a good fit for me anymore."

"Bree." She may be two feet from me, but I don't think I've ever felt so far away from her.

After what seems like minutes, she finally meets my gaze. "What?"

Something deep and painful flickers in her eyes. As I lean forward, I grab one of her hands. Her skin is soft and warm, and when I squeeze her fingers, she squeezes back. "What happened?"

She shrugs again, tugging her hand away. "Nothing. I was ready for a change, that's all."

I pull my head back in confusion. "Then why did you take the job here? It's the same kind of work, isn't it?"

She blinks rapidly as she takes a ragged breath. "I… I—"

The doorbell rings. Her eyes flash to mine like a deer caught in the headlights of my old Jeep on the ranch.

I'm pushing too hard, and I haven't even asked the big question of why she disappeared from my life for a year. And as much as I want to know the reason, cornering her will only make things worse. Kind of reminds me of the mustang that showed up one morning and joined our herd. She was fine in the group, but alone, she'd buck and snort at anyone who tried to get close.

Except for me. Took a while, but Luna finally let me get near enough to hand-feed her at first. Took most of the summer before my senior year of high school to get her to trust me and allow a saddle. Last I heard, she just had her first colt, bearing the same moon-shaped patch of white hair on his muzzle right below his eyes.

"That would be our pizza." I give her a reassuring smile before heading to the door.

Bree already has the plates and napkins arranged on the table when I return with the pizza box. Her laptop sits off to the side, open to some graphics program she's using to edit the video she took of Ethan and Elias. "The E-team" spans across the bottom in a banner with bold letters, with the Sun Kings logo centered, yet overlapping the top of the text.

I gesture toward the image. "Impressive."

To my relief, she smiles and lights up. "I'm creating a model to show Rebecca tomorrow so she can get a feel for the branding I'm working on. And I have some events in mind that will not only help the team's image but also work with the charities you guys are involved with."

When she takes a single slice of pizza, I add another because I know she's distracted. Even in high school, Bree would forget to eat during finals, so I always made sure I brought extra snacks in my backpack so she wouldn't pass out or become hangry.

"You've done your research." I slide three slices onto my plate.

She nods. "And I made a list of ideas to optimize your profiles."

"Should I be worried?"

Bree swats my arm. "Don't worry. I know how much you hate this kind of stuff. I'll only ask you to do the most important ones."

She's right, but when it comes to her, I'll do anything that will make her happy. "Whatever you need, Bree. I'm your guy."

The smile she beams at me as she tilts her head in that way she does to express her thanks deposits a familiar ache in my chest. I'm already hers. Have been for years. I just haven't figured out how to tell her.

The old feelings are very much there, if not stronger. I knew that the minute I had her in my arms earlier, and I relished the feel of her against me. Sensing her distress stirred a primal desire to protect her, which brought to the surface everything I thought I'd buried. And then some.

How am I going to survive this? I can't imagine my life without Bree, but somehow I have to be content with her being my best friend and nothing more.

Lost in thought, she chews and swallows. "Fans love meeting you guys in person, so I want to do something like that romcom 'Win a Date with Tad Hamilton.'" She gestures in the air at an unseen headline. "Win a Date with a Hockey Player, or we could use your names like 'Win a Date with Goaltender Wade Pierce.'"

I choke on the bite of pizza I was about to swallow and reach for one of the water bottles she thoughtfully put on the table to accompany our meal.

She jumps up, slapping my back like Nana would do whenever we choked on something, then resorts to rubbing her hand across my shoulders while her cornflower-blue eyes study me with concern. The warmth of her touch does crazy things to my pulse.

Once she's certain I'm not going to keel over and die, she returns to her seat. "I'm only asking the single guys if they want to take part, but don't feel you have to do it, okay? I mean, Rebecca may not even like the idea."

She's backpedaling because my reaction made her doubt her idea. And though I'm not keen on the thought of being fixed up on a date in such a public manner, if it helps a charity—and Bree—then I'll do it.

"You just surprised me, that's all. Like I said, I'm your guy."

I'd love more than anything, maybe even more than

hockey, to be hers in the most serious and intimate of ways. But Bree Sutton will never be mine. And I don't want to jeopardize our friendship.

Maybe this dating thing will not only benefit Bree but also help me get over her.

She's my best friend, and that will have to be enough.

Chapter Six

BREE

Wade was right—had I slept on the couch, I would have bitten his head off for waking me up so early. By the time I wandered out of the bedroom the last two mornings, bleary-eyed and in need of a serious caffeine fix, he'd already gone for a jog, made himself some green smoothie concoction that smelled like hay, and was waiting for me to wake up so he could make me breakfast.

I told him not to waste his time—I never eat breakfast. But he was insistent that I start my day with a hefty dose of protein.

The man definitely likes his routines. And eating healthy, which I get. His body is key to his profession. Mine is my brain, and it prefers mac and cheese. I hid the packages I purchased yesterday in one of the packing boxes in the living room so I wouldn't have to hear him razz me for dining on junk food. I know he's right, but a girl has to have some kind of vice.

Nevertheless, when he slid the plate in front of me, noting that he had added extra cheese for my benefit, I relented and ate. I'll admit, the man knows how to make a wicked omelet, hot sauce and all. But that may be what's turning the butterflies in my stomach into an angry swarm of bees as we leave his apartment today.

Or it could be the three cups of coffee loaded with a hefty dose of sugar fueling my first day at my new job jitters or this sense of impending doom that's still hovering over me like a lingering dark cloud. Even though I haven't heard a word from Chase and it's only been a week since I blocked his number, that feeling of dread sits in the back of my mind like an unwelcome guest standing at the door with a questionable casserole in hand.

What are the chances that the three states sitting between us will serve as a deterrent and that I'll never hear from him again? For once, I'd love to see things work out that easily in my life, so that the whole thing would magically go away.

Just call me an ostrich and show me the nearest pile of sand to hide my head.

From what I hear, Sarabella has lots of it—sand, that is. The nice powdery white kind, too. Maybe I can talk Wade into stopping at the beach on the way home tonight to see my first sunset here. Just the thought of walking by the water's edge as the sun sets and the waves lap around my ankles settles the anxiety tangling my insides.

Since the U-Haul's still hitched to my car, Wade suggested I ride to work with him—makes sense anyway since we're both going to the same place—and then he'll return the trailer for me after practice as I'll still be at work. Then he'll pick me up and take me home.

There he goes again, trying to make sure I'm okay. He hasn't pushed me for more details about what really happened in Texas, and I'm all for 'don't ask, don't tell' in this situation. The last thing I want is for Wade to see me as the fool that I am.

Blue sky and fluffy clouds reflect in the giant windows on the front of the arena as we approach the entrance. The way the sunlight glistens off the glass panes and the red metal trim of the building gives me an idea.

I stop on the sidewalk, shielding my face from the sun as I study my new workplace and its bare-minimum signage. "What do you call the arena?"

Wade glances up at the simple 'arena' sign and shoots me a confused look. "What do you mean?"

"Most arenas have corporate sponsors, except for Madison Square Garden, which is iconic. Just wondering what the deal is with this place." I make a general sweep of my hand, imagining the team logo filling one of the massive windows above the entrance, and a more elaborate name representing the team's home base.

"We just call it 'the arena.'" He opens the door, holding it open for me, then follows me in. "Rebecca could tell you more, I'm sure."

I tilt my head as I look up at him. "You call her by her first name?"

He nods. "She's really laid-back. You'll like her."

I don't tell Wade that I already do, or that she did tell me to call her Rebecca on the video interview. But hearing him call her by her first name makes me believe she meant it.

Wade walks with me, bypassing the door to the locker room. When I shoot him a questioning look, he shrugs.

"Didn't want you to get lost on your first day." His slanted grin returns, the one I've known my whole life, but this time, it hits me differently. As does the tenderness in his gaze. But he's always acted like this around his sisters and me. Ever the big brother taking care of us 'fillies' as he used to refer to us.

I suppress a smile. "Thanks, but I think I could have found it on my own."

The light in his eyes dims. "I know, I just thought…"

Now I feel like a heel. He's just looking out for me. I touch his forearm. "Thank you. I *am* a little nervous."

His expression brightens again. "Don't be. You're going to be amazing."

His belief in me sends a reassuring warmth through my entire being and settles those angry bees swarming in my stomach. Come to think of it, I don't recall Chase ever saying anything affirming to me. I was the one usually building him up.

As we approach what looks like a reception desk, the young woman sitting there smiles right away. "Hi, Wade." Her gaze shifts to me. "You must be Aubrey."

After I glance at Wade, I nod. "Call me Bree."

She jumps up and holds her hand out. "I'm Harper, Rebecca's assistant. If you need anything, just let me know."

Harper shows us into an office on the opposite side of the hallway. "Wade and Bree are here."

Rebecca rises from her chair and rounds the desk, hand extended to me. She's the picture of professionalism in her tailored black and white pantsuit, black heels, and a neat updo to her blonde hair. Her gray-blue eyes sparkle with genuine enthusiasm, which makes me smile and puts me somewhat at ease.

"A pleasure, Bree. We're so glad to have you with us." She raises a brow at Wade, then refocuses on me. "I understand you two have known each other for a long time."

"Yes, ma'am." I clasp my hands in front of me and try to remember to breathe. This woman's father was a legend in the hockey world, and Rebecca is fast becoming his counterpart in the builders aspect of the sport.

Her face pinches for a moment. "Please, call me Rebecca."

The sleeping bees in my stomach turn into an angry swarm. Did I offend my new boss already? "Of course. Glad to be here…Rebecca."

Her wide smile returns as she points to the man sitting on the small sectional on the other side of the room. "And this is Zach Keller, our general manager."

An older man with gray speckling the sides of his hair and dark, piercing eyes stands, buttoning his pin-stripe jacket as he approaches us. "And Rebecca's husband."

I shake his hand, fangirling a smidge. I've watched Zach Keller give analytical commentary on many games while on staff with the Texas Stars. "I know. I mean, I know who you are, and I heard you two got married."

Great, now I even sound like a fangirl. And over my boss' husband!

Rebecca rolls her eyes. "He likes to make sure everyone knows."

Zach lifts his chest as he tugs on the bottom of his suit jacket. "I don't want anyone to get the wrong idea if they see me kiss you in the hallway."

She shakes her head. "Hockey players…"

The look of adoration Zach gives Rebecca nearly melts me in my shoes. Chase never looked at me like that. No one's ever looked at me with anything near that level of affection.

Except for Wade… But he's my best friend.

I study him as he makes a comment that brings a laugh. Then he swings his warm gaze to me, making me second-guess everything. Has he always looked at me that way? He looks at his sisters the same way, too, doesn't he?

"Right, Bree?" Wade stares at me, waiting for a reply to something I didn't hear.

I startle back to the present. "Yeah, sure."

My eyes dart between Wade's puzzled expression and Rebecca's curious one as I try to figure out what they were talking about. Maybe I should just confess I zoned out because I was trying to figure out why Wade was looking at me with such affection…and pride.

Yeah, that will make a stellar first impression.

Not. "I'm sorry. Can you repeat the question?"

"See? She's thinking about her next great idea. She already hooked me into one of them. Win a date with a hockey player, right?" Wade raises a brow at me to let me know he's trying to help, as usual.

"Right! I have a presentation prepared to explain several projects I think will not only encourage the fans to connect with the team more but also benefit the charities you—we—support."

Rebecca flashes a smile at me. "Why don't I show you to your office first, and then we can talk about your ideas?"

I grin brightly…maybe too brightly. "Great. I'd love that."

And now I'm acutely aware of Wade's hand resting on my lower back. I'm sure he's done that a thousand times over the years, but this time his touch sends a warm tingle through me, and I find myself wanting to lean into the pressure and warmth of his palm.

He drops his hand. "That's my cue to get to practice."

I glance over my shoulder as he leaves, puzzled at the twinge of longing coursing through me as I miss his touch. Things between Chase and me were strained for months before I told him I was done. And it's not like he was that attentive to begin with. Even when he did pay attention to me, he always made me feel like he was doing me a favor.

Rebecca gestures toward the doorway. "Shall we?"

Zach waves, but then settles into a chair in front of Rebecca's desk while I follow her into the hallway.

A few quick steps down the hall, we reach a door, which Rebecca swings open, allowing me to enter first. The space is somewhat small with the bare bones of furniture—a metal desk, a simple chair like you'd see in a waiting room, and a bookshelf that's seen better days. It's basic, but I'm sure I can liven the space up.

"This is just temporary until you pick out your furniture." She approaches the desk and taps a manicured fingernail on the catalog sitting there. "Select whatever you need to make this a comfortable space, and Harper will order it for you. Don't worry about the cost."

The pointed look she gives me is convincing. "Wow, thanks. I appreciate that."

"I'm a firm believer in having the right tools to do a good job." She glances upward fondly. "This place needed a lot of work, but now it's finally taking shape."

I get the impression the structure isn't the only thing she's talking about. I've already noticed the vibe here is so different from what I'm used to. Something about it makes me want to settle in and stay forever. So far, so good.

Rebecca tilts her head. "If you don't mind my asking, exactly how long have you and Wade known each other?"

A tingle of nerves bursts through me. "Practically all our lives. We grew up together."

Her brows pop up for a moment in reaction to my reply. "You seem close."

I can't tell whether she meant that as a question or a statement. "He's like my brother."

There. That should settle any concerns she might have. I'm certain they have a policy about personal relationships between coworkers, although she *is* married to her general manager.

But it doesn't matter. Wade and I are just friends. Like brother and sister. No reason for me to concern myself with what the company policy says about dating the players, because I sure as hell won't make that mistake again.

Rebecca's expression gives a definitive 'if you say so' vibe but thankfully, she seems content to drop it. "I have an appointment in ten minutes, so why don't you get settled, pick out what you need, and then we'll regroup for a lunch meeting so you can show us your ideas."

"Sounds great."

She smiles and then leaves in a swish of elegance and floral perfume.

I pull out my laptop, place it on my desk, and then begin flipping the pages in the catalog as I push all thoughts of Wade out of my mind.

Or at least, I attempt to.

Chapter Seven

WADE

The minute I saw Ethan go right, I should have known he was pulling a deke. Instead, I went down to block, and he shot the puck into the top shelf.

He goes down on one knee, pumping his fist.

I groan at his exaggerated celly. "You got lucky, D-man."

But I know it's more than that—I'm distracted.

Ethan spins around and bows. "*Aaaaand* you're welcome."

With a grunt, I pull off my catcher, shove my helmet up, then grab my water bottle from the back of the net. Bree's first day has barely started, and I'm already feeling the tug on my attention. If she hadn't appeared off in Rebecca's office, I'd probably be fine. But something shifted…changed in her, and I can't figure it out. It's not like she's never looked at me before, but this time, her expression seemed different as if she were seeing me for the first time.

Maybe I'm reading too much into things, but it's like I'm on full alert, analyzing her every move. At this rate, I'll either go into mental overload or, worse, shut down. And that definitely won't help my career or advance us to the playoffs.

Luke skates over and comes to a stop at the crease. He says nothing, but he doesn't have to. His raised brow questions me louder than any words he might speak.

Still, I play dumb. "What? He got a lucky shot."

His jaw ticks. "If you say so."

I curse under my breath as he skates off, then tug my helmet off as I lay my stick across the top of the net. Next, I grab my water bottle and spray a stream into my mouth, which I swish and spit out. The second squirt I swallow, then douse my face and head—all the usual.

After I slick back my hair, I shove my helmet on, then my glove. I grasp my stick, give each side of the pipes a tap before smacking the center with the flat side. A deep breath, and then I spin around and move into position.

Normally, I save this for my pregame routine, but I need a reset. I focus everything I've got on the puck and block every shot for the rest of the drill.

Until Payton takes his turn. Pay is one of the fastest forwards I've ever seen, and he knows how to use his speed to advantage. Doesn't hurt that he's always changing up his moves, too—part of what keeps our team ranking in the top ten so far. We're seriously lucky to have a sniper like him.

He gets into position, then flies down the ice before I even have a chance to think about what he might do. But that's the reality during every game, and I welcome the challenge.

A rookie tries to steal the puck, but to no avail. He'll learn a vital lesson on this one as Payton gives the biscuit a gentle tap, sliding it between the kid's skates before charging at me like an angry bull barreling toward its perceived threat.

I drop into a butterfly, ready to block to my left, but he goes around the net, trying to pull a classic Gretzky move. When I realize what he's doing, I launch to the other side, glove in the air and right leg extended.

The puck bounces off my pad, but as my skate hits the pipe, I feel a pop in my groin area.

"Killer shot, Maxwell!" Mathéo pats him on the back.

Payton slips his helmet off. "Cheers, Barbie-man. Even better if I'd made it into the net."

I shift to my side, careful to stay prone on the ice a little longer, hoping the burn in my inner thigh backs off.

Luke's head fills my view. "You okay, Cowboy?"

"I'm good, Cap. Just give me a sec." I don't meet his probing stare because I know the minute I do, he'll figure out something's up. That's part of what makes Jameson such a great captain—he's always watching, checking on his team to make sure we're not hiding anything.

If I'm smart, I won't try to hide this. But we have a game tomorrow against our rival, and I really want to be there for the fellas, especially for Maxwell. But playing through a pull could lead to a tear.

As I roll onto my back, Luke calls Coach over.

Next thing I know, I'm surrounded by a bunch of studious heads. Coach Markelson hovers above me to my left. Next to him stand Luke, then Ethan, Elias, Payton, and Mathéo, surrounding me in that order.

Coach points to Luke and Ethan. "Jameson, McKennen, get him up and help him back to the locker room.

I push my helmet off. "I'm fine, Coach. Just need a minute."

Nonetheless, I'm hefted up by my teammates, who don't

seem to want to let go. I pull away to skate to the net, but a sharp twinge in my inner thigh makes me hiss through my teeth.

"Locker room. Now." Coach's acid tone cuts off any arguments I might have. Even if I had tried to argue, Luke's glare alone would have cut me off before I started.

After a nerve-racking assessment, I'm diagnosed with what I already knew—a groin pull. I'm relieved it's not a tear, but it means I can't practice or play for a week, possibly two. That part sucks because I need to be there for my team tomorrow night.

To make things worse, I can't attend the game because I have to keep my leg elevated for the first several days and do the whole RICE—rest, ice, compression, elevation—thing so I can get back to the net.

Plus, I'm not allowed to drive, which means I can't help Bree return her U-Haul. Just as that revelation hits, I hear the guys' voices as they file into the locker room. When Luke walks into the exam room, he takes one look at me with my leg up and an ice pack on my inner thigh and lets out a stream of curses that twists the dagger of guilt already hanging out of my chest.

I hate—and I do mean hate with a passion—letting my team down. Closing my eyes, I groan and tip my head back on the minuscule rectangle they call a pillow in this place. "Sorry."

Luke scrapes a hand down his face. "How bad?"

"Just a strain. But I'm out for at least a week."

He nods. "Guess our new backup goalie will get more playtime sooner than expected."

Rebecca and Zach did a trade for Mason Holt after last season, so he's still getting used to how we do things. I've worked with him a fair bit, and so far, he seems a good fit. But he hasn't had to perform under pressure yet.

"What?!" Ethan slides in from behind Luke. "Cowboy, say it ain't so."

"Wish I could, but you fellas will be fine." I'm the one who will turn into a nutcase because I won't be there.

Luke snorts. "In your dreams." He cringes when he looks at me and sees the remorse I'm feeling. "Sorry. I know you're probably more upset about it than we are."

I have no words, so I simply nod.

The room gets smaller when Elias and Payton squeeze in, along with Mathéo.

An awkward silence fills the small exam room as they bounce their gazes to one another in some secret communication I'm not privy to.

Payton's the first to speak. "What do you need, mate?"

My gaze coasts from one concerned face to another. "I told Bree I'd take her U-Haul back for her today."

Elias clears his throat. "I can handle that."

I lift my chin at him. "Thanks, man."

He holds his hand out for a bro-shake. "No problem."

Ethan shifts from one leg to the other. "What else?"

They surround me like an upside-down horseshoe. These guys aren't just my teammates; they're my best friends, and I'm letting them down when they need me the most.

I glance at the crutches the therapist brought in for me. This affects more than my position on the team. "Look out for Bree, okay?"

Mathéo lifts his brows.

I clench my jaw and speak through my teeth. "Hands off, Barbie-man, or you'll resemble a Ken doll, if you catch my meaning."

His face pales, matching the walls in the room. "I wouldn't dream of it. I was only going to suggest we help her get familiar with Sarabella, since you'll be laid up."

"Fine, but go in groups," I snarl.

Luke pats my shoulder. "Chill, man. We know better than to touch your girl."

"She's not mine." I drop my head onto the pathetic pillow with a groan.

He lifts that brow at me again. "Maybe not yet."

I brush off his comment. "Elias, my keys are in my locker. Make sure Bree gets them, and thank you for helping her with the trailer."

He nods, then leaves, along with Mathéo.

McKennen bounces a fist on my good leg. "I'll drive you home when they cut you loose."

"Thanks, man." We bro-shake before he walks out, leaving Luke and me alone again.

He settles onto the stool next to the exam table. "When are you going to tell her how you feel?"

I let out a sarcastic laugh. "Um, never. What's the point? She sees me only as a friend. More like a brother."

"Sometimes things change."

If he'd only been with me this morning when Bree looked at me as if I sprouted horns or something. I could use an objective opinion or someone to tell me to get over it. Over her.

I turn my head toward him. "I've known Bree since I was seven years old. We grew up together. Trust me when I say that's not going to happen."

He pats the vinyl exam table and stands. "Not with that attitude, it won't."

Before he reaches the door, I call him back. "I get what you're saying, but not everyone gets their dream girl, okay?

Bree's my best friend. I can't jeopardize that. Besides," I push up on my elbows, "I think she's been through something."

"You think?" His tone is borderline confrontational, as if he's surprised I haven't gotten the full story yet.

"I've asked, but she won't tell me anything."

"Then keep letting her know you're there when she's ready."

A weighty breath bleeds out between my lips. "Yeah, that."

One side of his mouth ticks up in a smirk. "Could open a door to something more."

He leaves before I can argue, and to be honest, I don't want to. More than anything, I'd like to believe he could be right.

Being there for Bree is easy. I'd do anything for her, but I'm not sure how long I can keep my feelings in check, especially when she's living with me.

Then, an idea hits me. If I'm going to be laid up for at least a week, I'll need something to occupy my time between physical therapy sessions and resting.

And finding Bree a place to live will be the perfect distraction.

Chapter Eight

BREE

When I get home, the first thing I observe is my car parked in a different spot, sans the trailer. I make a mental note to thank Elias. Maybe Wade knows what his teammate's favorite snacks are, so I can put together a basket for him to show my appreciation.

The next thing I notice when I walk into the apartment is Wade standing in the kitchen.

"Aren't you supposed to be resting?"

He's leaning on his crutches, stirring something on the stove. "I was, but my stomach started growling."

I set my purse and laptop bag on one of the dining room chairs, feeling a slight twinge of guilt for commandeering his kitchen table as a pseudo-office.

"Why didn't you just order takeout?"

He shakes his head. "My body needs the right fuel to heal."

I suppress an eye roll. "A supreme pizza has protein and veggies. Sounds healthy to me."

"Says the woman who thinks a box of macaroni and

powdered cheese is good for you." His tone is snarky, but he's not smiling.

"Hey now, that's not all I eat." I join him by the stove and peer down into the large pot. Aromatic herbs fill my nose as chunks of chicken, carrots, and celery chase after the spoon as he stirs.

"Glad to hear that." When bubbles break the surface of the broth, Wade pours in a box of elbow pasta.

"Pasta is dried." I roll my lips between my teeth, trying to contain the giggle welling up.

He shoots me a look so full of disdain, I think the hair follicles on my arms just retracted.

I nudge him aside. "Go sit. I'll finish this up for you."

He frowns at me. "Are you sure?"

An exasperated sigh escapes me before I can stop it. "I think I can handle this part."

After a moment of hesitation, he hobbles his way to the couch. "Thanks. Bowls are on the counter."

I glance over and note the large Fiesta Ware ceramic ware—one in bright green and the other purple.

Two, of course, because Wade always made it his mission to make sure I ate. "Interesting choice of dishes."

He grimaces as he lowers himself onto the cushions, then props his leg on the arm of the couch. "Nana ordered them for me. She insisted I have sturdy yet stylish dishes. You still like purple, right?"

A surge of tenderness fills me as I picture him selecting the bowl just for me. I run my finger over the rich indigo shade, which contrasts so well with the bright green, which I know is his favorite. "Yeah, I do."

His chuckle seems to lighten the mood somewhat. I can only imagine how frustrated he must feel, having to miss games and practices for at least a week. When Elias brought me Wade's keys and told me what happened, I wanted to race to the locker room, but Elias said Ethan was taking him home.

I want to ask Wade for details because I understand the ramifications of a groin pull turning into a tear if a player pushes too soon to get back into the game. And I know the looming question in every player's head that comes with an injury—will it be a career-ender?

Once I confirm the noodles are done with a taste test, I ladle soup into the green bowl, cradle it in a napkin, and take it to Wade, along with a spoon.

He thanks me as I return to the pot to fix mine. Since he has his leg stretched out on the couch, I settle into the chair off to the side of the sofa, folding my legs underneath me, and sample my first bite. A flood of memories hits me as the savory chicken and broth-soaked pasta hit my tongue, transporting me back to his grandmother's kitchen.

"Is this Nana's recipe?" I stir my spoon through the soup.

"Yeah, I texted her for it."

I take another bite and hum with pleasure. "Well, you nailed it."

He grins. "Make sure you tell her next time you see her."

My stomach hollows out at the thought. That would mean returning to Texas, and I've no intention of doing that anytime soon. The more distance I can keep between Chase and me, the safer I feel. At least until I know he's lost interest in making my life a living hell.

"What's that?"

"What was what?"

He points at me with his spoon. "That look of dread on your face."

I kind of forgot how Wade could always read me. I stare at my soup, scrambling for some excuse to circumvent having to tell him the truth. "There's celery in here."

First, he rolls his eyes, then dons an expression that says he's on to me. Because, of course, he is. This is Wade.

"You don't hate celery that much."

"Who says?" I shoot back, still determined to avoid his question and keep the mood light.

He places his bowl on the coffee table. "Come on, Bree. Since when do you hide things from me?"

Good grief, he's like that proverbial dog with a bone! For a guy who typically avoids confrontation, he sure is going after this with fresh gusto.

"I'm not hiding anything from you." Not completely true, but close enough. "I'm just not ready to talk about it, okay?"

His jaw locks, causing the muscle on the side to pulse.

I may never be able to tell him everything, but I can apologize. I rest my spoon in the bowl. "I'm sorry, Wade."

His brows dip in confusion. "For what?"

"For ghosting you for a year. I should have replied to your texts. I just…" I'm near tears again.

His shoulders relax, and his gaze softens. "It's okay, Bree-bear."

My breath hitches at the sound of his childhood nickname for me, and cracks form in the walls around my heart—walls I erected to protect myself against Chase. But now I'm realizing they shut me off from everyone, including one of the people who matters the most to me.

He swings his leg from the couch to the coffee table and pats the cushion next to him. "Come here."

Without second-guessing, I put my bowl near his and scoot into the crook of his arm. He's warm and solid, and I fit perfectly against him, just like always. When I lay my cheek against his chest, I inhale his clean, soapy sandalwood scent and exhale with a sigh against his T-shirt.

For the first time in I don't know how long, I feel a sense of peace, like I've found my center. All the noise and stress fade away, allowing me to breathe a little easier. That's always been Wade's grounding effect on me, and how I've missed it.

He rests his cheek against my forehead. "Whatever happened, when you're ready, you can tell me. No judgment, okay?"

Closing my eyes against the sting of unshed tears, I nod and let myself settle into him more. "Okay."

We stay like that for a while until Wade shifts. "I need to ice my leg again."

"I'll get it for you." I jump off the couch and scurry toward the kitchen.

He instructs me on which ice pack to retrieve from the freezer and to wrap it in the towel draped over the back of the barstool.

When I bring it over, a compelling instinct to take care of him hits me, so I lay the cold compress on his leg, then grab the pillows he tossed to the side and wedge them under his foot. Without thinking, I caress his shin, more out of concern, but when I look at him, our gazes collide and lock.

Something flashes in his eyes, but it leaves so fast, I'm not sure what I saw, if anything. But that doesn't stop the heated tingles shooting straight into my core.

I've always felt a stronger connection to Wade than to his sisters. He was the one I ran to first when I needed to talk something out, or the first person I called to share a win.

But this—this feels…different.

He drags a blue and green afghan off the back of the couch—one I'm sure Nana knitted for him because I have one just like it in pink and purple—and tosses it over his foot. "The ice pack makes my toes cold."

When he reaches for his soup, I hand it to him so he won't have to strain.

"Thanks." He won't look at me, just stares into his bowl, but doesn't eat. As if he flipped a switch, leaving me in the dark.

"Sure thing." I return to my chair, holding my bowl close but not feeling hungry anymore.

And here I thought my apology, followed by the hug, had restored our friendship, but the air between us feels thick, filled with tension again. I know it's my fault. What did I expect after I ghosted my best friend for a year? Did I think things would be the same?

Somehow, I have to make it up to Wade, *show him* I'm sorry for not taking better care of our friendship. I know he forgives me, but the damage to our relationship will take time to heal, something I'll have to accept and live with.

I hate that he's laid up with this injury, but maybe this could be my opportunity to prove to him how much he means to me.

He's always been there for me when I needed him. Now, I can do the same for him.

Chapter Nine

WADE

I grunt as the physical therapist works on the muscles in my thigh, hip, and glutes. It's less sore today, which is a good sign, but even that does little to ease my frustration over missing the game last night.

The team played well, and we won, so that's a relief. Pay-man got a break from dealing with his nemesis because Jennings wound up injured during a previous game. Holt, our backup goalie, held his own and blocked one shot that had the fans jumping to their feet. I'm glad Mason got some playtime, but I don't like this unmoored feeling sitting on my chest like a boulder. I *need* to get back on the ice.

Hannah hits a spot that makes me grunt. "Still tender?"

"What do you think?" I growl.

She raises a brow at me. Hannah is as tough as she is caring, but she'll let us know when we cross the line. Still cracks me up that she married a lifeguard with the surname Lawless because it totally fits her attitude sometimes. I can't speak to what she's like outside of the arena, but the woman is formidable when it comes to the recovery of the players she treats.

I drop my head. "Sorry."

She grabs an ice pack from the cooling unit, wraps it in a towel, and then lays it across my leg. "You can't rush this one, Wade."

"Yeah, yeah." I pinch the bridge of my nose, willing the ache to slide away into oblivion so I can get back to the crease.

Her blonde curls tickle my shoulder when she leans over me and gets right in my face. "I mean it. Push this, and you'll be benched for the season."

I blow out a breath. "Yes, ma'am."

Coach Markelson greets her as he walks in. "How's he doing?"

"I told him not to rush this one. And I mean it." She shoots him a razor-edged look as if to say he had better pay attention, too.

"Yes, ma'am." He holds his hands up as if to fend off an attack.

I snort. "That's what I said, Coach."

Hannah blows out a noisy breath, making the curl in front of her face dance to the side. "Don't make my job harder. That's all I'm saying."

She throws me a wink as she leaves, letting me know she's kidding. Hannah would go above and beyond for any of us, and she often has.

Coach strolls over and pats my shoulder. "I know it's hard to be benched, but do what she says. Take it slow so we know you're a hundred percent when you return."

"Sure thing, Coach." I put on my best agreeable face even though I'm seething inside.

He walks out, leaving me alone in the silence of the

therapy room. I drape my arm over my eyes as the lack of sleep due to a restless night settles into me. A sleepy doze relaxes my limbs, and I give in to it.

That is, until the sound of a knock jars me. "Yeah?"

Bree's soft voice filters through the closed door. "Can I come in?"

"Of course."

She peeks in as if she's checking for something. "Just want to make sure you're decent."

I blurt out a chuckle. Feels good to laugh. Bree and her bubbly take on life may be the exact thing I need at the moment. "I'm dressed but don't know about the decent part."

Her giggle affirms my suspicion as it seems to lift some of the heaviness harboring in my chest.

"You're the most decent man I know, Wade." She's smiling as she says this, but her blue eyes are razor sharp as if her life depended on every word.

I swallow down the knot in my throat. Moments like this make it twice as hard to hide my feelings for her. Bree's always been my biggest cheerleader, believing in me even when I doubted myself. And right now, this injury is making me feel especially vulnerable.

She sits on the wheeled stool Hannah vacated and lets her laptop bag puddle on the floor by her foot. "Since you're not busy," she spots the ice pack on my leg and groin area, then quickly glances away, "and you're a captive audience, I thought I'd start with you on the 'Date a Player' fundraiser."

I fold an arm under my head to see her better. "Rebecca went for it?"

"Yeah, as long as we don't objectify the players, so I'm

doing preliminary interviews with each player who wants to participate, so we can control the narrative."

"Sounds good. Shoot."

Bree tugs her laptop out and attempts to balance it on her lap, which doesn't work well. I shift on the table so she can use the corner by my foot like a desk.

After she taps on her keyboard, she lifts her face toward me. "Basics first. I assume your favorite color is still green?"

"Yes."

"Favorite movie or TV show." She readies her fingers to type.

"Ted Lasso."

She snorts. "Of course it is."

I push up on my elbows to stare her down. "Have you even watched it? The show is brilliant."

Her smile turns mischievous. "Oh, I agree. I just wanted you to prove yourself worthy of the biscuits."

A deep laugh rumbles up as I realize her double entendres—how she connected 'biscuits with the boss' from Ted Lasso to how hockey players refer to the puck as 'the biscuit.'

"Very clever." I've missed laughing with her more than I can say.

She giggles, but it hits in my chest like a magnet drawn to its opposite. "Okay, next question, but I'm afraid of your answer. Favorite food."

The cringe on her face is priceless. She probably thinks I'm going to say salad or roasted vegetables.

My turn to blow her mind. "Nachos."

Her brows dart up, and her eyes widen, emphasizing every detail of her gorgeous blue irises. I could drown in those depths like a man lost at sea.

"Seriously? What, are they loaded with vegetables, which is totally gross, you know?"

I agree, but I'm going to let her think the worst. "Not the way I do them."

She makes a barfing sound. "There is no way vegetables work on nachos."

"You'd be surprised. I'll make them sometime so you can see for yourself."

"Hard pass, bro." She waves her hand in a no-go motion between us.

I know it's just a colloquialism, but I've had enough of her thinking of me like a brother. "Is that how you treat your best friend after a grueling therapy sesh?"

She rolls her eyes at me. "Let's move on."

At first, I wasn't thrilled about doing this date with a hockey player idea, but I'm enjoying spending time with her and the comfortable banter between us—like things used to be.

But then she hits me with an unexpected question. "What's your favorite childhood memory?"

My thoughts flip through a plethora of scenes from the past like the old-fashioned Rolodexes Nana uses to organize her recipes. She also keeps it in a safe, if that tells you anything about how seriously she takes her cooking.

This journey down memory lane lands on a particular one I've held close for years. "That day you got caught on the barbed wire."

Her eyes go wide with surprise. "Seriously? I still have a scar." She leans to the left, pointing to the spot on the back of her leg, right below her rear.

Even though her pants more than cover the area, heat crawls up the back of my neck. Should I tell her that catching a glimpse of her pink panties was the highlight of my sixteenth summer?

Or the real reason that recollection stuck with me?

Bree had to trust me to lift her up, bride-style, in order to unhook her ripped jeans from the barb. I could have put her down after that, but instead, I insisted she let me carry her back to the house with the excuse that walking would make it hurt more. The image of her clinging to me, of holding her close against me, has taken permanent residence in my head ever since.

I scoff. "You were barely scratched. Didn't even need stitches."

"I had to get a tetanus shot!" Her exaggerated expression is plain adorable.

Biting my bottom lip does little to suppress my grin. I lower my voice to a conspiratorial whisper. "You were so pissed."

"Those were my favorite jeans, and you ruined them." She sounds breathy, flustered.

And I'm enjoying this way too much. I press my hand against my chest. "Me? You're the one who tried to do rodeo tricks off the side of your horse."

She leans in closer, giving me a hint of sweet floral, reminding me again of the honeysuckle bushes that grow wild on our property. "In case you've forgotten, Wade Pierce, you dared me."

For a moment, I get lost in her eyes as she stares me down. A dark blue circle rims the lighter blue of her irises, making them appear backlit as if she's filled with pure goodness and light.

I glance away for fear I'll reveal something I shouldn't. "Yeah, I suppose I did."

The silence in the room shifts, feeling awkward.

Bree pokes my bicep as she whispers, "I almost nailed it, though."

My gaze lifts, then gets snagged again with hers, much the same as that barbed wire did on her jeans. "I knew you could."

Her lips part slightly, drawing my attention there for a moment and making me wonder what it would be like to kiss their softness and that freckle. Not that I haven't thought about it a thousand times before, but this time feels more…real. Attainable. Although I've no idea why.

She jerks her gaze away and stares at her laptop screen. "Since I can't very well share that memory for obvious reasons, how about I just put the aroma of your Nana's baked bread filling the kitchen?"

My mouth fills with saliva and longing. I really should go home soon for a visit. There's not enough time at Thanksgiving since we play the day before and after, but I could make a quick trip for Christmas.

Maybe Bree would want to come, too.

"And her chocolate chip cookies."

She tilts her head back with a moan, which floods my head with inappropriate thoughts. "Those are the best."

"Okay, one more. What's your idea of romance?" Her fingers hover over the keyboard.

Her question confuses me at first because it's so broad. So, I venture into dangerous territory and pull upon the things I've imagined if Bree were mine.

I lean my head back on my arm again and stare at the ceiling tiles. "Let's see—a sunset walk on the beach, followed by her favorite ice cream. Cooking a special dinner and fussing over her for the rest of the evening and surprising her at work with her favorite treats. Having a hot bath ready for her when she gets home after a rough day. Buying her fuzzy socks for Christmas."

When I glance at Bree, she appears stunned.

My shoulders tense. Did I overshare? Sound like a dork?

She blinks, then lets out a nervous chuckle. "I meant a date, not a relationship."

"Then just the sunset and ice cream part."

She swallows and nods. "Adorably cliché, but I like it."

This is the first time I've ever seen Bree flustered, and I like *that*—a lot.

I give her a slow, deliberate smile, the kind that usually gets me in trouble. "Good to know."

Her eyes flash with something I can't read. Or maybe wishful thinking?

She shuts her laptop, then leans over, trying to shove it into the saggy bag that doesn't want to cooperate.

"I should go. More interviews to do." With a huff at her failed attempts, she grabs both, clutches them to her chest, and launches off the stool so fast that it slams against the wall.

She freezes in place, staring at the damaged paint, eyes wide like a possum caught in headlights.

"Sorry. Really gotta go." After giving me a horrified grimace, she rushes out the door, her cheeks flaming red.

This is more than my flustering her.

She's acting more like the clumsy, unsure girl she used to be in middle school. But then she bloomed in high school, becoming this amazing, confident young woman who didn't let anyone hold her back. That's when I truly fell for her—and hard.

A simmering rage courses through me at the thought of something or someone making her doubt herself, which makes me more determined to find out what happened to her in Texas.

When she got snagged on the barbed wire, Bree trusted me to handle her with care. Somehow, I'll convince her that she can do it again.

This time with her heart.

Chapter Ten

BREE

What is wrong with me? I can't believe I rushed out of the room like a skittish schoolgirl who bumped into her crush, behaving like a blathering idiot.

Maybe Wade didn't notice how weird I acted or the dent I left in the wall. I groan to myself as I beeline it to my office. Of course, he noticed. Wade's the one person in my life who's always seen me. All of me—the best and the worst.

Right now, I'm pretty much the least attractive version of myself. But I can't shake the way those three words made me feel…

Good to know.

It wasn't what he said so much as *how* he said it, his voice soft and steady, eyes fixed on me like it was a promise he intended to keep—with me. In all the years I've known him, Wade's never expressed any romantic interest in me. Nor I in him. We've just always been close…best friends.

He probably didn't mean anything by it. I'm the one making something out of nothing because, thanks to my dick of an ex, I'm wired tighter than a spring. My fight and flight reflexes are still amped up from what happened.

I close the door to my office, dump my laptop bag on my new desk, and sit in my comfy new desk chair. A few select pictures of my family sit on the matching bookshelf, a couple of which include Wade and his sisters, but I zero in on the one of just him and me.

Right after I graduated high school, I found out my parents had put up the ranch for sale. They'd divorced a year before, but reassured me nothing would change. What I didn't realize, though, was that they'd waited to sell until after I graduated.

My world—my dreams—shattered for a second time.

Wade understood because he was the only one who knew about my idea of turning the ranch into a destination for events like weddings and family vacations. He'd encouraged me that day to show my parents the vision book I'd created, which I did.

But to no avail. My parents couldn't afford to keep the ranch and pay for a small apartment in town for my dad. Plus, they had my tuition to cover. I argued I would skip college and implement my plan to turn things around, but they said the risk was too high since I didn't know what I was doing.

That's the ironic part. The whole reason I wanted to go to college was to gain the knowledge and skills I would need. But no ranch meant no dream.

I still got my marketing degree, but nothing felt the same after that until I landed the PR position with the Texas Stars. For the first time, I had a plan for my life that made sense. And my years of watching Wade play hockey and loving the sport turned into an invaluable skill for the job.

Maybe I'm just being overly sensitive, but I still feel like

I'm in a constant state of dread, waiting for the next 'Chase Files' to drop. That's what I've decided to call the emotional rollercoaster I've been on over the last year. I can only compare dating Chase to that analogy of a frog in a pot of water slowly heating to a boil. By the time I realized what a self-centered jerk he was, I was in too deep.

At first, I thought he was just…particular, which I found intriguing and sophisticated. For the first few months, he seemed like the perfect guy. Very attentive, always respectful, and super romantic. When he said he liked the secrecy of our relationship, I went along with it, even though I was pretty sure HR wouldn't have a problem with us dating since neither of us held any authority over the other.

Soon after, he asked me to help pump up his image on social media. I figured he was in it for the fans, wanting to connect more. But then he'd make these comments about how hard it was to find time to post, so I offered to do some for him. Chase gushed so much over me for helping that I offered to take it over for him. No one knew we were dating, and it wasn't like I didn't assist the other guys with their social media presences.

But then he wanted me to do more to catch the attention of their parent team, the Dallas Stars. Even then, he posed it as if we were a team and this was our 'end goal' to secure *our* future. Together.

And me? I was stupid enough to believe him. Until I caught him cheating on me, and told him we were over. No more relationship, and I sure as hell wasn't handling his social media anymore. He threatened to tell management that I pushed him to do all this stuff in order to build my own resume to go out on my own. And I believed him because he's best friends with the team owner's son. Apparently, they grew up together, so there's no way they'd believe me over Chase.

Yep. Just call me frog because I'm the one who got boiled in the pot.

My phone chirps. The muscles in my neck and shoulders tense, most likely because I was thinking of Chase and still live in perpetual fear of the creep working his way back into my life again. I check the screen and exhale my relief—it's from Wade.

Wade: Looks as if we'll be entertaining tonight. You okay with that?

Bree: Define 'entertaining.'

Wade: The guys are coming over to "cheer me up." Guess I looked like a sad sack during PT today.

Bree: You did seem kind of off earlier.

Wade: Sorry. Can't stand being sidelined.

Here I've been concerned about helping Wade with things like running errands for him or going to the grocery store so he can rest, but I didn't think about the emotional toll this is taking on him. Probably because Wade rarely shows that side of himself. He's always held his emotions close, making him difficult to read. His sisters and I have had many discussions about this.

Bree: I can stop at the store on the way home to pick up pizzas and beer.

Wade: The guys have it covered.

Bree: Okay. I'll stay out of the way.

My phone buzzes again, only it's not a text this time—Wade's calling me.

After a moment of hesitation, I hit the accept button. "Hello?"

"Why are you going to stay out of the way?" His words sound clipped and rushed.

"I just figured it was guy time." Chase and his buddies had a regular card night. Only guys. No girlfriends or wives allowed.

"We're just hanging out." He clears his throat. "Wives and girlfriends are coming, too, so you'll get to meet Sophie, Mia, and Lily."

Chase never included me in events like this since our relationship was a secret. Come to think of it, that's when I started feeling like I didn't fit anywhere.

"If you're sure..."

"Bree, you're my best friend. Of course, I want you there. Besides, it's your home, too."

Wow. Wade wants me to get to know his teammates and friends. But he isn't my boyfriend...just my best friend. That must be why. He wants me to make friends here, too, especially since we work together. I'm sure he doesn't want the job of my only friend in this cozy beach town.

"In that case, count me in. I'll take care of the dessert. Any special requests or no-nos?"

He snorts. "No-nos?"

"Yeah, anything you and your teammates won't eat because you worship your bodies with healthy food."

His laugh makes me smile. "A little indulgence here and there is okay. Besides, Ethan devours donuts like a police officer, and I have it on good authority that Barbie-man eats bonbons."

"Who wouldn't with that nickname?" I throw back.

Wade's chuckle fades into a sigh. "I really missed you, Bree. I'm glad you're here."

Now, why would my cheeks suddenly feel like they're on fire? Most likely residual embarrassment left over from being a horrible friend for the last year. "Me, too. Sorry again—"

"Don't." He clears his throat. "That's in the past. What matters is here and now, right?"

"Right." I don't deserve Wade's friendship, and I'm glad he's such a forgiving guy. I'm not sure how understanding I'd be if the tables were turned.

"Okay, gotta go. See you when you get home." He ends the call, leaving me alone again with my thoughts.

Not my favorite place to be these days, so I open my laptop and get busy uploading the new videos I took during practice. Ethan and Elias jumped in to do their latest rendition of the 'E-team.' Luke just skated away, which was an improvement since he didn't glare at me. I think he's warming up to the idea that this is my job, and it helps the team. Maybe I can pick his girlfriend's brain tonight for ideas on how to break through his grumpy facade.

The rest of the guys still seem a little wary, but Rebecca reassured me they'd come around. I hope she's right because I can't very well launch the 'Date a Hockey Player' event without hockey players. Another reminder of how generous and kind Wade is. He hates this kind of thing, yet he didn't even hesitate to volunteer.

I shouldn't compare, but Chase was always about what I could do for him.

How in the world did I put up with it—him—for as long as I did?

When I walk into Rebecca's office, she glances up at me with an immediate smile. A quick look to my right confirms that Zach is there, his expression welcoming as well. These two have to be the ultimate power couple of the hockey world, which gives me another idea.

"I wanted to run something by you two." I swing my gaze between them.

Zach unfolds himself from the couch and joins us at Rebecca's desk. "Shoot."

"Most arenas are named after corporate sponsors."

Rebecca shakes her head. "I'm not interested in going that direction." She glances toward Zach, who lifts a single brow but remains silent. "At least not yet."

I hold my hand out. "Right, but that's not where I was headed. The arena—your arena—still needs a name. What if the fans helped pick it out?"

Zach sits on the edge of Rebecca's desk. "You mean like the whole Boaty McBoatface incident?"

Rebecca's eyes widen with mild alarm.

"No, we won't let that happen," I reassure her. "We'll come up with a short list and have the fans vote. Creates a sense of ownership for them, too."

Zach and Rebecca pass a look. He gestures at me. "I like the way she thinks."

Rebecca's mouth quirks up on one side. "Perhaps because she just echoed my philosophy about ownership."

Dumbfounded, I bounce my gaze between them. "Then you like the idea?"

"Love it." Elbows on her desk, Rebecca clasps her hands under her chin. "Let the players give their thoughts and ideas, too."

"Of course. This is their home."

Again, they send each other knowing looks accompanied by grins this time.

Rebecca lowers her hands and widens her smile. "You've barely been here a week, and you already fit us like a glove, Bree. I love this idea. Let's get to work on that list, shall we?"

If I could do a happy dance and still look professional, I'd break out some moves. I'll save that for later, but I will use this budding confidence to propose my other idea.

"I have another proposal that I think would be fun and help build the team's profile overall."

Rebecca holds her hand out. "Go on."

"So far, Ethan and Elias are giving me great footage as the E-team. And the other players are slowly warming up to doing these videos to establish the team's social media presence."

They both nod.

"I'd like…I mean, I was wondering… Would you two be willing to do some videos as well?"

They stare at each other in a silent dialogue. Zach's smile quirks up, matching his lifted brow on that side of his face. Rebecca's blush turns several shades darker.

I wave my hands between them. "Oh, nothing embarrassing. I meant strictly professional. You two are like the power couple of the ECHL. We could show the fans some behind-the-scenes glimpses of your professional partnership."

Rebecca leans back in her seat as Zach pushes off the

desk and stands next to her, eyes completely focused on her. "Your team, your call."

She holds his hand, twining her fingers with his, and stares up at him. "Our team."

A knot forms in my throat at the love and respect defining their exchange. I get the semantics. Outsiders could easily assume he's the one running the show.

That he understands this, yet expresses his total support for Rebecca without pointing out the negative aspects, kind of blows my mind. An ache hits my heart along with a longing to have something like it in my life.

Someone who believes in me.

Chase said I was crazy for leaving the Texas Stars to work for myself. I thought it was because he wanted to keep control over me, which I'm sure was a big part of it. But maybe he thought I didn't have what it took to succeed.

Wade believed in me. So much so that he recommended me for a job where he lives and breathes hockey. He didn't seem that surprised when I got the position either. He had complete faith in me. Supported me. Let me move in with him, even though it meant he'd lose his bedroom.

Rebecca rises from her chair and leans into Zach. "We're a team. I think the fans would love to see that."

I literally bounce on my toes. "Yay! Oh my gosh, this is going to be amazing. Sarabella will not only be known for its beaches but for its hockey culture, too." I pause as another thought hits me. "Plus, the fans need to see what a woman in charge of a sports team looks like."

I think I almost made my boss cry.

Rebecca blinks, then smiles. "I'm all on board with that."

After a few more idea exchanges on how to handle that, I zip out of her office to work on concepts for both of my ideas. Before I get there, I pull out my phone and send a text to Wade's Nana.

Bree: Any chance you'd share your world-famous chocolate chip cookie recipe?

Nana: I could, but then I'd have to kill you.
And I love you too much to do that.
(laughing emoji)

Giggling, I glance up in time to avoid plowing into Wade, who's walking on his own. "No more crutches!"

He shakes his head. "Don't need them anymore." He points to my phone. "What's so funny?"

I press the screen against my chest so he can't see what I'm up to. "Nothing, just texting a friend."

"Oh?" He frowns at me. "Hope it's not your loser ex."

If he only knew how right he is about Chase, but I'm still not ready to talk to him about it. However, Wade's tone riles something up in me. "That's none of your business, Wade. And why do you assume he's a loser?"

His brows shoot up. "He let you go, didn't he?"

I open my mouth but can't find the words. I'm too taken aback by what he said.

Wade shakes his head. "Sorry. I shouldn't have said anything." He pushes a strand of hair behind my ear, cupping my face for a moment before dropping his hand. "You deserve better, Bree."

My heart pounds in my chest. All I can do is stare at him because my brain's still processing what he said. If Wade thinks I deserve better than Chase Langston, then I should believe him.

But my question?

Who exactly does he think deserves me?

Chapter Eleven

WADE

After that grueling PT session with Hannah, Barbier said he could run me home if I didn't mind a few stops on the way. I'd much rather go home and grab a nap before the entire crew shows up tonight, but I wasn't cleared to drive until today. So I guess I'm along for the ride.

I tap my fingers on the door handle, willing him to walk out of the store he zipped into ages ago. Why is a beer run taking this long? Just pick one and buy it, dude. It's that simple. And this better be his last stop because I'll barely have time to grab a shower at this rate.

Right when I'm about to crawl out of my skin, he finally walks out with a shopping cart filled with bags. The back of his car thumps as he loads everything, then he slides in behind the wheel.

I scowl at him. "I thought you were only buying beer."

"And snacks." He starts the engine.

"Is an entire pizza not enough for you?" My words drip with sarcasm because Barbie-man's appetite for pizza is legendary. I once saw him eat a whole pepperoni pizza and then snack on a few slices of cheese pizza as if they were his dessert. He must burn more calories than the rest of us because the man is a beanpole.

I tap my watch. "You might as well stay when we get to my place because everyone else will be there soon."

He gives me a sheepish grin. "That was kind of my plan."

A low growl slips through my lips. "I should have asked Bree to run me home or one of the other guys."

Barbier hesitates, scrubbing a hand over his mouth. "It was Bree's plan, too."

Bree? Why would she want to keep me out of the apartment all afternoon? "What are you talking about?"

He turns onto the street leading to my place. "You'll find out soon enough."

"Evasive much." Whatever this mystery is, I'm not a fan. I've never liked surprises, not really. I prefer to know what I'm walking into so I can at least prepare like when I'm in the crease. I can read the players, predict their moves, and anticipate what's coming. That patch of blue is my territory, and I know how to run interference.

Yet here I am, blind to whatever plan Bree's hatched.

When we finally—and I mean finally—reach my place, I'm in no mood for small talk when I walk in the door. I want a shower and a few minutes to myself before the place fills up with noise and chaos. Don't get me wrong, I love these guys like they're my brothers, which they are when you consider how much time we spend together on and off the ice.

But I need a hot shower to help my aching muscles and to relax my unsettled nerves. Things will get better once I'm back in the crease. I just have to ride this out until then.

As I walk inside, the sweet scent of chocolate chip

cookies slaps me in the face like a much-needed douse of cold water. Bree's hunched in front of the oven, staring through the glass window as if her life depended on it.

When she straightens and notices Barbier and me watching her, she startles in a way that's so frigging cute; it makes me clench inside.

"Oh, I didn't hear you come in." A smile grows on her face as she grabs a plate from the counter and approaches us. "Fresh out of the oven. Care to try one?"

She's smiling, but her eyes hold clear trepidation.

I pick one up and take a bite. Warm chocolate bathes my tongue and mixes with bits of crisp cookie as I chew. The entire sensation transports me home, back to my grandmother's kitchen.

"Is this Nana's recipe?" I drag my gaze from plotting my next mouthful to Bree's expectant face.

She nods. "I had to bribe her to give it to me."

I'm convinced my nana was a hostage negotiator in another life. Or ran her own country. "Did she require you to name your firstborn after her?"

"Something like that." Bree giggles.

Barbier grabs one and shoves the entire thing in his mouth instead of savoring it like Nana's cookies deserve. "Wow, these are delicious," he says in a spray of crumbs.

Bree pulls the plate out of his trajectory. "No sharing, thank you very much."

I close my eyes with the next bite and lose myself in the nostalgia it brings. The aromas filling the kitchen at the ranch, the sound of Nana singing some tune to herself while she shuffled trays of fresh-baked cookies from the oven with the next batch, and Bree and me sitting at the small dinette set, dunking them in tall glasses of milk.

The realization that Bree did this for me hits me square

in the chest and expands into a warm, fuzzy feeling. I'm like the Grinch when he realizes the true meaning of Christmas. "Thank you, Bree-bear."

When I open my eyes and look at her, I swear I see tears in hers. I take the plate, put it on the counter, and pull her into a hug. "Don't tell Nana, but I think you make them as good as she does."

"Bree-bear?" Barbier flashes a cocky grin.

I grab the collar of his shirt, then twist my fist, yanking him to me. "Don't even go there."

He bobs his head up and down like a scared rabbit. "Sure thing, Cowboy."

After a few seconds more of staring him down so he knows I'm dead serious, I let him go. He stumbles away, tossing a wary glance over his shoulder.

Bree shoots me a pointed look. "Be nice."

I hold my hands out to my sides. "I was. He can still talk."

"Go shower…*Cowboy*." She's mocking my hockey nickname, but the way she says it sounds almost flirtatious, and the look she gives me as she walks away twists my insides.

Good thing we're not alone, because if we were, I think I would have grabbed her hand and yanked her against me. And then I would kiss her until she couldn't talk for a long, long time. But those thoughts can only live in my head.

When I return to the main living area, freshly showered and wondering exactly what Bree promised my nana in exchange for her cookie recipe, everyone else has arrived. My first instinct is to find Bree and check if she's enjoying herself because she tends to play hostess while forgetting to enjoy herself.

That's not what this night is about. I want her to connect with the other wives and girlfriends—WAGs—so she'll have friends here—something she needs more now than ever.

The tension in my shoulders eases when I see Mia, Sophie, and Lily chatting with Bree in the kitchen. And she's smiling. Good sign. I had a feeling she'd like them, and I knew they'd like Bree—she's amazing. They already seem like friends.

How Ethan, Luke, and Payton landed such incredible women, I'll never know, but it's inspiring and depressing all at once. I want what they have, but I don't see how that's possible until I let go of these feelings for Bree.

Not that I'm trying to hold on to them—believe me, I've tried to let go. But I find myself even more drawn to her, even after a year of little to no contact, which doesn't help.

I take the seat near the couch where Luke's sitting with his love-consumed eyes pinned on Sophie. That deep ache hits me square in the chest again as I stare at Bree. My thoughts take a wayward direction, imagining what this same scenario would feel like if she were my girlfriend, hanging out with the other WAGs.

Luke clears his throat, leans toward me, and whispers, "Check your face, man."

Ethan, who's sitting next to him, nods his agreement. Elias and Mathéo sit huddled together on the floor with Mason, watching an NHL game, so they're oblivious.

Payton holds out a beer to me. "I recognize that look."

Glancing up at him, I take the proffered drink and then take a long pull. The fizz goes down my throat and lodges there.

"Thanks," I grunt.

"How's the groin?" He lifts his brows.

I'd have welcomed the change of subject if it had been

anything else, but I push a grin I don't feel onto my face. There. All fixed. "Getting better every day."

Luke and Pay exchanged glances.

I wave my half-empty beer between them. "What's that about?"

"Just concerned about you, man." Luke sets his nearly full bottle on the shell-shaped coaster sitting on the coffee table.

"I'm fine," I spit out. The last thing I need is these two acting like helicopter parents.

After a surreptitious glance toward the women, Payton sits on the arm of the couch. "Has Bree said anything to you?"

"About what?"

Luke's turn to chime in. "What happened in Texas?"

I shake my head. "Just that she went independent, but it didn't work out."

Again, they share this look like they know something but don't want to risk upsetting me.

A sigh mixed with a growl slips out of my mouth. "Stop pussy-footing around and spit it out already."

Luke scratches the side of his head. "Sophie did a little digging."

Judging by his demeanor, I'm not going to like this. I down the rest of my beer. "Why?"

He shrugs. "I shared your concerns over what happened to Bree, so she called a friend who does the coverage for the Texas Stars."

I about launch out of my chair. "I told you not to tell Sophie about my—"

He holds his hand out toward me. "Relax, man. I didn't say anything about that. Just that Bree's your best friend, and you're worried about her."

When I glance over to where Bree's standing with the others, my gaze collides with hers. She's watching me with a puzzled expression on her face, making me wonder if she overheard me. I'm glad Luke cut me off before I revealed my secret. That would have created an even bigger mess than I'm in right now.

I don a grin for her benefit. She returns the gesture before diverting her attention back to the group of women surrounding her.

She looks comfortable standing there with them, like she belongs. Like a vise, the pressure in my chest tightens a little more at the sight, and my head and my heart are having a full-blown argument at this point.

"Pierce!" Luke's growl yanks me back to what he's saying.

"What?"

He blows out a breath and rolls his eyes—something I know he's picked up from Sophie. "If you keep looking at your girl like that, she's going to figure it out."

"She hasn't so far. I might as well be a pane of glass." Sarcasm drips from my tone like a leaky faucet.

He knits his brows together.

"She looks right through me." Pains me to say it, but it's the truth. Always has been.

Understanding dawns in his eyes. "Do you want to know what Sophie found out or not?"

I take a minute to think about it because a part of me feels like I'm crossing a boundary or entering Peeping-Tom territory. "Do you believe this information is helpful?"

"Yes."

"Then shoot." I lean forward, resting my forearms on my knees, preparing myself for the worst.

"There was an unconfirmed rumor that she was secretly dating one of the players."

That would explain her evasive answers whenever I asked about her boyfriend. "Unconfirmed?"

He nods. "Yeah, some guy named Langston."

"Chase Langston?" I bite out.

Something deep inside me snaps at hearing the name. I know her choosing to date him isn't a rejection of me, but it sure feels that way.

"You know him?"

"Yeah, I know him." The bane of my existence during junior league, I once told him when he expressed interest in Bree, that she was off limits.

Clearly, the jerk didn't get the message. And knowing Chase, there's a good chance he did it to piss me off. He's lucky Texas isn't a short drive. Otherwise, I'd be grabbing my keys right about now and most likely spending the night in jail.

Instead, I do the next ridiculous thing—aka stupid. I push out of my chair and head straight for Bree. The heat simmering in my chest feels like a volcano about to erupt without warning, but there's no stopping it.

"Pierce!" Luke's bark grabs the attention of the knuckleheads playing video games, but does nothing to slow my stride.

Maxwell tries to step in front of me, but I shove him aside.

Bree's back is to me, but the other three? The closer I come, the more their eyes widen, so my face must be broadcasting my rage. As I reach Bree, I resist the urge to grab her wrist and drag her into a private place to talk. Instead, I tap her shoulder.

She spins around, all smiles, until she looks at me. I don't think I've ever seen her smile disappear so fast.

I unclench my jaw enough to force my words out. "Can we talk?"

She makes eye contact with Mia, Lily, and then Sophie before landing back on me. "Sure."

I'm almost positive Sophie just figured me out, judging by the way her brows lifted and her eyes sought out Luke. So much for keeping my secret from her. My reaction probably confirms what she already suspected.

But I don't care at this point. I take—not grab—Bree's wrist and tug—not drag—her into the bedroom. At least I'm using some restraint. And I'll be honest. I've imagined this many a time in the past, but never like this.

Bree's technically not the one I'm angry with—Chase gets that honor—and I'm mature enough to recognize that the hurt I'm feeling over her dating him instead of me is my problem, not hers. I've never told her how I feel.

But that doesn't answer the bigger question: What did the scumbag do to her? Because I know Chase, and I'm one hundred percent positive he's the one who messed with her head.

Once I shut the door, I face her. Before I can temper my tone, the words fly out. "Chase Langston? That's who you were dating?"

Chapter Twelve

BREE

How did Wade find out?

That's the first question that flies through my head.

The second?

Did I just lose my best friend?

At this stage in my life—let's just call it suckville, okay?—I can't afford to lose my one and only best friend. I had a few friends in Texas, but they were either staff like me or WAGs of the players. After I quit my job to start my own PR business—and to get away from Chase—I didn't hear a peep from any of them.

I later found out that one of those *friends*—Amber—turned out to be the one Chase was cheating on me with. And since she was the lynchpin of that friend group and I was the newbie, my phone didn't ring once after I left. Not surprising. I can only imagine what she told the others.

If there's such a thing as a mental groan, I think I just did one. How could I forget how *small* the hockey world is? I should have known he'd find out, eventually.

Did Chase say something? Did Amber? Are they

spreading rumors about me now? I didn't consider Chase stooping that low, but then again, I didn't realize what a manipulation mastermind he was until it was too late.

Wade's gaze bores into me harder, if that's even possible, making me realize I haven't said a word yet.

"How did you find out?" My voice squeaks as a burn hits me behind my eyes.

He must notice my distress because a wave of regret softens his features. "A little birdie told me."

The mention of his nana's expression is like a wrecking ball hitting the walls that have held my emotions in place for the last several months. And you know what they say? When the floodgates open…

Sobbing, I drop onto the edge of the bed. "See? I knew you wouldn't approve."

"That should have been your first clue. The guy's a scumbag."

My stomach twists into a knot as I take in his disgusted expression. Great. Now I repulse him.

I bury my face in my hands again. There's no stopping the tidal wave now. I don't know how to handle this version of Wade. And what a way to wreck an evening, right? I was really clicking with Sophie, Mia, and Lily. What will they think of me now? Will this be another repeat of what went down at my previous job?

Warm hands touch the sides of my knees, making me gasp in surprise. Wade's kneeling in front of me, his face a tortured mask of emotions. His mouth moves as if to speak, but nothing comes out.

But I know what he's asking, though.

Is Chase the real reason I left Texas…

I nod before falling forward into him, clutching his shirt and crying it out against the base of his neck. One of his hands presses me closer while the other runs up and down my back in a comforting caress. Between crying and the security of his warm embrace, some of the stress and hurt I've carried over the last few months melts away.

Finally, my tears dry up. But I'm still so embarrassed that I can't bring myself to look at him because of what I might see when he looks at me.

But as Wade does, he forces the issue by leaning back far enough to lift my chin. Even on his knees on the floor, I still have to look up at him from my perch on the end of the bed.

His eyes appear more cloudy brown than hazel green as he searches my face. "What did he do to you? Did he…?"

I shake my head. "Nothing like that." But almost as bad, right? How do I explain what happened without sounding like a naïve idiot for believing Chase? If I hadn't been so trusting…

"Then what? You know you can tell me anything, right?" The concern in his voice borders on pain.

A knock sounds on the bedroom door, saving me from jumping into the drama of my slow demise.

Wade strides over to open it, revealing Sophie standing there.

She blinks at him before refocusing on me. "Is everything okay? We heard crying."

This time, I groan audibly and flop back on the bed. It's bad enough having to tell Wade the entire story, but to share my dirty laundry with his friends, too? No, thank you.

He swivels his head between Sophie and me as if he's at a loss on what to do. "I think she's okay."

Okay? Hardly. I'm a walking and barely talking dumpster fire blazing out of control. Hot and stinky. That's me. Just call me *blazy-girl*.

Wiping my face, I sit up. "I'm fine now. Just worn out from moving and starting a new job. Really. It's nothing."

Wade shoots me an ironic look that makes it clear he sees right through me, as usual.

Sophie pushes past him, sits on the bed next to me, and pulls my left hand into her lap. "It's okay if you're not fine, Bree. I know we only recently met, but I'm happy to listen anytime."

I give her a watery smile. "I'm fine now. Just needed a good cry." I wipe away a lingering tear. "I'm sorry I ruined the evening."

Sophie shakes her head and smiles. "You didn't."

She's a better faker than I am. "But we didn't even order the pizza yet."

Sophie laughs. "We ate so many of your cookies and the snacks Mathéo brought that no one was hungry anymore." She raises her hands. "See? Not a disaster at all."

Wade leans out the doorway, then bobs back in. "Did everyone leave?"

"We figured you needed some privacy. But I wanted to check on you both before Luke and I left." She sends a pointed stare at Wade, her tone stern. "And you're okay, right?"

A blush runs up Wade's neck to his cheeks. "All good here."

Sophie faces me, smiling as she pats my hand. "Good. We're having a girls' night out tomorrow evening at the Turtle Tide after work. You'll come, won't you, Bree?"

How can I resist this woman, who seems to know exactly what I need without saying a word? "I wouldn't miss it."

"Great." She stands and walks toward Wade. "Luke said

you two had plans to hang out, too, so this works out perfectly."

"We do?" He looks like he did on the first day of high school after finding out that someone had accidentally changed his PE elective from weight training to interpretive dance. I tried to talk him into keeping it, telling him that it would help his moves on the ice, but he refused to believe me.

Sophie pats his arm like a mother hen. "You must have forgotten."

I think I'm in awe of Sophie now. She's this sweet, pink, petite bombshell on the exterior and a fierce mama bear on the inside. Her future children will be the luckiest kids in town.

In the bedroom doorway, she glances over her shoulder and waves. "See you tomorrow, Bree."

As I return her wave, I realize I'm smiling. Sure, there are things I need to say to Wade, but I'll tell him the rest when I'm ready.

Wade follows her into the main living area while I stay put on the bed. Muffled voices filter in, then the sound of the front door closing.

I jump up from the bed and start to shut the bedroom door.

Wade splays his big hand on the upper part to stop me. "We still need to talk."

As his broad shoulders fill the doorway, I take in the sharp angle of his jaw, his wavy auburn hair, and the intense look in his eyes. I know he's just trying to look out for me. "I'm not ready to talk about it, Wade. Not yet."

He scratches the side of his short beard. "Fine. I'm sorry. I should have waited until later." He lets out a long breath. "I guess I let my emotions get the best of me."

I glance toward the bathroom. "Need anything in there before I go to bed?"

He frowns. "It's early."

"I know, but I'm exhausted, and I want to be alone right now, okay?" Please let him understand. The hardest part in all of this was figuring out how to tell him I dated his rival. Now that he knows, I have to figure out exactly what to tell him about the rest.

He purses his lips together and nods. "Good night, Bree-bear."

"Good night, Wade." I close the door, feeling this odd mix of relief and guilt. He used his nickname for me, so he must not hate me. Like me still? That's a question for tomorrow-me.

And since he found out about Chase, I should probably tell him the entire story sooner rather than later. I'd hate for him to hear false rumors before he hears the truth from me. My ex has a knack for putting his spin on things and coming out smelling like a flower in the middle of a manure pile. Granted, the stench remains, but he still looks pretty.

There's a reason they call it gaslighting. When I realized Chase wasn't exactly who I thought, I did some research, and that's the word that kept showing up to explain how I would always feel like something was off, but when I confronted him about it, he would imply it was all in my head. The man is a master manipulator.

But no matter how many ways I try to spin it, I wind up looking like a stupid idiot, even to myself. How on earth can I explain it to Wade without appearing like that to him, too?

Chapter Thirteen

WADE

Luke: How's Bree doing?

Wade: Dunno. She wouldn't talk to me. Just went to bed.

Payton: Can you blame her?

Wade: What does that mean?

Ethan: Never force a woman to talk if she isn't ready. Want confirmation? Ask Mia.

Elias: Yeah, that's quite a story.

Ethan: Wait. When did she tell you about it?

Elias: Right after it happened.

Ethan: Bro, that was last month. Since when do you two talk about…things?

Elias: Since she started calling me your work wife. That's the name she gave me on her phone, too. She showed it to me.

Mathéo: Wow, tellement émasculant.

Elias: Masculine? Hey, I kind of like that.

Payton: It means emasculating, you pillock. I thought you understood some French.

Elias: Basic French. Not complicated words. And Barbie-man, I officially hate you now.

Mathéo: And how did you know what it means, Maxwell? Have you been holding back on me?

Payton: I have a brain, mate. And Google…

Luke: Now that we've established Elias doesn't understand as much French as he thought, and that Payton knows how to use Google, can we get back to helping Wade? What can we do to help, man?

Luke: Cowboy, you still there?

Ethan: Maybe he fell asleep.

Payton: Yawn. I almost did.

Ethan: I'm giving you the finger, Pay-man.

Payton: What I can't see can't hurt me.

Luke: What a bunch of knuckleheads.

After I catch up on the ridiculous bro chat, I switch to my conversation with Bree. She still hasn't answered any of my texts today—she's not engaging with me at all, which feels just like the last year of our friendship all over again.

Except this time, it's my fault. I may have checked out of the thread with the fellas last night, but they were right. I should have thought things through instead of embarrassing Bree by confronting her like that. She has every right to be mad at me. But I still wish she'd answer me, tell me if she's okay. And explain what happened so I know whether to book a flight to Texas so I can punch Chase's lights out.

But she won't be home until late because she's meeting the other WAGs at the Turtle Tide tonight after work, which is happening now. Wish I could be a fly on the wall because I'm almost certain those ladies will know more than I do by the end of the evening.

When I hear a knock, I check the peephole to find Luke's sour mug staring back.

I swing open the door. "What are you doing here?"

He brushes past me. "We have plans, remember?"

"I thought Sophie was joking."

"Nope. I have official orders to keep you company tonight. We can call the others and make a thing out of it."

"A thing?"

He shrugs. "Yeah, you know. Pizza. Beer. We never did get to order last night."

The ludicrousness of the situation makes me feel itchy. I rub my hand against the back of my neck. Bree's most likely pouring her heart out to Sophie, Mia, and Lily, which is great—I want her to have friends.

I just wish she'd talk to me.

Granted, now that I know Chase Langston, my long-time rival and all-around turd bag, was her mysterious boyfriend, and considering how I behaved when Luke dumped that detail in my lap, I can understand why she might feel more comfortable talking to them.

Even so, I'm her best friend. In the past, she's shared every part of her life with me. Some I could have gone without knowing.

With a resigned sigh, I close the door, saying goodbye to my evening alone. "You're all I can handle tonight."

Pressing a hand to his chest, he smirks. "Should I be flattered?"

"Hell no," I mumble and follow him to the couch.

He sits at one end, his arm stretched out toward me along the back of the sofa. I flop down on the other end, arms crossed, with a foot propped on the coffee table.

The silence in the place is deafening.

Luke clears his throat. "Want to talk about it?"

"Not really."

"Good." He leans forward and grabs the TV remote. "I think there's a baseball game on tonight."

I say nothing because all I can think about is Bree. "Am I difficult to talk to?"

He drops his head and puts the remote back on the table. "So, we're talking, then?"

"No...yeah, I guess." I sound like a whiny teenage boy, even to myself.

He doesn't reply. I glance over to see what's up, only to find him with his nose in his phone, fingers flying across the screen.

"What are you doing?"

"Texting Sophie."

"Why?"

He gives me an incredulous look. "Do you think I'm good at this, man?" He points to his screen. "I'm asking her what I should say next."

I snicker. "She'll probably tell you to just listen."

He lets out a classic Luke-style grunt, then holds his phone out for me to see.

The words 'just listen to him' sit in the last blue bubble.

"Told you." At least I'm right about something.

He puts his phone away and leans back. "Shoot."

I weigh my options before speaking. I'm emotionally intelligent enough to realize that keeping this stuff locked up inside is messing with my head and affecting my performance on the ice. Bree's the one I want to talk to, but she's not ready to fill me in. So I guess this brute—my team captain—is my best option. At least for now.

Like a spring, I snap into a sitting position to face him. "What chafes me most is that Chase is the reason she won't talk to me about what happened to her."

"No, man. That's on you. You're the one who's made this about you."

"What are you talking about? I want Bree to tell me what the prick did to her."

He bobs his head. "Yes, because you clearly hate the guy."

"I told him to stay away from her years ago," I grind out.

"Exactly." Brows raised, he holds his hand out as if he's made his point.

But I'm not getting it. "What?"

He takes a deep breath and slowly lets it out. "You made

it about you. Not Bree. You're mad because Chase went after your girl and hurt her."

"You bet I am!" I growl. I thought that was clear.

"Fine, but don't take your anger out on her. You need to set your ego aside on this one and quit thinking about how he pissed you off and start hurting for and with her."

Hurt for and with her? I'm not even sure what that means. I turn and sit back against the cushion and try to separate what I'm feeling and focus solely on what Bree's struggling with. Might help if I knew more about what happened, but do I need to know everything in order to sympathize with her? The image of her with her face in her hands, crying, deflates my anger.

I curse under my breath.

Luke picks up his phone, preening like he scored an impossible goal.

"Are you texting Sophie again?"

"First, I'm ordering pizza. Then I'm texting Sophie to tell her I listened and actually offered some sound advice."

"Then we're finished talking?" If he says no, I'll make him leave and eat the pizza by myself.

He side-eyes me. "Is there more you want to say?"

"No," I say with more force than I meant to.

He grunts. "Then my work here is done."

Chapter Fourteen

BREE

When I walk into the Turtle Tide, the aroma of fresh seafood, french fries, beer, and all the accompanying spices shifts my saliva glands into overdrive. Nautical-themed objects and signs cover the wood-paneled walls, and light blue tweedy fabric patterned with dark teal anchors or seashells covers the booth cushions.

Soft globe lights covered in rope dangle over the tables, and yacht music plays softly in the background. The place is warm and cozy, and I understand why it's such a popular hangout for the team.

A waving hand draws my attention to a table at the back of the restaurant. I recognize Sophie's big smile, pink top, and near-black bangs right away. Mia's blonde head and Lily's honey brown one both turn in my direction as well, both smiling as they wave me toward the table.

As I approach, I take in the French doors leading to a patio, which give a full view of powdery white sands and the aqua blue ocean beyond. I arrived almost a week ago, and I've yet to explore the beach, let alone the nuances of this cozy town. I'd planned to ask Wade to take me for that sunset walk, but he wound up getting injured. Perhaps this weekend I can go by myself. Or even better, perhaps my new friends might like to make a day of it.

I slide into the booth next to Sophie, letting my purse strap fall to the bench seat. She pulls me into a hug while the other two ladies continue to smile at me.

"I'm so glad you came." She squeezes me tighter before releasing me.

"Me too." I tuck my hair behind my ear, my nerves making me feel a bit on edge.

Or maybe I'm hangry? I wound up so busy working on the Date a Hockey Player event that I never ate lunch. And then Rebecca asked me to handle a social media hiccup involving one of the rookies, who took the crown from the team's new mascot, Stingin' Ray, and posted a video of himself parading around the locker room wearing it. When I explained he'd jumped the gun in revealing the new mascot, he frowned and said it was only the crown.

He had a point. Instead of taking the video down, I reposted it on the team feed as a small hint about the big reveals planned for the game on Saturday. The fans ate it up, reposting and sharing, while posting guesses what it could be in the comments. Nothing like a little intrigue to get our stats pumped up.

My favorite speculated that the crown was for Payton, along with an honorary title of royalty in Sarabella. The thread of replies had so many hilarious suggestions, I tucked it away for future reference, just in case.

Yeah, that was my day—crazy yet great, because Rebecca said my pivot to make a blunder appear intentional was *brilliant*. And I may have preened a little over her praise.

I pick up the menu. "What's good here?"

All three reply at the same time, "Everything."

We all erupt into giggles, which diffuses my nervousness about fitting in with these three women. They've done nothing to make me uncomfortable. Quite the opposite, actually. The shy girl I used to be in school returned with a vengeance after the whole Chase debacle, bringing back my insecurities in a major way, so this feels like an upgrade in comparison.

"We already ordered some hushpuppies." Just as she says this, the server arrives with a tray holding a red basket lined with checkered paper and three glasses of white wine.

Mia slides her glass closer. "We didn't know if you preferred wine or beer. Or water." She adds the latter as an afterthought.

"Wine sounds great." I smile at the server. "I'll have the same."

She nods and leaves.

After taking a sip, Lily lowers her glass. "So, Aubrey Marie Sutton, what's your story?"

How does she know my middle name? I'm almost positive that the subject didn't come up last night. "How did you know Marie was my middle name?"

Mia waves her off. "Don't mind her. She's a bodyguard—"

"*Former* bodyguard," Lily interjects.

"Whatever." Mia rolls her eyes. "As I was saying, don't mind her. She investigates everyone she meets."

I didn't have a chance to ask Lily about her profession last night. On that first day at the arena, Payton explained what had happened earlier in the season when his title as an heir apparent wound up leaked to the press. He kind of glossed over his fiancée being his bodyguard, though. "Payton mentioned you were his bodyguard."

Lily pauses mid-sip and puts her glass down. "He loves to pull that card out every chance he gets."

After I thank our server for the wine she places in front of me, I return my attention to Lily. "He didn't go into detail. Did you really have to protect him from a threat?"

"Only from himself and the press, thanks to a rival who has a bone to pick with him and revealed Payton's true identity to the paparazzi."

Sophie dips a hushpuppy into a creamy orange sauce. "You should have seen her take charge. Even I was shaking in my shoes."

Lily dons a maniacal grin. "Now I get to put all those skills to work for the team."

"Playing bodyguard?" I can easily imagine her bossing those guys around.

She snorts. "Sometimes. But not really. I handle security at the arena."

Mia groans.

We all turn to face her.

She bounces her gaze to each of us. "What?"

Sophie gives her a pointed stare. "Why are you upset?"

"I'm not." Her tone borders on a whine. Next, she lets out a harrumph and drops her chin into her hands. "Fine. I'm envious. You all have such exciting jobs. Sophie's a photojournalist. Lily's head of security over the arena, and the new girl here does PR for the team."

Sophie rolls her eyes. "Here we go again."

Mia sits up straight, stiff as a board. "What does that mean?"

"You're always complaining about how boring your job is, but you know you love it."

"I didn't say I hated it. Just that it sounds dull compared to you three."

Lily gives her a pointed look. "Then don't compare. Be proud of the fact that you're shaping minds for the future."

"True." Mia lifts her glass to take a sip.

Sophie takes it from her. "New girl?"

Mia cringes, then dons an apologetic expression. "Sorry, Bree. I was being sarcastic. Soph will tell you I'm a snark queen. Just my MO."

Appreciating her apology, I smile. "No worries. I get it. My job may sound glamorous, but it's not. Especially with hockey. The smell alone has me rethinking my career choice many a time."

All three laugh and nod their agreement because they know full well. I settle in, enjoying the camaraderie forming among us as we talk about everything and anything. The conversation never lags, not even when our meals arrive.

I'm on my second glass of wine, something I rarely do, when I notice Lily keeps staring at me. I focus on finishing my scrumptious fried shrimp and oysters, but she continues to study me.

Finally, I sit back and touch my cheek as I return her stare. "Do I have tartar sauce on my face?"

Lily shakes her head. "No, just wondering when you're going to tell us what happened last night."

Feeling pinned, I push my wine glass away.

Sophie rests her hand on my wrist. "The thing you have to understand about Lily is that she doesn't beat around the bush, but know that her directness always comes from a place of caring."

Emboldened by my liquid courage, I slide my eyes to Sophie. "Wow, I can see why you're a journalist."

"Photojournalist."

Lily leans catty-corner across the table toward Sophie.

"I still struggle to grasp the difference between the two, since you write the articles that go with your pictures."

Sophie waves her off, but faces me. "You don't have to share anything you're not ready to talk about, okay? We just want you to know we're here for you. And if we can help, I hope you'll let us."

Mia and Lily both nod at me with compassionate smiles.

Lily's brows lift. "Oh, I know. I could tell you about the time I had to help a client get dressed after I found them passed out naked in the bathroom. That was pretty bad."

Mia diverts her gaze to Lily. "You never mentioned that one. Male or female?"

"Male"

"Attractive?"

"Very."

"Then what made it so bad?"

"He totally missed the toilet."

"*Ewww*," all three of us say in unison.

I sigh. "Thanks for trying, but it's a long and complicated story."

Sophie slides my wine glass back to me. "We have all evening."

For the next hour, I tell the story of how Chase and I reconnected when I started working for the Texas Stars, and how things progressed to us secretly dating and the resulting toxic relationship. I gloss over some details because I'm still too embarrassed.

Sophie squeezes my arm. "Wait. Let me wrap my brain around this. He basically used your relationship to manipulate you into handling his social media to make him look better for sponsorships and to get the attention of the Dallas Stars management?"

I nod, leaving out how I willingly went along with it

until I quit my job and tried freelancing until I could figure out my life.

"And he cheated on you, too?" Mia jumps in.

Heat creeps up my neck and into my face, which I cover with my hands. "I know. I was so stupid. When I questioned things, he would reassure me that he loved me and that it was all for our future. But the more I did for him, the more he asked until I was just in too deep." I drop my hands. "I ended it the minute I found out he was cheating on me, though."

Adding that last part does nothing to lessen my extreme embarrassment. I didn't intend to share all the sordid details, including my mortification, but between the wine and their compassion, the spew just kept coming.

Lily's the one who reaches out and squeezes my wrist this time. "Do not blame yourself for what he did to you, Bree. He gaslighted you. That's worse than the cheating part in my book."

Mia nods her agreement, and I think she has tears in her eyes. "He sounds like a sociopath."

Sophie takes my other hand into hers and holds it. "We're here for you. Whatever you need to move past this, okay?"

A burn starts behind my eyes, more out of gratitude. I expected a little judgment, considering how irresponsible I feel for allowing myself to wind up in such an awful situation, but these women are completely on my side.

The massive weight I've been carrying sloughs off my shoulders and joins the fried crumbs on the floor. Talking about what happened and opening up feels so cathartic. Like, I can finally move past this and get on with my life.

Later that evening, we parted ways, saying our goodbyes

in the parking lot. As I head toward my car, Sophie calls out to me.

I stop and turn around to find her walking toward me at a fast pace.

She stops in front of me, glances down, and pushes her hair behind one ear. "Listen, I hope you're not mad at Luke for asking me to do some investigating."

So that's how Wade found out. I let this bit of information sink in, trying to decide how to feel about it. I'm not mad at Sophie, but I am very curious as to why Luke would ask her to do that.

She must take my silence as a sign that I'm upset with Luke because she suddenly looks bereft. "Luke takes his captain duties to the extreme sometimes. He said Wade was concerned about what happened to you in Texas, so he thought this might help."

"No, it's okay. I understand. I haven't talked to Wade about it yet. But I will," I add, but I don't know if I'm saying that for her or for me.

After sharing more than I intended and then being affirmed that it wasn't all in my head, I feel ready to talk to Wade. And I should before he hears any more rumors and does something ridiculous like ask one of his hockey buddies to rough Chase up. Or does it himself.

He wouldn't do that, would he?

A hesitant smile forms on her face. "Wade really cares about you a lot, Bree."

I let out a weary laugh. "Maybe too much sometimes. You should see how protective he is of his sisters, too."

She studies me for a moment. "Somehow, I don't think it's the same."

What is she talking about? "Why do you say that?"

"I saw the way he looked when he stormed over last night."

Stormed? I had my back to him, so I missed that, but he did drag me into the bedroom like a Neanderthal. Funny thing is, I kind of liked it.

"What—what did he look like?" My mouth goes dry as I try to imagine Wade in a protective fury…over me.

"Jealous."

I shake my head. "Not possible. Wade and I are like brother and sister."

Sophie barks out a short laugh. "Trust me. Brothers do *not* look at their sisters like *that*."

Chapter Fifteen

BREE

It's late by the time I get back to the apartment. A light breeze rustles through the nearby palms, carrying an earthy scent from a brief rain shower.

I pause in front of the door with Sophie's words repeating in my head, wreaking havoc with my frontal cortex. That's all I could think about on the ride home. I haven't known Sophie long, but I feel like I can trust her.

So, what if she's right? What if Wade does have feelings for me? I don't even know how to process that, but I can't deny the tingles running through my entire body at the thought. Sure, Wade's attractive—very attractive. Maybe I've noticed more so since I arrived, but I just assumed that was because he's bulked up over the last year, and I'm simply appreciating his male form.

But what if it's more than that? Am I developing *feelings* for Wade?

I jiggle my keys in my hand, noticing the feel of them against my skin, and take a deep breath. This is crazy. I'm behaving like a silly teenage girl who just found out a boy has a crush on her, and suddenly she has stars in her eyes for him.

Well, maybe not stars. More like curiosity or intrigue.

Wade and I are best friends. That's it. Whatever Sophie thinks she saw, she must be mistaken. Wade's always been fierce about the people he loves. There isn't a more loyal and caring person on this planet. I'm almost positive that's what Sophie witnessed on his face.

Well, mostly. That's the story I'm running with before my heart and my brain go to war with each other. The last thing I need right now is more romantic drama. I've had more than my fair share over the last year. Enough to consider staying single for the rest of my life. At this point, I'm content to become one of those cat women, except with Chihuahuas. I don't do cats.

I move to insert the key into the door when it flies open.

Wade stands there, filling the doorway with his broad shoulders sheathed in a very soft-looking heather gray T-shirt, black joggers that tug over his muscular thighs, and a concerned expression that makes him appear more broody than grumpy.

"I was starting to worry about you." He steps to the side so I can walk in.

As I brush by him, his musky, spicy scent wafts up my nose. I have this urge to wrap my arms around his waist and bury my face against his chest to see if his shirt's as soft as it looks and if his pecs feel as muscular and firm as I imagine.

It's like every cell in my body suddenly stood up and took notice of this man standing in front of me…worrying about me. I don't recall my heart beating this fast in reaction to Wade, except for the times we raced on our horses to see who got back to the barn first.

Now I'm starting to worry about me, too.

As he shuts and locks the door, I hold my arms out to my sides. "I'm fine. See?"

I'm not sure why I said that. Do I want him to look at me so I can search his face for something that may or may not be there? I've memorized the planes of his features, noticed how the color of his eyes shifts between hazel and green when he's happy, and catalogued every version of his smile, but I've never noticed him look at me in any other way than friendship.

But have I truly seen him?

Our gazes connect and lock. His eyes look greener than hazel at the moment, and the start of a smirk sits on his lips. "Looks like you had a good time."

I drape my purse over the dining room chair in front of my laptop and sit down. "I did. The girls are great. They've really made me feel welcome."

The smirk turns into a genuine smile, as if he likes whatever he's seeing. Or is that relief because he won't have to be my one and only friend during one of the most challenging times of my life?

"That's great. I had a feeling you would hit it off with them. You need friends here."

Guess that's enough confirmation right there. Feeling mischievous, I fold my leg under me and tilt my face toward him. "Why? I already have you."

His smile falters as he slips his hands into the pockets of his joggers. Are his ears turning red? His hair is on the longish side, so I can only see part of them, but they definitely appear darker right now.

I've never noticed that happening before. Ever.

"I know, but you should have some friends who are girls." His words tumble out in a rush.

"Are you afraid I'm going to talk about *girly things*

again?" I use air quotes, curious if he'll remember his words.

He may think I didn't notice his discomfort in middle school when I told him about my first period, but I did. What can I say? I was cramping and moody, and wanted someone else to be uncomfortable, too. Not my finest moment.

But I will say he made a stellar attempt to hide his unease. Kind of like he's doing right now…

He rubs a hand over his mouth, making a scratching sound that makes me curious what his short beard would feel like against my face…or my neck.

"No, not at all. You know you can talk to me about anything." The subtle raise of his brows implies the question he's trying not to ask.

Am I ready to discuss Chase? Ready to lay out the whole twisted story and risk Wade's reaction to it? To me?

Telling Sophie, Lily, and Mia about it helped more than I realized it would. Kind of ripped the Band-Aid off a healing wound in need of air. But this is Wade we're talking about, and I'm almost certain his dislike for Chase will turn into pure hatred when he hears the full story.

I do want to tell him, but there's still this small part of me that's afraid of what he'll think of me. The girls' reactions were so affirming and a relief to hear it wasn't all in my head, that I hadn't made the situation into more than it was.

My doubts about misreading Chase are gone. I know he manipulated and gaslighted me every step of the way.

But I still fell for it. Believed him. Doubted myself.

Since I arrived in Sarabella, I've felt a glimmer of my old self return. It's like I'm rediscovering who I am—as if I can breathe again and not live with giant question marks from my past hovering over my every move in the present.

Now, when I think about how I lost sight of myself, I get angry at myself and at Chase. Mad at myself for allowing him to manipulate me and at him for using me in that way. Again, which I allowed.

Talk about a vicious circle, and this one's eating me up like piranhas. But avoiding the topic will only prolong my misery. Might as well get this over with.

Despite the trembling in my body, I take a deep breath and square my shoulders.

Wade tilts his head, still waiting for me to say something.

So…here goes nothing. Or everything.

I point to the couch. "You should sit down for this."

I've lost count of how many times Wade either rubbed the back of his neck or scrubbed his hand over his mouth, most likely to prevent himself from swearing up a storm to match the one raging outside.

Right after I began filling him in on the Chase Files, a flash of lightning lit up the living room, followed by a rumble of thunder that shook the walls. It wasn't long before the sound of torrential rain beating on the roof complemented my dialogue.

Or diatribe. Once I started, my anger spilled out. More like spewed, to be honest, so I can only imagine what Wade's thinking as I finish my woeful tale. At this point, I'm not concerned about his opinion of Chase. I want to know how he feels about me.

Wade rises without saying a word, then paces behind the couch like a panther on the prowl. My insides quiver at the thought, marginally terrified that I could wind up his prey. Or worse. What if he goes to Texas and confronts Chase?

"Wade, please say something."

He stops, threads his fingers through his hair, then leans his hands on the back of the sofa. "I want to kill him." His dark expression matches his words.

Should I question my ethical moorings over the fact that I'm more relieved for myself than concerned over what he intends to do to Chase?

Actually, I'm terrified he'll do something foolish, jeopardizing his career. "Good thing he's not here, then."

He shoots me a scathing look.

Guess I'm not totally in the clear. To my surprise, I relayed a rough draft of the last year of my life without crying once, but now, I'm feeling the burn behind my eyes. Plus, I think my stomach just made a pit stop somewhere between my knees and the floor.

"I'm sorry, Wade." I swipe away a rogue tear.

His expression softens somewhat. "Why are you apologizing?"

"Because you're clearly angry with me."

He rounds the couch, sits back down, and faces me. "I'm not mad at you, Bree."

"I knew you two were rivals, but in my defense, I honestly thought your beef with him was only on the ice."

Wade turns his head, revealing the pulse of his jaw muscle. "Chase is the one at fault here. I told him to stay away from you."

I pull my head back. "You what? When?"

"The last time you came to a game, right before I got drafted. He asked if you and I were an item. I told him you were my best friend and that if he ever went near you, I'd rearrange his face."

I guess some part of me wanted to believe Chase's pursuit of me was genuine on some level, even if only at the beginning. But now I see I was never more than a tool to him—a double whammy of a lifetime to advance his career and get a dig into Wade.

My turn to stand up. "Great. So I was just some pawn you two could flex your Neanderthal muscles over?"

He jumps to his feet, but winces as he grabs his upper thigh. "What? No! I saw how he treated women as if they were disposable. I didn't want him near you."

His voice grates with his agitation, or because of his pulled groin. Maybe both. But he's right. That's exactly how Chase treated me, but I can't bring myself to admit that to Wade, even though it's obvious.

I grab an ice pack from the freezer, wrap it in a towel, and hold it out to him. "I'm a grown-ass woman, Wade. I think I can handle myself."

After accepting the cold pack, he drops onto the couch. "Like you handled Chase?"

Stunned that he actually threw it in my face, I'm left speechless aside from the squeak that comes out when I search for a comeback.

He diverts his eyes, placing the pack over his inner thigh. "Sorry. That was unnecessary."

This is one of those moments of complete clarity, when the answer you didn't even realize you needed materializes. If Wade felt anything other than friendship for me, I'm pretty sure that ship has sailed. And he may not want to be my friend anymore.

I should find somewhere else to live, even if it's just temporarily. Staying here will only cause more tension between us, which neither of us wants right now. He needs to heal and refocus on getting back on the ice, and I need to focus on my new job and getting my head—and my heart—straight.

In the morning, I'll pack my bag and call the Sandpiper Inn to see if they have any availability. Worst-case scenario, I'll stay at a cheap hotel off the interstate and deal with the longer commute to work until I find something closer and more permanent.

"I'm going to bed. Do you need anything in the bedroom?"

He shakes his head.

"Good night, Wade." I'm halfway through the doorway when I finally hear him speak again.

"'Night."

Once I finish my nightly routine and crawl into bed, I let the emotions I held back earlier spill out in a flood of tears onto my pillow—Wade's pillow.

I thought discovering my boyfriend used and cheated on me was the worst thing that could have happened to me.

But losing Wade, my best friend, hurts even more.

Chapter Sixteen

WADE

Wade: I blew it.

Luke: Bro, it's late. Why are you up?

Wade: Can't sleep, obviously.

Ethan: I'm guessing this has to do with Bree.

Wade: Give the man a gold star. (Snicker)

About a month ago, after an away game and a few beers, Ethan let it slip to me that his wife, Mia, who's a schoolteacher, found another use for the gold stars she gives her students. The implication was clear, and I can't resist throwing in a little snark of my own.

Ethan: The vault, man. Did you forget?

Wade: My bad. Sorry, not sorry?

Elias: I already knew, so cool your jets.

Ethan: Excuse me while I wake up my wife.

Mathéo: What happened, Pierce?

Wade: Bree told me what went down with her ex. I want to frigging kill him.

Luke: I understand that you're feeling jealous as hell, but this seems like more than that.

Mathéo: So insightful. Those therapy sessions are really expanding you, Jammer.

Luke: Shut up, Barbie-man. Anybody could tell Pierce's beef with this guy goes way back.

Zayne: I agree with Mathéo. Very insightful.

Ethan: Who added the rookie? (No offense, Z.)

Mathéo: I did. After that stunt he played with the new mascot, I figured Zanie earned a probationary trial with the big guns.

Elias: Big Guns? I like that. We needed a name for our chat group. Adding it now.

Ethan: Seriously? I think we can do better.

Luke: Zanie? What the hell is that?

Mathéo: His new nickname. The kid's a prankster. It suits him.

Zayne: Not the worst I've been called.

Wade: This is useless. Forget I said anything.

Luke: Not going to happen, man. Guys, shut up and listen.

Wade: I didn't handle it well.

Ethan: As in…?

Wade: As in, I blew up. I don't mind competition, but this guy, Langston, took it to a whole new level after junior league.

Luke: For what?

Wade: Being better. He wanted to be a goalie, but couldn't cut it. I did. He's had it out for me ever since. He used Bree to advance his career and cheated on her. I know he did this to get back at me.

Elias: Sounds like you made this about you and not what he did to your girl.

Wade: What? No. And she's not my girl.

Elias: Yet. Did you reassure her? Tell her it wasn't her fault?

Wade: I told her I wasn't mad at her.

Ethan: Pierce, I say this with love, but that was a douchey move, man. Brunner's right. You should have been there for her.

Elias: E, thank you for affirming my insight.

Ethan: Don't even. I'm still pissed at you, man.

Elias: Why? Wade's the one who spilled the tea.

Ethan: Spilled the tea? Bro, you really need to stop reading those gossip columns.

Elias: Is Mia mad at me, too?

Ethan: I've officially banned you from talking to Mia EVER AGAIN.

While the E-team hashes it out in our thread—and I'll take that I like the name "Big Guns" to my grave—I rehash my discussion with Bree in my head. Even before I screwed up by implying Bree wasn't mature enough to make a solid choice about who she dated, I did nothing to make her feel heard or seen. Instead, I made her feel worse.

Deep down, I think I am a little mad at Bree, too. And hurt.

But only because she didn't choose me.

Wade: Like I said, I blew it. I have to fix this.

Luke: Tomorrow's another day.

Elias: See? So insightful.

Luke: I need a grunting emoji.

Zayne: I'll get right on that, Cap.

Luke: And brown-nosing will get you booted out, Zanie.

Zayne: ...

Too exhausted to read any more of the fellas' antics, I plug my phone into my charger and turn it face down on the coffee table. I toss the room-temperature ice pack to the floor with an unsatisfying thump, wishing I could go for a run instead of sitting alone on my couch.

I'm not sure yet how I'm going to fix things with Bree. But one thing I do know?

It's going to be a long night.

What is that sound?

I crack open an eyelid enough to note my living room is filled with light. Normally, I wake up on my own long before now, but after the night I had, I set an alarm, just in case I overslept.

That's what I'm hearing—my stupid alarm. I reach out to smack my screen, but the blaring sound continues. Then I remember I turned it face down last night because I didn't want to read any more texts in the Big Guns chat.

Guess the name stuck with me.

As I sit up, I grab my phone and stop the torture device. That's when I notice an unread message from Bree.

Bree: Hey, I didn't want to wake you this morning. So I'm sending a text. I'll either be at the Sandpiper Inn or, if they're still full, I'll find a cheap hotel for a few nights. I think it's better this way. Really. You need your bed back, especially now that you're recovering.

I know she's using my recovery as an excuse for the real reason. And I don't blame her. I acted like a jerk last night when she needed her best friend. I'm such an idiot—how could I do that to her?

Despite the slight protest in my thigh, I launch off the couch toward my bedroom. The door stands ajar, and the light's off. When I flick it on, I note the pile of sheets sitting on the floor, yet the bed is neatly made. I open one of her drawers, but it's filled with my socks and underwear again.

The empty side of the closet and the lack of her toiletries in the bathroom confirm the unsettling reality that she's gone. And that I'm the biggest tool on the planet. Ethan's right. I'm a douchebag.

But I'm not a big enough one to let Bree wind up at some fleabag motel. We need to talk. I take the quickest shower of my life, dress, and shoot out the door to go to the arena.

Like I told the fellas, I have to make things right between Bree and me. Not to mention my nana will have my hide if I don't. But more importantly, and at the very least, I need my best friend back.

I arrive at the arena well after the rest of the guys get there for practice, but with time to spare before my physical therapy session with Hannah. It takes forever for the elevator to reach the third floor. I thrum my fingers on the side of my leg, waiting for what seems an eternity for those doors to open.

Our general manager stops me on the way to Bree's office. "Wade, how's the groin?"

In normal circles, this would be an awkward question, but not in the hockey world. Zach Keller was a killer on the ice and dealt with several injuries himself until a knee injury ended his career, so I know he understands.

"Getting better every day. I'm hoping Hannah will clear me for the game on Saturday." I glance down the hallway for any sign of Bree.

"Good. I'm looking forward to seeing you back out there." He pats my arm and then continues toward the elevator.

When I reach Bree's office, she's not there, so I head to Harper's desk to see if Bree's in a meeting with Rebecca, the owner.

"Hi, Wade! How are you feeling?" Harper stares up at me with genuine concern pinching her face.

"I'm good. Thanks for asking." Attempting to appear cool, I tap my index finger on her desk. "Is Bree in a meeting?"

She shakes her head. "She went downstairs to grab us coffee. She'll be right back."

"Great. Okay if I wait in her office?"

"Sure. I'll let her know you're waiting for her."

Harper's next words stop me in my tracks.

"I'm really looking forward to having Bree as a roommate. Do you know what her favorite snack is? I thought I'd stop at the store on the way home and grab a few things to make her feel welcome."

I turn to face her. "Roommate?"

"Yeah, we just figured it out. The timing was perfect, too. My roommate moved to California with her boyfriend last month. I was about to give up my apartment and move back in with my parents, which would have been a nightmare."

She shudders at this, reminding me of what went down with our former GM, who's also Harper's father. The man treated his own daughter like trash while he tried to manipulate the team for his own gain.

She gives me a sheepish look. "Hope you don't mind my stealing her."

Feeling the air in my arguments deflate, I pull on the back of my neck. "No, that's okay. I knew she couldn't stay with me long since I don't have a spare room."

Holding her hands up, Harper smiles. "And I do! See? It's perfect."

I nod, then turn around to head to the elevators. There's no point in talking to Bree now. She landed in what I hope is a safe place, and something in my gut says I need to let her go—let her find her own way, no matter how much I want to jump in and fix things for her.

Harper's voice calls from behind. "I thought you wanted to talk to her. Should I tell her you were looking for her?"

I turn briefly, shaking my head. "Don't bother. I'll catch her later."

"Okay." Her expression turns puzzled.

She can imagine whatever she wants. And I'm sure she'll mention that I stopped by.

Not certain what I'll say to Bree now, aside from a very sincere and necessary apology. And I'm the one who wanted to find her a place as soon as possible, so I didn't have to constantly hide my feelings for her when she was so close.

Close enough to touch but not available…or interested.

I should be relieved. *Really*.

Too bad I'm not.

Chapter Seventeen

BREE

I arrange the decorative pillows on the bed for the third time, and then step back to take in the full effect of my new bedroom. After work, I stopped at Wade's place and grabbed a few of my boxes so I could make the space my own. I knew he wouldn't be there because of a team meeting, so I took advantage of the opportunity to grab some of my things without running into him.

Fine. I know I'll have to talk to him at some point, considering we work in the same place. But for now, I need time and space to figure out my life…and how to be around him without feeling like an epic failure.

When I arrived early this morning, Harper was the only one there, thank goodness. My biggest fear was running into Rebecca with puffy, red-rimmed eyes because of lack of sleep and crying most of the night. In my short time here, I've come to know my boss as smart, bold, and very empathetic.

But I'd rather not explain to her why I'm upset. That would raise too many questions, including the dynamics of my friendship with Wade, which I'm not even sure I understand anymore.

Because something's changing…different.

I knew my dating Chase would set Wade off, but to imply I'm incapable of making good choices as to who I date?

That hit me hard. Possibly because I still blame myself for being stupid enough to believe Chase actually cared about me, but I'm pretty sure at least fifty percent of the female population has made the same mistake.

No, it was the way Wade looked at me right before he made that remark, and then wouldn't look at me as if he was dismissing me—I think that gutted me worse than anything Chase did.

Normally, Wade would pull me into his arms and reassure me that everything would be okay. He's done it at least a thousand times during our friendship, through every teen heartbreak, life disappointment, and especially after my parents got divorced. And that's what I wanted more than anything, for the old Wade to tell me everything would be okay.

But he didn't. Instead, it felt like he judged me when I needed him most.

That's the part that feels different, though. I didn't just need Wade, my best friend. I wanted Wade, the man who would protect me, hold me, and…

I don't even know how to explain it, other than this is the deepest ache I've ever felt in my life.

Like I said, Harper was the only one there, and despite my attempt to get to my office without being seen, she swooped in after me with a box of tissues, sat in the cute polka dot upholstered chair in front of my desk, and coaxed me into telling her what's wrong.

I didn't go into all the details about my ex, but told her the crux of the issue and my decision to move out of Wade's place. That's when she turned into a human pogo stick, bouncing in the seat with excitement over the idea of me moving in with her.

Perfect timing, for sure. I actually smiled and hugged Harper out of relief. At least I won't be in some stale, worn-down hotel room—the Sandpiper Inn was still booked—while I cry and binge-watch Emily in Paris for the umpteenth time, eating a tub of Chunky Monkey ice cream.

Before Harper left my office, she told me Wade had stopped by, looking for me. I thought about going downstairs to look for him and find out what he wanted, but I'm guessing he just wanted to make sure I didn't wind up in some sleazy hotel. His not bothering to wait for me after Harper told him I was moving in with her confirms I made the right decision.

He's off the hook, and now he doesn't need to worry about me anymore.

My phone pings on the nightstand. When I pick it up, I see Wade's name.

> Wade: Glad you found a place to land. Harper seems ecstatic to have you. Since we don't have practice tomorrow, the guys will bring your boxes over in the morning. Sorry I can't be there to help—still not cleared for anything more strenuous than sporting an ice pack.

I start to type a reply, but I can't think of what to say. 'Okay' sounds borderline pathetic, as if I'm sulking, which I'm not. And "thanks" sounds like I'm admitting he's right, that I'm in this position due to poor judgment on my part, and grateful for any help I can get.

With I sigh, I revert to a thumbs-up emoji. Let him read whatever he wants into that. I have more important things to focus on.

Like why is Wade's sister calling me—I check my watch and deduct three hours for California—when she should either be at practice or getting ready for a game? Wade wouldn't have said anything to his sister. I'm sure of it. Unless…

Nerves rattled, I take a deep breath, attempting to sound normal. "Hey, Piper, what's up?"

"What is going on with my brother?" Her clipped tone leaves no doubt in my mind that she's on a warpath, but after whom?

"Do you mean his groin pull? I think he'll be cleared to play—"

"I already know about that. Is he there? He hasn't returned my texts for two days. Did something happen?"

Did something happen? How the hell do I answer that one? I cringe, trying to think of a way to answer her question without saying anything about the last two days.

"I'm not at his place at the moment. Are you sure your calls are getting through? Maybe he's just super busy with physical therapy. And stuff." I close my eyes and press my hand against my forehead. Even I can hear how lame I sound.

"If he's too busy to answer my texts, then he's not taking his recovery seriously enough." She should know. Piper's a professional hockey player herself and knows what the sport gives and takes intimately.

But even in the state I'm in, I can tell something's off with her. "Piper, is something wrong?"

Her loud exhale filters through the connection. "It's Nana."

The hair on the back of my neck stands up. "Is she okay?"

"Yes, sorry. She's fine, but she's, well, she wants to *retire*."

"Retire?" How does one *retire* from a horse ranch? Wade helped her find a part-time foreman two years ago to lighten her load. If Nana doesn't want to run it at all… "Do you mean sell?"

Her silence answers my question.

"Oh, no." That burn hits behind my eyes as the memory of my parents telling me they were selling our ranch flashes front and center, but I push it away. Piper doesn't need to add my distress to her burden at the moment.

"Don't say anything to Wade. I need to be the one to tell him."

"Of course. I understand." I certainly won't have any problems not mentioning it, considering he and I are barely talking. "Does Ellie know?"

"No. Not yet. She's getting ready for midterms and doesn't need the distraction."

Message received. "I won't say a word."

"Thanks, Bree. Please tell my brother to call me."

I cringe again. "I will. And I'm here, Piper. Whatever you need, let me know if I can help?"

"Sure thing. And thank you."

Still staring at my phone, I sink onto the edge of the bed, my heart heavy for Wade and his sisters. My dad often said things came in threes. Mostly, he meant the good stuff, but I know he meant both.

First, I disappointed Wade by dating his nemesis. Then

he winds up with a groin pull, and now this. He'll be crushed.

I open up my chat, hoping he'll reply to me this way so I won't have to actually call him.

Yes, coward is now my middle name.

Bree: Hey, Piper just called. She really needs to talk to you.

Wade: Why?

I roll my eyes. Typical male response, but I won't break my promise to Piper.

Bree: She sounded upset.

Three dots appear, then disappear. I wait for them to show up again, but they never do.

And my heart aches, because my best friend is about to get the worst news of his life, and there's nothing I can do about it.

Chapter Eighteen

WADE

I didn't sign up for this.

That's the only thought going through my head right now. And it's selfish, I know.

When I called Piper, I filled her in about Bree, the part Langston played, because she knows who the guy is, and how I didn't exactly handle things as well as I should have.

Yeah, Piper ripped me a good one. I may not sit comfortably for weeks.

Then she told me about Nana's decision to sell the ranch. Not right away, but soon because…she's met someone. Who knew geriatric romance was a thing?

This shouldn't surprise me, though. Nana's as feisty as they come. Already a young widow, she didn't sign up to raise her three grandkids alone. My mother left when my sisters and I were little because she couldn't picture herself strapped to a ranch for the rest of her life. To mitigate his pain, my father threw everything he had into running the ranch that killed him in the end.

By the time they found him on the back side of the

property, he'd already slipped into a coma from a severe stroke. He passed away two weeks later, leaving Nana to raise three children on her own.

And she did it with passion and dedication, doing whatever it took to keep the ranch running so we didn't lose our home, too. When I discovered my love for hockey, she made sure I had the equipment and lessons I needed to pursue the sport I loved, even to the point of selling one of our stallions to pay for it all.

She deserves to have a life of her own, no matter her age.

That's why I'm a selfish jerk, worrying about whether I have to give up hockey to keep the ranch in the family. Piper just got drafted into the PWHL, and Ellie's still in college. I, on the other hand, have had several years to pursue and live my dream of playing professional hockey.

Do I want to take a shot at the NHL? Hell, yes.

And no…

Or maybe I should say I don't know anymore.

I'm not sure of anything at the moment. My world feels like a listing ship about to keel over at the moment.

But I can't think about any of it right now because I'm lying on the table as the team doctor does an evaluation of my condition while Coach Markelson hovers in the doorway. As much as he wants me back in the crease, I need it more—need the distraction.

From my family's situation, and from Bree.

She and I have exchanged basic texts over the last few days, but that's been it. It's like we're dancing around each other, avoiding the rift forming between us. I didn't get to help move her boxes, which may have been a good thing, since I haven't been in a great headspace. The guys said all I did was scowl at them while they loaded their SUVs.

"Well?" Coach's voice grates from my right.

The doctor glances his way before zeroing in on me. "You're not feeling any pain whatsoever?"

I shake my head. The last time I felt a twinge was a couple of days ago when I got up too fast from the couch—the last time I saw Bree. If I mention that, though, the doc might think it's too soon for me to play, but I need to get back out there—for me and for the team.

Perched on a rolling stool, Doc pushes away from the table and coasts backward as he crosses his arms. "I'll clear him for tomorrow night's game."

"Yes!" I sit up, feeling the weight of anticipation slough off of me.

Coach shoves off the doorjamb, appearing relieved.

"But on one condition."

I freeze in place. So does Coach.

Doc continues, "If you feel even a hint of a tickle, you tell a trainer right away. Deal?"

"Deal," Coach and I both reply to him at the same time.

I don't expect that will be an issue. I'm feeling back to normal, and I'll make sure I'm intentional with my stretching, which I normally am, but I'll add a few more reps to play it safe.

Swinging my legs over the side, I perch on the edge of the table. Coach stands there, arms crossed and silent, but I read the warning in his eyes—sitting out one more game won't make or break our season and isn't worth the risk.

I hold a hand up. "I'll be careful."

Coach nods. "Good. See you out there."

He turns and walks out. I head to the locker room to get ready for practice. My insides buzz with the anticipation of getting back on the ice after almost two weeks of sitting around with ice packs on my leg.

I still worked with my goalie coach during that time to implement some new eye movement exercises and focused on my upper-body workouts, but I missed being out there.

With my guys. With my team. Classic case of FOMO.

Putting on my equipment felt more akin to a ritual, a form of worship. I almost luxuriate in the weight of my gear as I head down the tunnel to the rink, like a familiar friend I haven't seen for far too long. The irony of that thought lands deeper than expected.

But when my skate touches the ice, that listing sensation fades away. My world as a goalie rights itself again.

And for the next few hours, that's enough.

Coach runs us through some demanding defense scenarios to check for any weak spots in anticipation of Saturday's game. The E-team—Ethan and Elias—look like they're ready to drop from exhaustion.

After an hour and a half, I'm feeling the strain myself since it's my first full day back on the ice. Coach had me take a couple of breaks, but overall, I feel good. By Saturday, I know I'll be ready.

Coach blows his whistle. "Head in."

The relief on Ethan's and Elias's faces is palpable.

Luke glides over as I pull my helmet off. "How'd that feel, Cowboy?"

I couldn't suppress my grin even if I tried. "Like a pig reunited with its mud."

Luke shakes his head. "I'll take your word for it."

As I leave the ice, I notice Bree standing at the end of

the tunnel. She's dressed in wide-legged black slacks and a tight-fitting white top with a black and white cropped jacket that reveals her small waist. She's also wearing some kind of black platform shoes, making her taller. Her hair is swept back into a high ponytail, which accentuates her cheekbones and makes her gorgeous blue eyes the focal point of one incredible smokeshow.

My gut twists at the sight of her—that familiar feeling I always get when I see her, but even more so. She's stunning. Eloquent. Perfection.

"Bree." Her name floats from my mouth on a breath filled with relief. Only then do I realize just how much I've missed her. But then I remember I owe her an apology.

The corners of her lips lift in a slow smile as I come closer. "I heard you're cleared to play."

I stop in front of her, sweat dripping down the sides of my face, jersey soaked, and wishing I could hold her as if she were mine. "Doc gave me the go-ahead today."

Eyes glassy with moisture, she glances away, her expression guarded. "I bet you loved being back out there."

"Understatement of the year."

We both laugh softly, but a foreign awkwardness lingers between us.

I swipe my sleeve along the side of my face, wiping off the sweat tickling my cheek. "Listen, Bree, I owe you an apology."

She rolls her lips inward, then nods for me to continue.

"I got caught up in my head about Langston when I should have been more concerned about what he did to you. I never meant to imply that you couldn't handle yourself."

Smile gone, her gaze darts back and forth as if she's

studying me in an entirely different way. "But you did, Wade."

"I know. I was wrong, and I'm sorry. I, um… I made it about me instead of being there for you."

She blinks away the sudden moisture in her eyes, but her grin returns. "Thank you. I appreciate that."

"So, are we okay?" I swallow the emotion in my throat. "Because I really miss my best friend. A lot."

Her expression warms, and her shoulders settle. She bobs her head. "Right as rain. But I'm not letting you hug me."

I snicker, then hold my arms open and take a step toward her, catching a whiff of my stench. "You mean you don't want a piece of this?"

She wags her hand in front of her as she backs away. "No, thank you."

Turning serious, I lower my arms. "Want to hang out tonight? I can make dinner for us?"

"Will it entail vegetables?" She side-eyes me.

"Most definitely."

"I'll bring a pizza." She smiles, and then something… different happens.

As Bree stares at me, I get lost in her cornflower blue eyes. I can't—and don't—look away. And I'm done hiding what I feel for her. If it's written all over my face, so be it.

We stand there, looking at each other as if we're in our own little world until Ethan comes up from behind and pats me on the shoulder as he walks by, bursting our time bubble.

"Hey." I barely give him a glance, loath to break the connection with Bree, but she's staring down at her hands now. "See you around six?"

She gives me a vigorous nod and a small smile. "Sounds good."

Walking away from her feels as if I'm trudging through water, each step a strain against the pull and the desire to recapture that look in her eyes. Did I glimpse something more than friendship swirling in their depths? Is Bree feeling drawn to me like I am to her?

Hope blooms in my chest. Before the turn leading toward the locker rooms, I look back at where she's standing, but she's gone. Yet the sense of something developing between us lingers like a promise.

Or did I just imagine it?

Chapter Nineteen

BREE

What just happened?

That's the question I keep asking myself every step of the way back to my office.

All I know is I couldn't tear my gaze away from Wade, despite the significant odor coming from his sweaty body. Whoever said there's no stink like hockey stench wasn't exaggerating.

I've seen him dressed in his goalie equipment many a time, but it's not just his on-ice workout that made him such a hottie this time. The curl of his damp, unruly hair framing his face, along with his short beard and green eyes—I couldn't look away.

Not to mention how he stared at me as if I rocked his entire world.

Has he looked at me like that before, and am I only noticing now? Maybe it's the uniform—he fills it out better than he used to, that's for sure. Or perhaps how he appeared so large and in charge on the ice during practice when I snuck down the tunnel to shoot some footage for the team's social media channels? The man definitely has moves.

That has to be it. I'm simply impressed by how much he's improved and mastered his skills and abilities. There's a reason he's the starting goalie for the Sun Kings.

When I reach my office, I settle into my chair to create some posts highlighting Saturday's game and the three special events we have planned. I've posted teasers over the last week, but this one will motivate and excite the fans about voting on a name for the arena.

And I love the list of names I've curated from the players and staff. I open the email from Rebecca to read what she and Zach came up with in addition to the ones I sent them, and add their two suggestions to the final list.

A zing of excitement shoots through me as I prep the post for the team's various social media channels. I enjoyed working for the Texas Stars—minus Chase, of course—but I *love* working for Rebecca and Zach. I never imagined I'd find a workplace that's so exciting and affirming all at once. Rebecca and Zach have made a point of telling me many times how much they appreciate my work and that I'm making a difference.

The Sun Kings—and Sarabella—feel more like home than Cedar Park. And now that Wade and I are back on a good footing, I feel like my life is finally coming together. No more dumpster fire.

As I'm about to upload my first post, which turned out super clever, my phone chirps. Most likely Wade trying to talk me out of bringing a pizza tonight. I'll make sure I order a supreme so he sees I am consuming some veggies.

Only, it isn't Wade.

Chase: Hey, doll. I know it's been a while. Wanted to give you some space while you settled. Just checking up on the profile piece you promised me.

My pulse jumps into full overdrive, beating so hard, I swear my heart is halfway up my throat. My entire body clenches with panic, making it difficult to breathe.

Why is he texting me? I glance at the last text I sent that made it clear I was moving and never wanted to hear from him again. I should have blocked his number, but I thought for sure he got the message since I haven't heard a peep out of him in weeks.

Bree: I told you that was a long shot. My connection at the magazine is no longer there. And I told you not to contact me anymore.

Chase: You owe me.

Bree: I owe you nothing, you cheating scumbag.

Chase: Wow. Seems the little kitten found her claws.

I bristle at the use of his nickname for me. The first time he called me 'kitten,' I thought it was endearing, until I realized how demeaning he actually intended it to be.

Bree: We. Are. Done. BYEEEEE!

I find his contact information, intending to block him

like I should have to begin with, but then his next message pops up at the top of the screen.

Chase: Then I guess I'll have to tell Carrington about this.

I swipe back to the chat and see an image of a half-naked woman, entangled in the arms of a man, in the throes of passion. I recognize the Texas Stars locker room, but not the player.

The woman has my face, but that is *not* my body. My cheeks flame with heat, and my eyes fill with tears. I wipe them away and look closer. I'd never—and I mean never—do something like that.

He must have used an actual image and instructed AI or Photoshop to change the face. But it looks so real… How am I going to prove that it's not me without showing it to someone?

If he brings this to the team owner, my reputation will be ruined, regardless of whether I expose it as a fake, because Chase will blab about all the extra coverage I did for him.

A fresh wave of shame overwhelms me, making me queasy. Why did I let him manipulate me like that? I was so stupid and naïve, blind to who and what he really is. But even so, I never imagined him capable of this.

I can't block him now. If I do, he'll show the image to the team owner, and I wasn't lying when I said my contact at the hockey magazine doesn't work there anymore. I have to figure out a way to appease Chase, even temporarily, until I find a way out of this.

Bree: You really did climb out of a manure pile.

Chase: Now, now, kitten. Watch those claws. I've already drafted the email. Just have to hit send.

My stomach lurches to the point where I nearly vomit into my garbage can. Sweat breaks out on my face. Taking deep breaths, I push my hair back and grab my phone from where I dropped it on my desk.

Bree: Fine. I do this, and we're done. And I mean it, Chase. This is the last time.

Chase: So glad you see things my way. I'll be in touch.

I slap my phone screen down on my desk and shove it away like it's a pariah as the full reality hits me.

Even if I succeed in landing an interview for him, Chase will never leave me alone. Somehow, I have to end his hold over me.

After I calm down—and thank goodness no one came into my office during that nightmare—I finish uploading the rest of the posts I planned, grateful for the distraction. Thirty minutes later, we have over a hundred votes already on the 'Name the Arena' project.

And five o'clock never looked so good. Then I remember I'm supposed to go to Wade's tonight and consider canceling. How can I keep this from him? He'll take one look at me and figure out something's wrong. Wade knows how to read me better than anyone.

But the thought of going home and wearing a brave

face for Harper doesn't feel any better. Can I hold it together in front of Wade?

The question plagues me the entire ride to his place, and especially up the walk to his apartment. A cool breeze rustles the nearby palms as I vacillate in front of his door, questioning my decisions now more than I ever have. Normally, this is my favorite time of year. Still, my mind is as far from appreciating the subtle change of season as I am from Texas—a distance that didn't make any difference in removing Chase permanently from my life.

The ramifications of my situation make my eyes burn all over again as I debate leaving. And instead of making my mouth water, the aroma wafting from the pizza I picked up on my way from work makes me queasy.

I still have a key and could let myself in, but that feels wrong. It's not like I stayed here long enough to think of his place as my home, and besides, I don't want to push the tenuous thread of reconciliation we've established.

Seeing no other choice but to power through, I lift my hand to knock, only to have the door whipped away before I can touch it. Wade fills the doorway with his broad shoulders, firm jawline, and piercing green eyes—an image that sucks the air right out of me.

When did he get so devastatingly attractive? Has he changed that much, or am I just seeing him now?

"Are you coming in or not?" He lifts a brow in tandem with his lopsided grin.

"I was about to knock." I brush past him, catching his clean, musky scent, which has quite the opposite effect of the pizza. Unlike the unappealing aromas of cheese and tomato, I want to bury my face against his heather gray T-shirt, bawl my eyes out, and feel secure in his muscular arms again. Wade's hugs have always been a place of comfort for me, although the thought of holding me makes my entire body hum.

"Why did you stand out there for so long?" He closes the door, studying me.

Looking away, because if I stare into those eyes any longer, I'll spill everything, I slide the pizza box onto the counter and drape my bag over the back of the stool. "Hard day at work. I was debating going home."

He smirks. "You would be home if you still lived here."

I sigh. "You and I both know this is a much better arrangement. You need your bed, and I need…"

His brows draw together with concern, and he closes the distance between us so fast that I take a step back.

"What's going on, Bree?"

I knew this would be difficult, but wow, am I in trouble. If I share the latest in the Chase Files drama, there's no telling what Wade would do, considering how much he hates him, a detail I'm fully cognizant of now. But I have to tell him something.

"Nothing I can't handle, okay?"

"Is it the job? Rebecca seems like she'd be amazing to work closely with. Is it Zach? I don't interact with him much, but if he—"

"It's not Zach." Realizing at his shocked expression that I raised my voice, I take a deep breath. "I love my job. It's great. No complaints whatsoever."

He brushes my hair back, something he's done many a time, but the urge to push my face into his palm nearly makes my eyes close with a desire I've never felt toward him before, until now.

"Do you miss Texas?" His caring tone pushes me to the edge of spilling everything.

Miss Texas? Not on your life, but maybe I can use that

as a shield. "Not really, but I miss your nana, and her wanting to sell the ranch makes my heart ache."

All true, but not the reason I'm cracking apart. Nana would have my hide for fibbing, too, but I brush that thought away because sometimes a girl has to do what a girl has to do.

He cringes. "Piper told you?"

I nod.

Watching his reaction is like looking in a mirror. He sinks onto a stool in front of the kitchen island, then drags his hands through his hair, appearing utterly bereft.

With slow, measured steps, I move closer until I'm standing next to him, placing my hand on his shoulder. Just the light touch sends my pulse into a spin, but when he lifts his tortured eyes to mine, every cell in my body buzzes with a longing I've never felt before.

Normally, he would be the one to pull me into a comforting hug, but this time, I do it. I slip an arm around his shoulders as he pulls me closer, and hold his head against my chest with my other hand.

"I didn't see this coming." His warm breath seeps through my shirt, warming the spot right over my heart.

"I know." I run my fingers through his hair above his ear, relishing the gesture of touching him in such a familiar way.

He lifts his chin to look at me. "I know you do."

Our eyes connect, and I swear I can almost hear the snap of sparks. Only Wade truly understands the heartbreak I experienced when, first, my parents divorced and then sold our farm—the loss of my past and my future.

His irises expand as his gaze drops to my mouth, and I do the same. Has he always found me attractive? Or is this new for him, too?

As if I'm not in control of my body, I lower my face until our lips touch. He stiffens, and a reality switch flips in me.

What have I done?

But before I can pull away, he pulls me against him as he stands, moving his lips over mine with a demand for more. And I want that, too, which blows my mind because I never pictured this between us.

He intensifies the kiss, greedy and demanding. At first, I match his fervor and cling to him, but then the reality of who I'm kissing rushes over me like a bucket of cold water.

He must read my body language because he shifts to something gentle, more pleading, yearning, then draws back. His curious eyes rove over me, greener than I've ever seen them.

And filled with questions.

But I don't know if I have the answers to any of them.

Chapter Twenty

WADE

Fireworks? Explosions? More like a total mind blow?

Bree…kissed me. And it transcended anything I had ever imagined. Soft. Passionate. She fit in my arms as if she belonged there.

But why? Why did she kiss me?

Her gorgeous blue eyes bounce back and forth as she stares up at me like a scared rabbit. She looks as if she's ready to bolt, too.

The wheels in my head spin, searching for a way to backtrack. Given how long I've wanted Bree, I shouldn't be surprised by how hard it hit me. After years of fantasizing about kissing her—and pining after her like a lovesick idiot—restraint was never going to be my strong suit.

If only life had an undo button, which I seem to say a lot these days. I take a step back, rub my hand over my mouth, then stop. What if she thinks I did that to remove the feel of her lips on mine? Not possible, even if I tried. Her touch and taste have branded me now—sweet and unforgettable.

I need to say something before she leaves, and we wind up avoiding each other again. "Bree, I'm sorry. I—"

"No, it's my fault. Really. Lousy day, bad timing. And we're both upset about Nana, right? It's fine. *Really*. Just. Fine." Her voice gets higher as she backs up, turns to the right, then to the left, like a malfunctioning robot, only cuter.

"It just happened. It's okay." I want to hold her, reassure her that nothing's changed between us, but that feels like a lie. I know what I want, and I want Bree. I always have.

Now that I've experienced that mind-blowing kiss, I don't want to go back to being friends. But what does she want? Until she figures that out, it's best if I back off and let her call the shots. What else can I do?

Her bottom lip trembles. "I'm exhausted. I think I'll go home." She grabs her purse and slings it over her shoulder, making a beeline for the door.

If she leaves, who knows how long it will take for her to talk to me again. Using my well-honed goalie reflexes, I bolt into action and make it to the front door before her, blocking her path like a shot on goal.

"You're right. This thing with Nana has me all messed up." I pull at the back of my neck as I search for the right things to say. "Let's start the evening over. You just got here with your smelly pizza. I'll grab some plates, and we'll chill, eat pizza, and talk about whatever you want, okay?"

She nods and whispers. "Okay."

Putting my hand on the small of her back, I lead her over to where we started—simply two friends about to have dinner together.

She slings her purse over the barstool again and lifts her pizza box. "You really think my pizza is stinky?"

A smile creeps onto her face, making us both laugh, and the tension straining between us breaks. However, the ache in my chest clicks into place where it's always lived, only stronger.

At least she's still here, talking to me.

"On a scale of one to ten, I'd say a seven," I add a tilted grin for effect.

She lands a light swat on my abdomen. "You're drooling for a slice, and you know it."

Warmth mixed with relief spreads through me. We're back to our usual banter. That's a good sign, right? I can work with this, salvage our connection because the only thing worse than not being with Bree is not having her in my life at all.

"Take your odoriferous box and sit down on the couch. I'll get plates and napkins.

"Odoriferous?" She eyes me. "Are you bringing out big words today?"

"Blame Nana."

"Does she still forward the word of the day to you?"

"Yeah, she does." The plates clink as I snatch two from the cabinet, grab the roll of paper towels—what Nana calls 'Pierce napkins'—and sit next to Bree on the couch.

She puts a slice on her plate. I slide one onto mine. It's as if that kiss never happened, but I know I'll revisit it every chance I get.

Bree does a double-take. "Taking a walk on the dark side?"

Shifting the plate back and forth, I make a show of examining the chunks of olives, peppers, and onions intermingled with sausage, pepperoni, and cheese. "I can work with this."

And with resuming our best-friends-only status.

But can I? Can I really?

"Pierce! Get your head in the game!" Coach Markelson rarely barks at us, but when he does, you better believe we listen.

The problem, though? It's not the first time he's said—or shouted—this at me today.

Remembering the manners my nana drilled into me, I give him a nod. "Yes, sir."

But like a dog with its tail between its legs, I skate over to the crease. Today's our last practice for tomorrow night's game. I have twenty-four hours to get my head straight and get back on track.

But all I can think about is Bree and the kiss I keep reliving in my thoughts and my dreams. In seconds, she confirmed what I had suspected for years—we could be good together. Very good. If only she could see that—see me that way.

The clink of the puck hitting the pipes jars me back to the present. Luke comes to a stop in front of the crease, snowing me—his warning shot.

He grunts. "We need to talk."

"I'm fine," I growl.

"No, you're not. After practice. Not an option." He stares me down like a bull positioning to charge.

He's not letting this go. I drop my gaze to the blue paint beneath my skates—the place I used to feel centered and connected. "Whatever."

Jammer skates off, joining the rest of the Big Guns, who keep casting concerned looks my way.

I rip my helmet off, tossing it on the net, then grab my water and douse my face and head. The cold liquid is bracing but doesn't help clear the tangled thoughts cluttering my brain. I don't know how to compartmentalize Bree. And this situation with Nana. I still need to call and talk to her about it and discuss other options. There has to be another solution than selling the ranch.

My salary is decent, enough to live on, but I can't afford to make her current foreman a full-time employee with benefits. He manages two ranches, so I know what the cost would be. The ranch doesn't bring in enough to cover it either.

Unless we sell some of the horses and cattle, or maybe part of the back property, but that would be a temporary solution.

An unexpected relief washes over me when practice ends. Usually, I'm happier in the rink than in the weight room, but after my performance today, I can't get off the ice fast enough.

I shed my gear and head off to work with my goalie coach on some new reaction drills for eye-hand coordination—a valid reason to avoid their questioning stares and scrutiny. But procrastination only takes me until the end of the day. Then it's back to the locker room to shower and clean up. And judging by the unusual silence of my guys, they're dreading this discussion as much as I am.

As we leave, Coach gives me a wary look, then lifts his chin at Luke, silently communicating who knows what.

If Coach is in on this, it can't be good. This feels more like an intervention at this point.

When I head to my car, Luke grabs me by the shoulders. "You're riding with me, Cowboy."

"What, are you worried I'm a flight risk?" I say with a

joking tone, but I can see myself pulling a deke and going home to hide. But they'd follow me and break down my front door.

Luke grunts, then shrugs. "Figured a beer or two might help loosen your tongue."

I stop. "But we play tomorrow."

"One beer, then. I'll drive you back to pick up your car."

Gritting my jaw, I grind out, "Fine."

Normally, we hang out at the Turtle Tide, grab drinks and baskets of their hushpuppies, but not the night before a game. So, I'm guessing we're heading to Steamers, a new place that opened last year that has a full bar, pool tables, and darts.

Luke and I arrive at the same time as the others. Ethan stops at the bar and puts in an order for a pitcher of beer while the rest of us claim a dart room. More like enclosed alcoves than rooms. Kind of like those ax-throwing places with partitioned walls, which give us some privacy.

I stand with my back to the dartboard while the rest make a J-shape formation like we do on the ranch when we're herding and sorting cattle. Guess that makes me a cow tonight, but I'm not liking it. At all.

Ethan grabs a set of darts and hands them to me as he joins the ranks. "Shoot and start talking, Pierce."

Heat bristles up my neck. I assess the situation, parsing out any potential escape routes, but they're like an impenetrable wall. That's hockey players for you. But with the headspace I'm in right now, I'd rather throw punches than darts.

Resigned to my fate, I spin around and throw the first dart, hitting a bullseye with a loud thump. The next two darts land dead center, too, smacking just as hard.

Payton lets out a soft whistle. "Impressive hat trick, Cowboy. Now talk."

The fight seeps out of me as I turn, meeting their eyes one after another. Do I give them details or just the highlights?

Here goes nothing.

"Bree kissed me."

Chapter Twenty-One

WADE

The smack of darts hitting boards brackets us on both sides, along with the chatter of voices and the aromas of burgers and fries. Our server walks over with the pitcher of beer Ethan ordered, deposits it and several glasses on a nearby high-top. She takes one look at us standing there, staring at each other, and hightails it back to the bar.

Elias glances to his left and then to his right as if he wants to know if the others are as shocked as he is. "I did not see that coming."

Mouth hanging wide enough to catch flies, Ethan nods in agreement.

Pay-man drags a hand down the side of his face. "I've experienced a bit of that myself, mate."

He has my full attention now. Maybe he can help me figure out what to do next. He fell hard for his bodyguard—way before she showed anything for him.

"Lily?"

He snickers. "Never saw it coming."

Could that be what happened to Bree? Did she catch

unexpected and sudden feelings for me? "Did it make you want to run?"

"No, quite the opposite." His expression turns sheepish as if he's embarrassed. "She's the one who resisted."

"Sophie did, too. When I screwed up." Luke growls and stares at his feet.

Things definitely got tense around here when Sophie came on the scene, and Luke had to agree to an interview—Rebecca had requested a series of profiles on the team for the local paper to help bring the fans back after the scandal with the previous owner.

Come to think of it, I do recall him being grumpier than usual through all of that.

But my situation is different. I know exactly what I want. Or rather, who. My problem is that I don't know how Bree feels about me. Beyond the whole best-friend status, I mean. "Not very encouraging, fellas."

"Yeah, but once we got our heads on straight, we went after our girls." Luke glances at Payton and Ethan, who nod reflectively.

"When you know, you know." Ethan shrugs, grinning.

Pay-man lifts a finger as if to push pause on Luke. "If I recall correctly, my head remained quite straight and very much focused on winning Lily over."

"More like out of your mind." Ethan gawks at him.

Payton flashes a cheeky grin. "I think of it as determination."

Sighing, Ethan tilts his head back. "Whatever helps you look in the mirror, Your Highness."

Payton's smile drops faster than a flying puck hitting the ice.

I'm about to lose my patience with these two when Zayne—or Zanie as Mathéo calls him—walks up to the group, hands in his pockets with a skittish expression on his face. "Sorry I'm late."

Mathéo smacks him on the chest with the back of his hand. "Got any experience with *amour*?"

"More what?" Zayne frowns.

I'm pretty sure Mathéo's cursing in French under his breath, and that his affection for the prankster slid down a few notches. "Love, you idiot. No one appreciates my language."

Mason rocks back on his heels. "I thought we were playing darts."

"This is useless." I take a step forward, heading for the gap between Elias and Mason, who also showed up for this throw-down because it's the clearest shot at an escape.

They close ranks on me. The rookie already looks terrified, so I stare Elias down. "You really want to get in my way?"

He doesn't back down. "We're trying to help you, bro."

Luke tugs on my shoulder from behind, forcing me to turn around. "How about this? We have a beer, play some darts, and if you feel like talking, we'll listen."

I consider, then give a tight nod. Coach must be more concerned about me than I realized to pull this stunt. So, for the sake of my job, I'd better go along. Or at least try to.

Payton grabs the darts from the board, steps behind the line, and shoots two in the red bullseye and the last in the green outer ring. "Blast. Can't believe a Texan outshot me."

The weight in my chest lifts some. They may feel a little too much in my face at the moment, but these guys have my back on the ice, and apparently outside of the arena, too. Maybe I don't have to figure this thing out on my own.

Snickering, I spin around and face Pay-man. "We'll always outshoot you…*mate*."

I wind up having two beers instead of one, but I figure the activity of throwing darts will help burn off the alcohol more than if we were sitting and talking. Plus, we're hockey players, so we have to put some moves into how we throw—that's part of the challenge.

Funny thing is, keeping my hands busy and my brain distracted made it easier to open up. I have to give Luke kudos for suggesting we come here instead of the Turtle Tide. Every team has a captain, but Luke seems even more vested in us since he reunited with his father. He's older than most of the other fellas, so it makes sense. I'm the one closest to his age, though.

By the end of our first round of 301—which I won despite Pay-man's posturing—I'd filled them in on what went down last night with Bree and our kiss—the full rundown.

"Let me get this straight," Ethan pauses, "you're back to being best friends…"

"Even though you kissed?" Elias chirps in, finishing Ethan's sentence.

I think those two have become a team off the ice, too. I'm beginning to understand why Mia calls Elias Ethan's work wife.

"Yeah." I thought I made that obvious.

Mason tilts his head at me. "But are you really?"

"What's your point?" I take a step in his direction, leaving less than two feet between us. I'm a few inches taller than Mason—taller than most of the guys—so staring him down is easy.

He shoots a nervous glance at Luke, who nods at him to continue.

Mason swallows as he returns his attention to me. "Does it feel the same? Like before?"

Talk about a truth gut-punch. I take a step back and rub a hand over my face. Less than twenty-four hours have passed, but the longing, the hunger I have for her is stronger than ever. "It's worse."

"You have to find a way to put that aside when we're on ice, Cowboy." Compassion fills Payton's expression.

Or is that commiseration? We all had a front-row seat, watching the Pay-man's reserved exterior crumble into a love-sick puppy, pining over his bodyguard.

But the implication that I could fail them hits a sensitive spot, like I just got cross-checked by my entire team.

I whirl to face him. "Don't you think I know that?"

Leaning away, he holds his hands up. "Whoa there, partner."

He's trying to defuse my anger—I get that, but it only makes this feel worse. It's as if all the things that matter the most to me are at risk—my relationship with Bree, my family ranch, and now hockey. I'd avoided a groin pull my entire career, but every hockey player knows our time in this game runs on a clock. I have some great years under my belt, but I'm in the second half of my run. So, I can't help worrying that this is just the first injury of many to come.

There's also the situation with my family. I still haven't told them about Nana wanting to sell our ranch. When I finally worked up the courage to call and ask her why she'd made this decision without talking to us, she told me she didn't want any of us to give up what we loved doing.

Still, it didn't sit right with me to let go of something that had been in our family for several generations, but Nana said it was time, and that was the end of the discussion. Like I said before, I get the part about her meeting someone and wanting to enjoy the remaining years of her life traveling and doing things she didn't get to do when she was younger. And I'm pretty sure her refusal to consider any other alternative is her way of ensuring my sisters and I don't sacrifice our dreams to fulfill some sense of duty.

But what if there's something more going on? What if she's sick and not telling us? Or is it about money? I don't make the big bucks like the NHL players, but I could tighten my budget, rent a cheaper place with a roommate, and delegate some of my income to help.

But would it be enough?

I can't find out for myself, though. Not yet, anyway. Our schedule is too tight until Christmas. Next week is Thanksgiving, but we have a game the day before and after, so there's no time to go home. Nana said she didn't plan to move forward until after the holidays, but waiting until Christmas to figure this out is almost torture.

"Is there something you're not telling us, Wade?" Luke's use of my first name grabs my attention.

Might as well get it all out in one go. "Nana—my grandmother—wants to sell our ranch."

A series of noisy breaths and low whistles fills the air.

Except for Luke. He grunts. "That's rough, man."

"Thank you for stating the obvious," I snap back.

His shoulders rise, and his jaw tightens.

I'm pushing his patience. Might as well say what's been banging around in my head like a ping-pong machine. "I may have to choose."

That's as much as I can say out loud, but judging by their faces, they know exactly what I mean. Even Mason gets it. And something in his expression makes me think he's dealt with a tough choice like this one in his past.

Pay-man hands me the darts. "Keep playing. Keep talking. We're going to help you figure this out, mate."

Chapter Twenty-Two

BREE

Somehow, I managed to avoid Wade at work today. After I went down to shoot some footage of the guys at practice, I zipped back to my office before they headed into the locker room for weight training. Except for the goofy video I filmed of Zayne loosening the tops of the water bottles at the players' bench, I made sure I stayed in the shadows so Wade didn't see me.

But if I don't talk to someone about what happened last night—not to mention Chase blackmailing me—I'm going to spiral down like I did after I found he was cheating on me.

Not that kissing Wade compared to my cheating ex—Chase never held me like that. Not by a long shot. Wade kissed me like a man suffocating, and I was the air his lungs desperately needed. A shiver runs through me just thinking about it.

I just wish I knew what it meant, if anything. Or *why* I kissed him. What was I thinking? I know the threat from

Chase has me reeling, but anytime I've needed comfort from Wade, a hug has sufficed. But in that crazy moment, I wanted more—needed more. And what really scares me? I still do.

Before I left his place last night, we talked about hanging out again tonight, but I think that was his way of reassuring me that we were fine, back to normal, even.

When Wade sent me a text earlier, telling me that he planned to go out with his teammates instead—that it was mandatory, whatever that means—I felt a little disappointed but also relieved. Until I can figure things out, figure *me* out, I don't know how to act around him.

We left things in a good place last night, mostly thanks to him. But I kind of hoped he'd bring it up, perhaps tell me he couldn't stop thinking about our kiss, too—in a good way because I can't stop thinking about it. About him. And I might as well confess that my thoughts don't resemble best-friend behavior.

Maybe he's avoiding me, too. I can't blame him, since I'm the one who practically threw myself at him. Did he kiss me back just to be nice? A pity kiss?

I can totally imagine him doing that, but then wouldn't the kiss have felt forced or stiff? If anything, it felt natural… inevitable. Like we'd kissed each other a thousand times before, yet new and exciting at the same time.

Not to mention hot. I had no idea he could kiss so passionately. Why would I? I never thought of him in that light except for a brief time in high school. It was fleeting, no big deal. I made myself get over it then, and I can do it again.

I'll rein in all these overwhelming emotions and return to my blissful state of thinking of Wade as only my best friend. Not a hot hockey player whose kiss set my world on fire.

That's why I need to talk to someone about 'the incident.'

I could text the girls. They added me to their group chat, The Puck Babes, despite my argument that I'm not in a relationship with a hockey player. Sophie argued that technically I was, since Wade and I are—were?—best friends, and Mia said I didn't have a choice because she liked the name too much to change it. Lily rolled her eyes at that one.

Trying not to overthink, I pick up my phone and open the chat, noting their tiny images sitting next to previous messages. They're amazing women, all of them. Strong and determined, yet compassionate and authentic. Even though I haven't known them that long, I feel like I can trust them to keep it between us.

But how do I text-splain I kissed Wade without them turning it into a thing? I put the phone down again. Maybe it *is* a big deal? Or maybe it just feels that way to me?

Groaning, I cover my face with my hands. I can't stop thinking about how my entire body came to life when Wade pulled me against him as a surge of excitement shot through me. How his lips felt—firm and commanding—over mine as he not only returned the kiss but took over like he owned me. And how much I liked every touch, every sensation. I've lost track of how many times I found myself staring at nothing, distracted at my desk while I relived every detail.

I pick up my phone again. I'll suggest a girls' night out and work it into the conversation organically. That'll make it easier, right?

After putting down and picking up my phone two more

times, I tap out a message to the group and hit send before I chicken out.

Bree: Feel like hanging out tonight?

Sophie: I'm always up for girl time!

Mia: And wine. Let's not forget the wine. I'm in the mood to celebrate.

Lily: What are we celebrating?

Mia: It's almost Thanksgiving, which means I get a break.

Lily: Sounds a little premature…

Mia: Trust me, it's not.

Sophie: Mia, you love your job, and you know it.

Mia: Whatever

Bree: So, is that a yes?

Sophie: Definitely

Mia: Packing up to leave work now.

Sophie: It's almost six on a Friday, and you're still at school. See? You love your job.

Mia: So do you, but even you said you need a break from time to time.

Sophie: Touché

I admit, these women can go off the rails sometimes, but I'm desperate to get this weight off my chest in exchange for some perspective.

Bree: Can we finish this conversation at the TT?

Lily: On my way. I'll get us a booth.

Sophie: Order hushpuppies.

Mia: And wine!

When I arrive, Lily's already here. She waves at me from the same booth we sat in last time. Four long-stem glasses of white wine stand like soldiers, guarding a basket of golden hushpuppies and several mini tubs of creamy tartar sauce. I grab the closest glass and gulp down half of it. Probably should have eaten one of those fried balls of dough they like so much first, since I skipped lunch, but I need some serious liquid courage right now.

Lily's brows shoot up. "That bad, huh?"

I nod, studying the varnished wood grain of the tabletop.

A distinctive giggle reaches us from the front of the restaurant. I spin around and watch Mia laugh over something Sophie said as they approach. Mia slides in next to me, and Sophie sits by Lily.

Like me, Mia grabs a glass and takes a gulp, then sets it down with a flourish and a sigh. "That's better. The world can carry on now."

Sophie rolls her eyes. "Good to know."

All business, Lily points at me. "She's in trouble."

The other two quickly sober and stare at me with concern.

Mia grabs my arm. "Are you pregnant?"

I jerk my head back. "What? No!"

She shrugs. "Lily said you were in trouble."

Sophie lets out an exaggerated snort. "Were you born in the fifties? *Being in trouble* doesn't have to mean that. And why would being pregnant automatically imply she's in crisis?"

Mia smirks. "I work with children all day long. Trust me, they're trouble."

Shaking her head, Sophie points at her. "And you love it because they're tiny versions of you."

Donning a winsome smile, Mia glances upward and shrugs. "Yeah, and I really love the mischievous ones."

I frown at her. "Why? Doesn't that make your job harder?"

She shakes her head. "More interesting. The pay sucks, so I have to find other perks."

"If you say so." Lily swings her attention to me and lasers in like an interrogator. "Now, spill."

Picturing how intense an encounter with her must've been back when she worked as a bodyguard makes me squirm in my seat. Normally, I don't see her at the arena unless she's running security for a game, and even then, she's in full 'don't-mess-with-me' mode.

I'd planned to bring up the whole "I kissed a Wade, and I liked it" topic organically. You know, a kind of drive-by admission you throw out the window and then speed away, hoping no one will actually hear you. But I need help to figure this out, and Lily just gave me the spotlight.

But in order to do that, I have to tell them the rest of

the story, about what led to the kiss, because out of context, my decision seems reckless at best and careless at worst. I may have already wrecked my friendship with Wade.

A deep breath for courage. Closed eyes to center myself. A long exhale of determination.

I bring up the incriminating photo on my phone and place it in the middle of the table. "That's not me."

Sophie gasps. "Who sent this to you?"

"My ex."

Mia drags it closer, studying the picture longer than I feel comfortable with. "I don't think it's completely AI-generated. Maybe photoshopped?"

Lily grabs my phone and pinches the screen in various places, enlarging parts of the image. I want to crawl under the table, even though I'm certain that body isn't mine, which makes me wonder about who the woman really is. Was she a willing participant? And if not, does she even know someone photographed her in such a compromising position? Chase would have no problem using this woman to get what he wants, just like he used me.

She hands my phone to me. "Can you email it to me at its original size? I suspect the man's face was altered, too."

When I first saw the picture, I was so focused on the woman wearing my face that I didn't even think to look closely at the player. Since I didn't recognize his face, I assumed he was a recent addition to the team.

I enlarge the image to see for myself. The profile of the man's face reveals only so much, which makes identifying him difficult. But when I move the picture down, I notice a piece of a tattoo on his torso below where the woman's side is pressing into him.

The moment I recognize it, my blood boils. "That's Chase."

All three lean in as I put the phone down and point to the partial design almost hidden in shadow. "Chase has a full-chest tattoo. Whoever did this missed that part. And I'm guessing the woman is Amber, the one he cheated on me with."

Mia's face twists into a frown. "*Eww*. So either he's using her, too, or she's a willing participant."

Sophie cringes. "Double *eww*."

Lily appears thoughtful. "What does he want from you?"

"A profile piece in USA Hockey Magazine. I used to have a contact there. I'd told Chase before I found out he was a jerk—"

"Scumbag," Mia interjects.

"Total douchebag," Sophie agrees.

"Sociopath," Lily adds, pointedly.

That one hits home because I know she's right. How could someone so easily play with the lives and emotions of others without having some remorse, unless they were incapable of feeling guilty on some level?

"He claims I still owe him that profile piece, even though I told him I don't have a contact there anymore."

Sophie straightens in her seat. "Technically, you do. Kind of."

"Oh?" I stare at her as if my life depends upon what she says next, and in a way, it does.

"They picked up the article I wrote about Luke last season, and Rebecca introduced me to Peter Orion, their chief editor, during a game."

I frown at her. "You'd be willing to write one about Chase?"

Her mouth slides into a maniacal grin. "Yes, but not the article he's expecting."

She swings her gaze to Lily in a silent exchange, then lifts a brow in question.

"I still have some contacts. I can get you a detailed analysis of the image by a known expert," Lily asserts.

Mia holds her hand up. "I'll proofread and handle moral support."

Tears cloud my eyes before I feel the burn. I've felt so alone and isolated in my attempts to deal with Chase and cut him permanently out of my life. And just when I was about to lose hope of ever being free of him, I'm discovering I'm not. I have a group of women who not only believe me, but are jumping in to help without hesitation.

I glance at each of them. "Thank you. I was going out of my mind trying to figure out how to deal with this alone."

Sophie reaches for my hand. "We've got your back, Bree."

Mia slings an arm over my shoulders. "Nobody messes with our girl. Right, ladies?"

Lily's smile turns calculating, as if she already has ideas. "Not without seriously regretting it."

Again, so glad that woman is on my side. Relief washes over me like the cool waves lapping the beach below the restaurant. I didn't expect to get help with Chase, just with figuring out my situation with Wade.

Might as well tell them that, too. "There's one more thing."

Lily narrows her eyes. "More?"

I let out a nervous laugh. "Yeah…something happened the day Chase sent me that image. With Wade."

Sophie gasps. "Oh no, did you tell him?"

Mia groans. "Did you show him the picture?"

I shake my head emphatically. "Good grief, no. I was too afraid of what he might do."

"Smart girl," Lily chimes in.

Mia side-eyes me. "Then what happened with Wade?"

I swallow down the ginormous lump in my throat and hunch my shoulders. "I kind of…kissed him."

Chapter Twenty-Three

BREE

"What!?!" Mia shrieks, drawing the attention of half of the restaurant.

"Kind of?" Sophie giggles, but then throws Lily an 'I-told-you-so' look.

Lily does an eye roll that starts from one side of her head to the other in a grand flourish before narrowing in on me.

I get the message, or rather, the command to explain myself. "I was so upset, and Wade was messed up about his nana selling the ranch. I guess we had a shared moment." I hold my hands up as if to assert my innocence, which I'm not. Innocent, that is. I was the one who instigated the kiss, after all.

They all sobered quickly, staring at me as if I dropped a bombshell, which I kind of did.

Sophie speaks first, concern coating her voice. "Why is his grandmother selling their ranch?"

The gawkers resume enjoying their meals, but three

very intent sets of eyes stare at me in expectation, demanding I explain.

I've done it now. Waving it off, I lean against the back of the booth. "I shouldn't have mentioned that. Not my story to tell."

Lily lifts a finely shaped brow. "But you did."

She's right. I did. "Then forget I said anything. Please?"

All three of them shake their heads.

Wade will have a cow if he finds out I told anyone before he's had a chance to process things and figure something out. I could pose it as if I were simply trying to help him. In all honesty, that's all it would be, anyway.

I've been banging around ideas to solve this predicament. I even dug through my boxes to find the album I'd created when I dreamed of opening up my family's ranch to the public for weekend events like horseback riding and a petting zoo during the spring and summer. My plan included event hosting for reunions and weddings all year long, and, in autumn, we'd rent part of the apple orchard on Wade's property for apple picking, which would include a stand selling apple fritters, hot apple cider, and apple cider donuts, of course.

I never had the chance to bring that dream to life, but who says this couldn't work now? It would take a lot, though, and since Nana doesn't want to run the ranch anymore, I doubt she'd be interested in doing it, anyway. Still, my heart aches to see the last connection to my family's history go away, too.

Mia turns in the booth to face me. "Is his grandmother sick or something?"

"No, nothing like that." I tug a hand from each of them into a knot of fingers on the table and cover them with mine. “Promise you won’t say anything to Wade, Ethan, Luke, or Payton. Swear?”

They all nod.

“She wants to sell the ranch and retire. That’s all I know.”

“Wade didn’t tell you what’s going on?” Mia asks.

I pull my hands to my lap and stare at them. “He didn’t really have a chance.”

Sophie mouths a silent ‘oh.’ “Because of the kiss.”

I shrug. “I guess.”

Still facing me, Mia leans her chin in her hand. “Yeah, let’s talk about that. Was it a good kiss? You know, the kind that’s nice and sweet. Or was it as hot as blazes?”

My cheeks burst into flames. I don’t have to see my face to know it’s beet red, giving her an answer without saying a word.

Sophie gasps yet again as she turns toward Mia, who’s wearing the biggest smile I’ve ever seen on her.

Mia holds her hand out toward Sophie. “Pay up.”

After digging into a bright pink wallet, Sophie hands over a dollar bill. “I hate it when you’re right.”

“I know.” Mia snatches and tucks the bill into her purse, grinning with satisfaction.

“A dollar? That’s it?” I don’t know why I’m offended. A dollar bet seems so minuscule compared to the impact this kiss could have on my friendship with Wade.

Lily holds her hands up in innocence. “I had nothing to do with it.”

I prop my elbows on the table and cover my face. “You guys, I don’t know what to do. I left Texas to get away from the mess there and start over. But all I’ve done is drag it here with me and create a new one as well.” I cross my arms on the surface. “What is wrong with me?”

Sophie's expression softens with compassion. "Nothing, Bree. We've noticed how Wade looks at you, and it's obvious that he feels more for you than just friendship."

Mia snorts. "So obvious. The man stares at you as if you're his next meal."

Could she be right? Has he always looked at me that way? And if so, why didn't I notice?

I reflect on the way Wade stiffened at first when I kissed him, making me realize what I'd done. But then he kissed me back, taking complete control. The memory zings through me to my core and makes my whole body heat. I never expected to feel anything for him again because I locked that part of my heart away years ago to protect our friendship.

How many times had I seen a high school romance flare and then fizzle by the time prom rolled around? I'd watched my parents, who started out as high-school sweethearts, do the same thing. Just took a couple of decades to reach the same conclusion.

But Wade and I aren't in school anymore. We're adulting, going after our dreams, and living our lives the best way we know how. This isn't peer pressure or a broken heart I'm afraid of. It's blowing up my life again and losing the one person who's always supported, encouraged, and believed in me.

Without Wade's compassion and gentle guidance, I don't know if I would have found a new direction or passion after my parents made it clear that selling the ranch—our home—wasn't up for discussion. They already had an offer by the time they told me, and I suspected then, as I do now, that they planned it that way so I couldn't talk them out of it.

"Hmmm." Mia dons a studious expression. "Why do you call Wade's grandmother Nana?"

I frown. "That's what he calls her."

"So do you." Her blue eyes pin me down faster than a bird with a worm.

"I think everyone calls her that." I snicker, trying to break the tension.

Sophie leans her face toward me. "Define everyone."

Wade, his sisters, me…

As hard as I try, I can't think of anyone else. Not the ranch hands. Not even my parents when we lived next door.

Just me.

Just me?

Appearing very satisfied with herself, Mia rests her chin on her hand. "Sounds like you two acted like family for a long time."

I frown again. "What's wrong with that?"

Leaning back, she shakes her head. "Nothing at all. But don't you see it? You two operate like a couple in so many ways already that I'm not sure why you seem so determined to keep Wade friend-zoned when he's clearly into you, and you've had a thing for him all along."

"What?! No… We're like brother and sister." I shake my head emphatically.

Judging by the disbelief on their faces, they're not buying it.

"Okay, maybe I had a crush on him briefly in high school."

Sophie's turn to examine me. "How brief?"

"Very." I shrug. "I knew it wasn't a possibility, so I shut it down. Fast."

Lily tilts her head. "Why?"

A nervous laugh bursts out of me. "Because it's Wade."

They all raise their brows at me like some symbiotic species.

"He's always been my best friend." I lift my hands in frustration. Why is this so hard for them to understand?

Sophie clasps my wrist. "Statistically speaking, about two-thirds of romantic relationships start as friendships, many falling in love before they even realize it."

"She did the research for an article," Mia interjects, "so she knows what she's talking about."

Lily leans over the table toward me. "You already kissed him, Bree. As much as you may want to, you can't undo that. So why not consider exploring what's clearly sitting between you two?"

Mia gives the other two women a knowing look. "I say there's no turning back now."

Sophie giggles. "Oh, this will be fun."

Lily chortles like a woman in the know and about to do harm.

The hair on my arms stands up. "What are you talking about?"

As if she's extremely proud of herself, Mia lifts her chin and purses her lips. "We're going to help you get your man."

My man? Are they nuts?

I can't even bring myself to talk to Wade, let alone flirt with him.

That's on the list, by the way. Lots of flirting. And not just the how, but the when, where, and what. I had no idea that many ways to flirt with a guy existed. By the time we finished dinner, the three of them had created a spreadsheet, using an app on Sophie's phone, that entailed a complete timeline, which she had already emailed to me. Of course.

Seriously, they're out of their minds.

There's no way I can do this. One, I've never had a serious boyfriend until Chase, and look where that got me. Two, this is Wade we're talking about. My best friend, as far back as I can remember.

And three? This is Wade! I wasn't in his league in high school, and I'm not now either. Not this gullible, stupid version of myself, anyway. The last two days have proven I'm still a blazing mess.

But I can't think that right now. As much as I want to fix things before I even consider something more between us, that's not happening tonight.

The puck drops in thirty minutes, and before that, we're revealing our new mascot, the results of the 'Name Our Arena' fan poll, and the 'Date a Hockey Player' charity event. And by we, I mean Rebecca, Zach, and me.

So, here I am, racing toward my boss's office to review the script one last time, while sweat trickles down my back. I had the perfect schedule planned until Zayne pulled another prank by detaching the oversized sunglasses from the new mascot costume and taping them to the Sun Kings logo in the locker room.

The guys thought it was great and asked if we could leave them there because it 'made them feel more connected to their identity as Sun Kings.' I mimicked a gag over that one as I ripped them off the wall, imagining the horrific expression on children's faces in the audience when they saw Stingin' Ray had no eyes.

Yeah, not on my watch.

Thankfully, we reattached Ray's glasses with no issues. I

just hope they don't fall off during his intermission appearances.

I shove that out of my mind as I push open the door to Rebecca's office, who's standing in the circle of Zach's arms and engaging in a rather sweet and intimate moment. They're both wearing the Sun Kings jerseys I had specially made for them for the event. Zach's has his old number on it from his playing days and 'Rebecca' across the back, while Rebecca is wearing her father's number and 'Zachary' on her shoulders.

"Oh, sorry!" I whirl around. "Should have knocked first."

Rebecca's laugh jerks me back. "No need to apologize. Zach seems to think the rules cease at five o'clock."

"If they didn't, I'd never get to kiss you until after the games."

"You two are so stinkin' cute, you know that?" I approach them, enjoying how easy it is to be around them, let alone work for them. "But you're going to be late if you don't go downstairs now for the presentation. The IT team has your mics ready."

"Tell them to get a third one ready." Rebecca eyes me.

Did they plan something without telling me? I have all the post and video reel templates ready to pop in images and upload them during the game. This could throw all my planning sideways. "What's going on? Who's it for?"

"You," she replies, her smile growing wider by the second as she holds what appears to be a folded jersey. "And you'll need this."

"You want me to help with the presentation?" I take the jersey, bunching the thick fabric in my hand as every nerve in my body fires with warning. This wasn't part of the plan.

"Yes. The fans should see the mastermind behind all the excitement. I think it's great for our brand, too, don't you?"

A surge of panic floods me, but this is the job I signed up for. "Sure," my voice squeaks out.

Rebecca glances at her watch. "She's right. We need to hustle."

I tuck the jersey into the crook of my arm as I text the crew downstairs to prep a third mic.

"Oh, Zach and I had another idea. Let's expand the 'Date a Hockey Player' to be part of a weekend extravaganza that will include an All Goalies game."

"Oh, I love that!" I flip open my tablet and start taking notes.

Zach grins in response to my excitement. "We know it's last-minute, but we can leave that part out of our announcements until we have an official event name."

Ideas flash through my mind, causing my fingers to fly over the virtual keyboard on my screen as I take notes. I stop tapping when an idea hits. "What if we called it 'Fire & Ice? Then we can add whatever events we want and make it a full-blown extravaganza."

Rebecca snaps her fingers and points at me. "Yes! I love that." She glances at Zach. "See? I had a feeling she'd be as excited as we are. Zach thought you might get overwhelmed making changes like this right before the announcements."

I shake my head. "Not at all. Things move and change fast in PR. Either you adapt or get caught with your pants down."

While Zach tries to hide his grin, Rebecca bursts out laughing. "I couldn't have said it any better myself."

Once we reach the staging area, I hand my tablet to one of the crew so I can pull on the jersey Rebecca had given me in the office.

A small gasp escapes my lips as I unfold it.

Rebecca gives me a semi-apologetic smile. "I wish I'd thought of this sooner, so we could have done something cute for your jersey like you did for Zach and me. But I figured this would work for now, and I don't think he'll mind."

She smiles and shoots Zach a knowing glance as I slip the jersey over my shirt. The hem falls just above my knees, making me glad I wore leggings today. Otherwise, I'd look like a baggy mess. Tingles dance through my body.

I can't believe I'm about to walk out on the ice, in front of a packed arena and every player on the team, with the name 'Pierce' branded across my shoulders.

Chapter Twenty-Four

WADE

I shift my weight from side to side, scanning the rest of the team as we stand in a circle at center ice. Spotlights dance all around us, except for the middle, where the Sun Kings logo—a blazing sun wearing a crown—remains dark. No idea what's about to happen because all we were told was to stay at center ice until instructed otherwise.

This must be Bree's design to make a proper show out of tonight's events for the fans, and for us, apparently. If we were communicating like we used to, I'd know. But we haven't talked since the evening she kissed me, despite my text asking her to call me so we could talk. She reassured me that everything was fine, adding a 'really' at the end of her reply with a promise to chat soon.

Yeah, nothing's fine anymore. She's avoiding me.

I get it. She's embarrassed. I am, too, to be honest. Not because she kissed me, but because I should have just told her how I felt instead of backpedaling and letting her friend-zone us again. Now I'm worried that if we don't talk about this soon, she'll do something impulsive like run away like she did in Texas.

A sour taste fills my mouth. Probably a good thing that several states separate me from Langston. If he lived closer, I'd likely be suspended from the league for inappropriate behavior by now, or worse. I still can't let that go. Not completely. What that asshat did to her…

The lights snap off, and the arena plunges into near darkness. I swear I can hear my own heartbeat over the crowd. The crescendoing notes of the song"*Radioactive*" fill the stadium until the bass kicks in, vibrating the place as if the ice has a pulse. Low lighting snaps on to reveal fog snaking across the rink, swirling with a life of its own.

The logo flickers and then…*boom*. Projected from above, flames burst out and dance around it, making center ice appear on fire. Gold and red blaze everywhere, bathing us in the onslaught as pyrotechnics explode from the nets on both ends of the rink, causing us to squint.

I raise a hand like I'm waving at the sun itself.

Totally radioactive.

The fans lose it.

Sudden bright lights illuminate the rink near the Zamboni door, where a red carpet covers the ice. Bree's voice carries through the speakers, presenting Rebecca and Zach as they step into the spotlight.

And then Bree walks out. "Ladies and gentlemen, welcome! I'm Bree Sutton, head of PR, and your Sun Kings have not one, not two, but *three* surprises lined up for you!"

Caught up in the hype, the crowd goes bonkers again.

With the biggest grin splitting her face, she pumps her fist in the air, daring them to get louder. And I'm totally enrapt. I've never witnessed her operating in her element, and she's incredible. I can't tear my eyes away as she makes a full circle, her full attention focused on the fans.

As her back comes into view, the shouts and cheers fade, leaving only the sound of my blood rushing through my ears.

She's wearing a Sun Kings jersey.

My jersey.

Why mine? And what does that mean?

The next thing I know, Stingin' Ray skates circles around us, making a big show of it as our arena ushers walk down the steps between the seats, handing out stickers and miniature plushies of our new mascot.

Most of the guys have neutral expressions on their faces, except for Ethan and Elias, who high-five Stingin' Ray when he skates past. I don't know who's in that suit, but the guy—or gal—is borderline psychotic. Kind of reminds me of the Flyers mascot, Gritty. I hope Stingin' Ray doesn't have freaky googly eyes behind those oversized sunglasses.

Bree's voice breaks into the music again. "And now the results of our 'Name the Arena' contest. We had nearly five thousand votes with one clear winner."

Whistles and cheers fill the stands. The upper-level LED boards flicker to life in a synchronistic wave, circling the arena with flashing waves and hints at the official name until the lights gather into letters, form the words, and flash as she declares the winner.

"Welcome to the Sunfire Arena!" Mic still in hand, she claps before handing things over to Rebecca.

"Good evening, everyone. We are so proud of our team and what we are building here in Sarabella. Of course, none of this would matter without the love and support of you, our fans."

More cheers erupt. The LED banners pulse with the words 'thank you' in all caps.

Rebecca smiles and waves as she waits for the crowd to quiet.

"You've all given us so much, and now we want to give something back to our beautiful community. Next month, we will hold our very first Fire & Ice Fundraiser Event." She winks at Bree, who beams at her, making me ache for that same smile to be directed at me again. The distance between us is killing me.

Standing to my right, Luke elbows me in the side. When I glance at him, he hovers a hand over his face. I get the message loud and clear. *School your expression.* I give him a quick nod and tuck my chin.

Rebecca continues, "We have an entire weekend of events planned for you, including a Date a Hockey Player auction fundraiser."

A series of gasps lead into an all-out riot of excited cheers. As I scan the fellas' reactions to that one, I see a mix of mocking leers to mild dread on their faces.

Rebecca hands the mic to Zach, who flashes a very broad white smile. "I'm so glad I'm spoken for."

Laughter peals out, then quiets, allowing him to continue. "As you all know, we have one of the best goalies in the league—Wade Pierce."

My gaze darts to Zach, who waves me over. I glance at Luke, who shrugs as if to say he has no idea about this, then tips his head in that direction, telling me to get moving.

I swallow the bile in the back of my throat and push off my left skate, leaving the circle to glide toward Zach.

He watches me as I get closer and spin around to stand next to him.

"Goalies are supposed to stay in the crease…but not this

time!" He pauses, letting the crowd hang on every word. "During the Fire & Ice event, we're throwing the ultimate challenge: an All Goalies Game! The best netminders from all over the country will form teams and face off in a mini playoff for a trophy. And if you've never seen it, picture our very own Wade Pierce, fully geared up," he gestures down my uniform, from leg pads to helmet, "fighting for the puck, taking shots on goal, and showing what it really means to defend the net!"

This time, the crowd not only cheers, but stomps their feet, too.

Zach mouths, "Thank you." Then he nods toward the team, letting me know I can retake my place.

As I skate toward the fellas, a chant breaks out from the stands.

Pierce! Pierce! Pierce!

Surprised, I slow my roll and lift my stick in acknowledgement. I've heard them do it for the Pay-man for obvious reasons, and for Jammer, but never for me.

As I get closer, the fellas tap their sticks on the ice in front of them, and several chant along.

I glide to a stop next to Luke, who lifts his chin, letting me know I should bask in the moment. To my left, Pay-man elbows me in the side while a cheeky grin spreads over his face.

Bree's voice booms through the arena as the rest of the lights turn on. "Let's play hockey!"

We skate off the ice, giving the crew time to clear the rink while they get ready to bring both teams out and do the national anthem.

Bree stands at the end of the tunnel with a huge smile. Her blue eyes appear glassy with unshed tears. And she's still wearing my jersey. It's not like she hasn't before. She wore one whenever she came to a game when I was in the junior league.

But it's different this time. Maybe because of the kiss I've replayed in my head more times than I can count. Or that she looked so confident and sure of herself out there. Like my old Bree.

Something primal crouches low in my gut, wanting the jersey she's wearing to be the truth, so everyone knows that Aubrey Sutton belongs to me.

When I'm about three feet away, she rushes forward and wraps her arms around me. "Wade, I'm so proud of you."

Without a care for who's watching, I drop my stick and pull her as tight as possible against my padding. "Did you guys plan that?"

She lifts her chin and stares up at me. "No, Zach just ran with it. The All Goalies Game was his idea—a last-minute addition. Isn't it great?"

I'm lost in the depths of her blue eyes and can barely remember my name, let alone give her an answer.

"Yeah, it is," I mumble.

She's so close—close enough to kiss. And I want to more than anything. Like a horse without water for too long and seeing the trough for the first time, I'd love nothing more than to dip my lips to hers and claim what I crave most.

But she's not mine.

Yet.

Something shifts inside me. A resolve to do whatever it takes to win her heart and make her happy. "You're wearing my jersey."

She pats my chest. "Rebecca sprung it on me at the last minute. I didn't even know I would be out there tonight, but she insisted."

I grin. "How could she not? You're amazing."

An adorable blush pinks her cheeks. Unless that was there before, from the coldness at this level. Either way, she's gorgeous.

She pulls away. "I have work to do, and so do you."

"Can we hang out after the game?" I know I'm pushing, but I need time with her.

She tugs the side of her lip in between her teeth, which only makes me want to pull her back and feel her mouth against mine again and kiss that freckle on her bottom lip that teases me all the time.

"Hang out or *talk*?"

"What's the difference?"

She snark-eyes me.

"Whatever you want, Bree. I miss you." I hadn't intended to say that, but I'm not sorry I did either. If I want her to know how I feel, I need to start telling her.

Her lips part as if she's surprised. Her chest rises and falls rapidly. Is it possible she misses me, too?

She nods. "Sure. We can hang out. I'll be waiting for you after the game."

And then she walks off without looking back while her words hum through my head like a promise.

I'll be waiting for you…

Chapter Twenty-Five

WADE

The fellas keep eyeing me as I rush through shedding my gear, showering, and putting my game-day suit back on. When they changed this requirement in the NHL, I'd hoped they would for the ECHL as well, but not yet. However, I'm kind of glad for it tonight. I want to look my best for Bree.

The sight of her in my Sun Kings jersey is seared into my memory. Seeing my name stretched across her back did something to me. Like every save I'd ever made, every hit I'd taken, was worth it just to see her wear something that said she was mine, even if she didn't mean it that way.

Luke eyes me as I slip on my jacket. "In a hurry?"

I shrug my shoulders to settle the fabric. "Just ready to celebrate our win."

We fought hard for that last winning point. Keeping my focus took everything I had not to let my thoughts wander to Bree and search the seats to see if she was still wearing my jersey.

But I resisted. Proved to myself that I can keep control of my mind and stay focused.

Towel wrapped around his waist, Ethan strolls by, punching me lightly in my side. "Cowboy's on a mission to wrangle his girl."

With a groan, I roll my eyes and stare at the ceiling. "Is this how it's going to be?"

All of them say yes at the same time. It's like they've made some kind of pact to orchestrate my love life.

"I appreciate the sentiment, fellas, but I think I can handle this on my own."

Pay-man and Jammer exchange looks.

I know what they're thinking, but just because their relationships started under complicated circumstances that seemed impossible at first doesn't mean they know how things should go for Bree and me.

Payton rises from the bench. "We disagree."

"We?" I gawk at him.

"Oui." Barbie-man winks as he says this.

Elias simply nods.

Grin tilted, Ethan shrugs.

Mason won't look me in the eye, and Zayne snorts.

Great. Just great. I'm surrounded by cocky toddlers.

"I'm out of here." I turn on my booted heels and head straight for the exit. Forget those guys. I'm going to take Bree wearing my jersey as a sign that her feelings for me are changing, growing into something more.

When I walk out of the door leading to the back hallway and the family waiting area, my gaze collides with her sparkling blue eyes. Her blonde hair frames her face, making her look like an angel.

But she's not wearing my jersey.

The anticipation I carried from the locker room turns to

sludge in my gut. I guess I thought if she still had it on, it could mean something more than a last-minute idea Rebecca threw at her.

But then I notice how her eyes are traveling up and down my suit in appreciation.

That's a good sign, right? Baby steps, and all that?

"Wade!" She rushes to me and takes my arm. "I'm so glad you're cleaned up and dressed already. The press is eager to ask you questions about tonight's game. Zach highlighting you caught their attention."

Disappointment wraps my chest like a belt and tightens. That's why she was assessing me when I walked out.

I remember Luke's gesture to control my face and take a deep breath. "Sure. No problem."

She walks with me into the press room, but waits by the door as I head to the front and take a seat behind the mic that's sitting on a narrow table. Beyond that, reporters fill most of the seats. It's not a large space, and the place isn't packed like an NHL press room, but the Sun Kings have drawn a lot of attention in the region.

"Wade, you looked surprised when Zach called you up tonight."

They read that right. The heat of that moment crawls up the back of my neck again as I lean in toward the mic. "I was."

A rumble of soft laughter breaks out.

The reporter's smile lifts on one side. "Care to expand on that?"

I run a hand over my mouth while I collect my thoughts. "The team is like an organism. We operate best as a whole. I guess I'm just used to sharing a spotlight with the fellas. Not on my own."

One of the female reporters lets out an *awww,* which

draws my attention to the back...and to Bree, who's watching me with an expression I've never seen before.

Curiosity for sure, but something other than intense interest. Could that be attraction—is she attracted to me? I vaguely recollect a time in high school when she looked at me like that, but before I could gather my courage and tell how I felt about her, she had a date with some other guy. I figured I'd just imagined it.

Another reporter asks me about my projections for the team, which leads to other questions about what challenges the Sun Kings might face this season. I give them the usual answers that basically say we're expecting a great season and plan to do our best to make the fans proud.

"Wade, will you be one of the players up for auction at the Fire & Ice event?" A dark brunette with eyes to match grins in anticipation as she waits for my answer.

I glance at Bree, whose smile appears forced now. "Yes, I'm happy to be part of something that gives back to the community that's given us so much."

"And what about the All Goalies Game. Can you tell us more about who will be there?"

Bree strides up and stands to the side of the table. "Those details will be released over the next few weeks as we formalize plans. Thank you, everyone."

Soft chatter fills the room. I join Bree by the door before following her into the hallway. The rest of the fellas stand by the exit, probably waiting for me to go out with them. I haven't had a chance to tell them I have plans with Bree.

But there's a question burning inside me that I have to ask. "Why'd you take off my jersey?"

Her eyes flash to mine, curious and questioning. "I took it off right after the game started. I didn't think it would look right for the team's PR person to show favoritism to one of the players."

I don't miss the caution making her sound guarded, and I groan at myself. Of course, she'd be more wary of something like that after what happened with Chase. "I didn't even think about that. I'm sorry."

She stops and grabs my elbow. "It's okay. It's just…"

"What, Bree-bear?"

Her gaze warms and settles on me. "I have to be careful, Wade. This is my reputation we're talking about. I love my job, and I don't want to do anything to jeopardize it."

Message received. She can't risk getting involved with a player again. I swallow down the shriveling hope clogging my throat. "I understand."

And I do. But what Bree doesn't understand is that I will do whatever it takes to show her we're meant to be together. That this wouldn't be some fling between a player and a staff member, and I'm almost certain Rebecca and Zach would support us.

I've loved her for years. Even though she's never seen me as more than a friend, I saw how she watched me during the interview, and I recognize attraction when I see it.

One way or another, we will be together. She just doesn't know it yet.

There's a reason they call it liquid courage. Two beers in, and I feel great. Confident. I've got this. That's what I'm telling myself, anyway.

I grab the darts from Ethan, who bombed his throw by hitting a triple nineteen, sending him over the amount he needed to win. And catch a distinct whiff of onion rings—

I've lost count of how many baskets he and Elias have put away.

All I need to win this game of 301 is twenty-four points. I bump fists with Luke for luck, because that's his number—24.

He obliges because he gets the connection. Plus, he knows there's no way he can garner a W. Besides, I'm pretty sure he'd rather I win than give Ethan bragging rights over Payton, who wound up more interested in his fiancée, Lily, and played distracted. Good thing he knows how to keep his focus when he's holding a hockey stick instead of a dart.

Mia and Sophie arrived a few minutes ago, so they're playing smoochy-face with Ethan and Luke. I can't help but chuckle at Mia's disgusted expression when she gets the full effect of Ethan's onion breath.

Since it's a weeknight, Steamers isn't as packed as it was last time we were here, although a low chatter of voices and clanking glasses creates a constant hum in the background. I'd hoped to spend a quiet evening at my place, hanging out with Bree. But when we caught up with the rest of the fellas after our brief chat in the hallway, she agreed to meet them without hesitation.

And a look of relief. But that told me all I needed to know—she's nervous about being alone with me. I'm not entirely sure why, but I have an idea, and I can work with that.

As Bree and Harper greet Mia and Sophie with smiles and hugs, I set the darts down on the nearby high-top table so I can roll up my sleeves. I left my jacket in the car when we arrived, but kept my sleeves down because of the chill in the air outside.

Bree mentioned once years ago that one of the things she found most attractive in men was a muscular forearm with tats. I happen to have both. And tonight, they are my weapons of choice.

As I finish, I catch her staring at me in my peripheral vision. I retrieve the darts, take my place at the line in front of the board, and plan my first throw. I could easily end this with one dart by hitting a triple eight. But then, she wouldn't get a full show, and we can't have that now, can we?

However, the fellas know me well enough, so I shouldn't make it obvious that I'm milking this for all its worth. Taking aim, I snap the dart loose, hitting the spot near the triple eight—a sixteen.

Ethan's eyes and mouth both widen as he guffaws. "He missed! Give the man another beer so we have a fighting chance."

With a dirty grin, Elias offers up his half-drunk beer to me, which I ignore.

I ready my next shot, keenly aware of Bree's eyes on me. This could go several ways. I could hit an eight and win, which is the expectation. If I were to change sides of the board, say to hit a four, six, or two so that I have a third throw, they'll think I'm just showing off.

Or I could hit a double eight, pretending to miss again, and give the rest of these idiots another shot at winning, but I'm too competitive for that.

The night's young, though. Plenty of time to work my magic on her. I flick the dart and hit the eight. Groans and snorts surround me as the fellas complain.

Yet Bree stands there, openly staring at me with narrowed eyes. I may have overplayed my hand. She knows how good I am at darts. That's because she's almost as good as I am. She'd probably tell you she's better, and she might be right.

But not tonight.

While I retrieve the darts from the board, she pulls the other four women into a huddle, which has the rest of us glancing at each other in confusion. Ethan appears amused after a minute, but Luke's expression mirrors the concern on Payton's face.

Not worry. More like dread. As in, what fresh hell are these women about to let loose?

I think we're about to find out.

Their huddle breaks with Bree at the lead. "We challenge you."

"Excuse me?" Anticipation tingles through me, much like when I'm in the crease and an opposing player heads toward me in a breakaway. The muscle memory makes my thighs and shoulders tense.

Mia crosses her arms. "You heard our girl. We're ready to show you guys who rules that board."

Payton snickers. "Wouldn't exactly be a fair fight, ladies. Wade and I are quite good."

Bree shakes her head. "One on one. I go against Wade. One round of Cricket."

As kids, we'd spend Saturday afternoons in the barn, holding our own dart tournaments. Ellie and Piper would last a few rounds before wandering off to more interesting endeavors, while Bree and I would keep the challenges going until we needed a bathroom break or food.

I don a slow smile as I tap a dart against the other two in my hand. "You're on."

She examines the various sets of darts provided by the establishment, most likely searching for the best weight for her smaller hands.

Barbie-man pulls me off to the side, a huddle of our own. "There's definitely a vibe between you two."

The hope I've held close pulses in my chest and grows. If they can see what I'm feeling, then I'm not off base.

But I don't want to jinx it either. "Just some friendly rivalry."

Elias snorts. "More like foreplay."

Luke jabs his elbow into his side, making Elias hunch over with an *oof*.

With a furtive glance toward Bree, who's standing at the throw line, practicing a few shots, Ethan leans toward me. "Is she any good?"

I nod. "Almost as good as me."

Zayne holds his hand out, revealing a twenty-dollar bill. "Let's make it interesting."

Luke grunts, pushes his hand away. "Not the time, man."

Even Mason's shaking his head.

Zayne splays his hands out, the twenty tucked between two fingers. "What? They have their *girl*. We're betting on our *guy*."

Before we can argue, he walks over to the women, who jump for their wallets, shocking all of us.

"They're vested." Luke pulls at the back of his neck.

Payton snickers. "Understatement of the year, mate. Lily's the most competitive person I've ever met." He wags his eyebrows. "Certainly keeps the relationship interesting."

We all groan.

Ethan drapes an arm over Payton's shoulders. "Happy for you, but TMI, bro."

While they continue to chirp at each other, I move to stand by Bree.

She lifts her chin, her blue eyes flashing with challenge and something else—desire perhaps?—I haven't seen before. "Ready to lose?"

Her sweet honeysuckle fragrance invades my nose, teasing me just like her words. I inhale her scent slowly, so she won't notice, and keep my expression steady. "I seem to recall winning the last time we played."

"That was a long time ago. I've gotten better."

Heat rides up the back of my neck and down my arms. Maybe Elias's comment about foreplay isn't too far off, but I can't let my head go there.

I lift my chin toward the board. "Prove it. Ladies first."

Her jaw clenches in that stubborn way she does when she's about to launch into a full-blown argument.

"For the bull-off." I hold up a dart to stop her retort. If she feels the need to prove something, I'm willing to play this out, her way, so she'll have no doubts about it being a fair game.

I win the throw to see who goes first, which rankles Bree but also seems to spur her on. The shouts of encouragement and ribbing from our friends fade into the background as I watch her every move. I'm tracking the board and our scores, of course, but I'm also stealing glances at how her jeans hug her hips and how her fitted T-shirt accentuates the curve of her waist.

She's so graceful, yet strong. Her throws are poised and targeted, hitting her intended mark with precision. She's right—she has gotten better at this game. Did she play darts with Chase?

The thought sticks in the back of my throat and sours. My next throw goes wide because of it, too.

She raises a brow at me. "What's wrong, Wade? Are you nervous about losing? I promise I won't rub it in your face too much."

I clench my jaw. Not because her comment bothers me, which it does, just not in the way she intended. I'm trying to control how my body is reacting to her. I may have been in love with this woman for most of my adult life—correction, *all* of my adult life—but I don't think I've ever seen her like this.

Sexy, bold, daring…

We continue this dance of precise throws and challenging barbs until we're both down to one throw to close our numbers. We both need an inner bullseye, something I can do easily.

However, I also know it's the most difficult one for Bree. It's the smallest space on the board to hit, and she used to always get it in her head if she didn't get those out of the way early on. My chest tightens at the thought of the pressure she's feeling right now, battling with my desire to win.

If she makes her shot, she wins because we're tied in points. If she misses, but I don't, which I know I won't, I'll win. And part of me wants to let her win—let her have her moment—so I can watch her strut a little more.

She takes position, wiggling her hips to get her feet right—and driving me crazy—then throws her shot.

And hits it.

The other ladies squeal, bouncing up and down as they hug each other. My cheeks tighten with my grin as they praise Bree.

Mia holds her hand in an 'L' shape to her forehead and then points at me. "Loser."

Worth it.

Behind me, the fellas intermingle some swears with their complaining.

I face Zayne. "Pay up."

With his tail tucked between his legs, he shuffles over to the women, roping an arm over Harper's shoulders, who then blushes as she shoots him a shy glance.

Interesting… But more so, Mason looks like he's ready to throttle him.

Not sure if this has happened before, but I make a mental note to mention it to Luke. We don't need *Zanie's* antics to wreak havoc with the family dynamics we have with the team and staff. We've worked too hard to recover from the scandal last year.

Ethan grabs my shoulder and leans in so he can whisper in my ear, "Did you let her win?"

I shove him off. "No, you bonehead."

Although I do feel a slight pinch of guilt that I had considered it, but Bree did this all on her own. She deserves the win.

And I intend to tell her that. I walk toward their group. Bree's back is to me, but her head is down. Mia, Sophie, and Lily stand around her, their smiles shifting to something else as I step closer, catching a glimpse of her phone.

A text pops up.

> Chase: I'm glad you came around. This will be good for both of us, don't you think?

I freeze in place, heart pounding so hard I can hear it in my ears. Is she getting back together with him? How could she do that after everything that creep did to her?

Sophie notices me standing there and quickly pushes her hand over Bree's phone. "Did you come to congratulate our girl?"

The happiness I felt for Bree's win turns cold in my chest. I force a smile when I'd rather grab her phone and toss it at the dartboard. Then I'd revel in watching it smash into pieces on the floor, joining what's left of my hope that I could ever make her see me as more than a friend.

"Of course. She got lucky, I guess." I hate myself for the barb, but I'm barely holding in my anger at this point.

Bree glares at me. "Never imagined you as a sore loser."

With a shrug, I turn away, tell the fellas I need to go, and then leave the bar, agreeing with Bree's statement every step to my car and on the ride home.

Because she's right, I am a sore loser. More than she'll ever know.

Chapter Twenty-Six

BREE

I still haven't answered Chase's last text.

Weary to the bone, I fall back on my bed. Harper's thumping around, getting settled for the night. I'll do the same as soon as she's done. Rooming with her has worked out great, despite sharing a bathroom. As an only child, I never had to share one growing up—not until college when I had an assigned roommate. And I had my own place before moving to Sarabella.

We lingered at the bar for a while after the guys left. Thankfully, Mia and Sophie came separately, and Sophie offered Lily a ride home so she could stay longer, too. After swearing Harper to secrecy, I gave her a semi-brief rundown of the Chase Files so we could talk strategy.

At first, I thought Harper would find the Chase Files unbelievable. She's so nice and innocent, but when I got to the part about Chase's latest attempt to blackmail me, this fierce side of her showed up, telling Sophie to annihilate him. That's when they filled me in on how Harper's father treated her as GM of the Sun Kings. She totally understood, which made me love her even more. She understands what it feels like to be used by someone who supposedly cares about you. I guess you could say we're bonding over our traumas.

After we brought Harper up to steam, Sophie helped me craft a reply to Chase, telling him I found a new contact—a photojournalist who freelanced for the magazine. All true. And that she would reach out to him to set up an interview. Also true.

When he didn't text back right away, Sophie instructed me to share her contact information with him when he did. My own dread compelled me to ask if she was sure about doing this, because I knew how awful listening to Chase's self-absorbed rhetoric was. She replied she couldn't wait to tear the scumbag apart with a gleam in her eye that made me even more nervous.

But now I'm second-guessing everything—even my friendship with Wade.

The heat between us tonight was undeniable, I'll say that. And unexpected. Wade's never acted like that toward me before—sexy…flirting…

I recognized it, too, from the times I watched him flirt with a girl in high school or with the puck bunnies when he played in junior league. But never with me. That's how I knew he wasn't into me, so I pushed those feelings away until they vanished. Until I only saw Wade as my best friend.

But what if those *feelings* never went away? How else can I explain the intense emotions I'm experiencing now? They seem so sudden, yet familiar at the same time.

A shiver runs through me as I remember how Wade leaned in to tease or taunt me during our darts faceoff, his lips grazing my ear as his warm breath caressed my neck.

His clean, spicy scent wreaked havoc with my resolve to keep us in the friend zone. As much as I love how the girls have encouraged me to take the risk and made that crazy spreadsheet to help, I still feel an intense need to protect our friendship. But after tonight, I don't know anymore.

Wade lost despite his efforts to unhinge me. I'm sure he only did all that to mess with my game, which only made me more determined to win. He always knew how to bring out my competitive side.

But the way he left…

The rest of the guys didn't stay long after that either. I think they picked up on the weirdness there at the end. Maybe they agreed with me that Wade was being a sore loser, but I suspect they're as concerned about him as I am.

He seemed fine until he walked over to our group. Good thing Sophie saw him before I did and covered my phone, or that could have turned into a very awkward—

I bolt up into a sitting position, eyes frantically searching but not seeing. Could Wade have seen Chase's text before Sophie hid it? That would explain the sudden shift in his attitude.

After I reply to Chase, giving him Sophie's contact information and telling him she'll be in touch, I switch to the Puck Babes chat.

Bree: He replied. I sent your info, Soph. He confirmed it, too.

Sophie: I'll call him early tomorrow and sound eager. That way, he thinks he's hot news and won't suspect a thing.

Mia: And you thought I was the maniacal one?

Bree: I hope this works.

Sophie: It will. Trust me.

Mia: If anyone can expose that poor excuse of a man for what he truly is, Sophie can.

Sophie: Why do I feel like we need a jingle to go with that?

Bree: (laughing emoji) Do your worst, Soph. Or should I say best?

Sophie: Both work (heart emoji)

Now, to ask the more important question.

Bree: Do you think Wade could have seen Chase's text before Sophie put her hand over my phone?

Mia: Still stressing over how he reacted to losing?

Bree: Yeah… That's not like Wade. He's usually more excited about my wins than his.

Sophie: Maybe it didn't matter as much then.

Bree: What do you mean?

Mia: Can I explain this one?

Sophie: Please do! I have an article to prepare (winky face). I'll keep checking back, though.

Mia: That was about more than a dart game, Bree. You were so focused on beating him, you didn't see the way he watched you more than the board.

Bree: He did?

Mia: Oh, yeah. The man is a total goner for you. Trust me, I know that look. Ethan stared at me the same way the first time we met, as if his brain turned to mush when he looked at me. He said he had never believed in love at first sight until he saw me.

Bree: Wow. This would be so much easier if Wade and I didn't know each other so well already. I can't read between the lines because they're all blurred.

Sophie: Oh, sweet analogy, Bree!

Mia: Such a word nerd.

Sophie: You know it, Diva!

Bree: What should I do?

Mia: Fight fire with fire.

Sophie: Hmmm, not sure I agree. Might be better if they were honest with each other rather than playing games.

Mia: I think the games are the best part.

An image of a phone number written larger than life in red lipstick across the arena plexiglass pops into the text thread. When I first met Mia and asked how she and Ethan met, she showed me the picture—one Ethan took and has kept ever since—telling me the entire story of their movie-worthy meet-cute at the arena and how she wrote her phone number, backward no less, after practice.

Mia: My favorite game of all.

Seriously impressive, but she's as bold and daring as they come, despite her insistence that she's a boring school teacher. As if. I think she uses her profession to hide the wild child she really is.

Bree: I'm not good at games.

Mia: Girlfriend, you totally disproved that theory tonight.

Bree: That was a real game. Not flirting.

Sophie: You forgot we had a front-row seat to the whole thing. And you, my friend, were flirt-challenging him as much as he was you.

Lowering my phone, I take a moment to reflect on the evening.

I did. I flirted with Wade and loved it. Too much, maybe.

Bree: Okay, I need moves, ladies.

Sophie: Opening the spreadsheet now.

Mia: Did we forget to add Harper to our chat? Or is she asleep already?

Bree: I'll fill her in. Again.

Which I do when we cross paths in the hallway, along with a promise to add her to the chat group. I think Harper needed friends as much as I did. And do.

Especially if things don't work out with Wade, and I lose my best friend for good.

Chapter Twenty-Seven

WADE

Ethan: Wade. Wade! (Mic tap) Anybody out there? Where are you, dude?

Matéo: Maybe he's asleep already.

Luke: Hey, man, you know you can talk to us, right?

Elias: Yeah, come on. Talk to us, buddy.

Ethan: Buddy? Since when do you call him that?

Elias: Just trying something new.

Ethan: Try again.

Deciding to ignore those idiots, I toss my cell onto the couch. Leaving the bar like I did—probably not a great idea. Because now I have to explain myself.

My phone chimes again. But this time, I know it's Bree because I assigned a unique sound for her texts and phone calls.

Bree: Are you okay?

Am I okay? Not really. The temptation to jump in my car, drive to Texas, and pound Chase into the ground so he won't bother Bree ever again overwhelms me to distraction. I have to keep reminding myself I can't let my team down. Regardless of the likelihood of winding up suspended or worse, incarcerated, for tearing that bastard limb from limb, we leave tomorrow for a six-game stretch lasting close to two weeks.

I want to tell her the truth, that the idea of her starting things back up with that scumbag shreds me to pieces. But that's not a conversation I can have with her right now. I'm too angry. Anything I'd say would sound more like an attack, and I refuse to subject her to that.

Dropping on the edge of the couch, I push my hands into my hair and hold my head. Everything feels like it's spinning out of control. First, seeing that text on Bree's phone, and then, during the ride home, Piper called to tell me Nana already has a potential offer for the ranch. Piper reassured me she's not doing anything until after the holidays, so we still have time to figure something out.

What, I have no idea, but add that to the steaming pile of crap living in my head that needs a bigger shovel than I can muster at the moment. I suppress a growl when my cell dings again.

Bree: Wade?

If I don't answer her, she'll keep texting or, knowing her, show up at my door, and I'm still too mad about that text I saw to have a reasonable conversation.

Wade: I'm fine.

Bree: Liar! Talk to me.

I start typing a reply, confessing I saw the text and asking her why she would want anything to do with him anymore. But nothing sounds right. No matter how I word it, I sound like a jealous boyfriend in a rage or a pathetic wimp dancing around my feelings.

One thing I know, Bree deserves better. She also deserves a reply. I latch onto the situation with the ranch as an excuse.

Wade: Piper called. Nana already has a potential offer.

Bree: Oh, wow. I'm so sorry. That has to be killing you. Why didn't you say something at the bar?

Easier to let her assume Piper called before I went to the bar to explain why I showed up in a crappy mood instead of admitting I text-dropped and can't handle the thought of her getting back with *him*.

Man, I can't even stand to think of his name, let alone say it.

Wade: Didn't mean to ruin the evening. I'm sorry.

The three dots appear, then go away. This happens several times, so either she's unsure what to reply, or she's writing a long message, telling me I had every right to be upset—a typical Bree-thing to say because she's so empathetic and caring.

Bree: You didn't. Want me to come over?

Short and sweet, and not at all what I expected. I'm guessing she hesitated adding that second line because she's still in avoidance mode. And I don't blame her, considering how I reacted when I first found out she was dating Langston. I need time to process this, so when she works up the nerve to tell me, I don't go ballistic and do something stupid that ends our friendship.

Wade: No, I'm going to bed. We have early practice, and then we hit the road afterward.

Bree: I forgot about that. Guess I won't see you for a while.

Is she relieved? She can figure things out with *him* without me giving her a hard time about it. That thought only pushes the knife in deeper. But at least I won't be around to see it.

Wade: Yeah, guess so.

Before she can reply, I send a text to make it clear I'm done talking. It's better for her…and for me.

Wade: Night, Bree-bear. I'll call you when I get back.

More cycles of bouncing dots. Part of me wants her to

push for answers. The other part doesn't want to risk losing her. This kind of conversation is hard enough to navigate without seeing her face to gauge her reaction, so telling her the truth in a text is a solid no. But I also know I can't pretend I'm not in love with her anymore, and I certainly can't lie. Probably a good thing that I'll be gone for a while so I can work on getting my head straight.

And come up with a plan.

Bree: Okay. Night.

I toss my phone down again, contemplating going to bed like I told Bree or running on the treadmill to relieve the powder keg building in my chest. The TV catches my attention, so I pick up the remote, searching for something distracting to stream, but nothing appeals. I'm too amped up to sleep, so treadmill it is. Better yet, the air felt crisp and clear when I got home. A nighttime jog should do the trick. I'll run until I'm ready to drop, shower, and then pass out for the night.

As I head to my bedroom to change, a knock at my front door stops me in my tracks. With a growl, I pivot in that direction. What if it's Bree? Can I face her right now when all I want to do every time I see her is crush her against me and taste her lips again? To whisper in her ear how long I've waited for her to see me as more than a surrogate brother, delegated to the best friend zone and that I go out of my mind when I think of her back with *him*.

Another knock, this time heavier and followed by Ethan's muffled voice. "Come on, Wade! We know you're home. Your car's here."

I yank open the door. All the fellas stand there, staring back at me—even Zayne and Mason.

"Shouldn't you idiots be asleep by now? We have practice in the morning." I shoot a scathing look at Luke, our captain, who should be the one saying that. Not me.

He grunts.

Well, isn't that great. Instead of facing Bree, I get to deal with these goons.

Zayne brandishes a toothy grin. "Aww, he called us idiots. Guess he likes us after all."

Mason elbows him in the side. "Not the time, man."

Hands in his pockets, Ethan shrugs. "You didn't answer our texts."

"I was going to bed." I shoot back.

Elias points to my clothes. "But you're still dressed."

"I would be undressed and in bed by now if I didn't have a bunch of mother hens clucking at my door." I don my best glare, telling them to leave me alone, but they're not moving.

"We didn't cluck, we knocked," he tosses back.

With a sigh, I open the door wider. "Whatever."

Ethan brushes by first, then the rest file in, making chicken noises under their breath.

As Payton would say, 'cheeky bastards.'

I shut the door and turn around. Again, they all stare at me like I'm Humpty Dumpty about to take a great fall. Maybe I am. And they're waiting to pick up the pieces as we do for each other.

But not like this. These cracks are deep, and I'm not sure there will be anything left worth reassembling. "I'm fine."

Elias shakes his head. "No, you're not."

I clench my jaw. What's the point of talking about it? Nothing I say will change the situation, and rehashing it hurts too much.

With another grunt, Luke crosses his arms, making his point without saying a word.

"I don't want to talk about it. I'm going for a jog."

Mason frowns at me. "I thought you were going to bed."

"Changed my mind." I disappear into my room to change, hoping they take the hint and leave.

Ten minutes later, I walk out of my bedroom to find a group of men changing clothes in my living room. Several gym bags dot the floor at their feet as they replace shirts and pants with athletic attire. Last spring, Luke, Ethan, Elias, Mathéo, and I started keeping duffels in our trunks for evening runs on the beach after we went out.

"What are you doing?" I growl.

Elias gives me an incredulous look. "Going with you, bro. What else?"

Still in his button-down but wearing a pair of gym shorts, Zayne holds his hands out to his sides. "Barbie-man loaned me a pair."

With obvious distaste on his face, Mathéo tosses him a worn T-shirt. "They're yours now, man. I *do not* want them back."

Mason sheds his dress shirt, leaving him in a white undershirt and jeans. He lifts a shoebox holding a pair of new running shoes. "Glad I forgot to take these out of my trunk."

How can a moment be ridiculous and meaningful all at once? I pause to take in the sight of these guys changing clothes in the middle of my living room, trading a quiet night at home to go for a run with my sorry ass. They said before that they had my back. Guess I need to believe it.

I duck into my bedroom and grab an extra pair of shorts, then toss them at Mason when I return. "Here. And I don't want them back either."

They exchange grins, thankfully acknowledging my acceptance of their presence without my having to say it.

Grabbing the single key I keep handy for when I go for runs, I hold open the front door. "Bree's getting back with her ex. And that's all I'm going to say."

Their faces go slack. The looks they give me aren't pity, which would have sent me over the edge, to be honest. They simply get it. Zayne appears to be the most affected, leaving me to wonder what he's been through with a woman.

As each one files past, they bump fists with me. No words. Just solidarity.

And then we jog into the night, in silence.

Chapter Twenty-Eight

BREE

"I don't think this will work." I stare at my reflection in the dressing room mirror, taking in the full effect of the very short, form-fitting dress the girls talked me into trying on.

According to the tag hanging from my left armpit, it's a micromini that covers less than some bathing suits I've owned. The hem barely reaches below my nether regions, so bending over would be a definite no-no for obvious reasons.

And don't even get me started on the top part of the dress. One wrong move and I'll end up charged with indecent exposure. I feel like a Barbie doll in this thing because the only way I can move without exposing myself is to remain straight as a board.

Since Wade and the rest of the team are traveling through Thanksgiving, the girls and I decided to do some shopping today, and then do our own version of Friendsgiving tomorrow that includes homemade pizzas, our favorite chips and dips, and boatloads of ice cream with not a single turkey or pumpkin pie in sight.

Needing a break, Mia's parents opted for a cruise this year. Sophie's 'funcle'—favorite uncle—is out of town on an assignment, covering for the paper's lead reporter who just had a baby. And Lily doesn't have any other family, except for her former partner, who is at some undisclosed location, working as a bodyguard for a foreign dignitary. Sometimes I wonder if Lily misses that life, but she assures us she has her hands more than full with Payton.

And then there's Harper, who isn't on good terms with her father and has no desire to entrench herself in her family's drama. When she found out I didn't have to travel with the team this trip, she attached herself to my hip.

I'm not complaining, though—quite the contrary. I'm grateful for each one of these women—my girls, as I've come to think of them. Otherwise, I'd be completely alone tomorrow, feeling nostalgic about Nana's juicy turkey and fixings.

Technically, I could have gone back to Texas. Wade's Nana has invited me for Thanksgiving dinner every year since my parents divorced and sold our place. I didn't go last year because Chase insisted we go to his parents, and no way would I go this year and put myself in close proximity to him.

The jerk already texted me earlier in the week to let me know—aka gloat—about the article Sophie's writing about him. Wish I could be a fly on the wall to see his face when that piece drops. And then he had the nerve to invite me to join him and Amber for his family's annual deep-fried turkey dinner. I'm sure he was fishing around, trying to find out if I was returning to Texas so he could drop in unannounced just to torture me.

So, here I am, wearing this ridiculous dress for some

vague purpose that involves Wade and an event that Sophie has yet to explain.

"Seriously, this is a joke, right?" I try to imagine Wade's reaction if he saw me in this. He'd rip off his shirt—better yet, his jersey—and pull it over my head.

Why does that thought make my pulse skyrocket, and my stomach flutter? Maybe because I noticed how Wade's eyes scorched and then devoured me when he saw me in his jersey for the big mascot and arena name reveal. I've tried to forget the way he looked at me, but his expression haunts my dreams of late.

On my right, Sophie's reflection blinks back at me.

Mia stands on my left. "You need weapons."

From behind us, Harper bounces up, trying to get a better look. "Girl, you *have* to buy that one. You'll have his eyes bugging out faster than a half-naked pirate gawking at a virgin."

We all turn around to stare at her, me holding the top of the dress in place so that my *other* girls don't try to make an appearance.

Sophie clears her throat. "I think we just learned something new about you, Harper."

Mia gives her a sassy appraisal. "Girl, we need to talk."

Ready to bail, I grab the hem, ready to pull it off right in the middle of the open area of the dressing room.

All three jump to stop me while Lily's reflection in the background leaps up from the chair where she was observing from and stands guard at the dressing room entrance. A woman with an armload of clothes approaches but scurries away when Lily barks at her to leave.

Sophie tugs me toward my dressing room, where a stack of sexy clothing I would never choose for myself waits for me to try on. "I get it. You're nervous, but do you want to live the rest of your life wondering?"

Feeling a tad mischievous, I turn her words on her. "Wonderland could be fun. Ask Alice."

She snorts. "Sometimes I think you missed your calling to be a writer."

Mia shakes her head. "She makes good money in PR. Why would she pursue that?"

Pointing at herself, Sophie scowls at her. "Excuse me. Writer here, and I make a decent living."

"Yes, but you report on needed information, both visually and in writing. Most authors have to keep a day job to pay the bills. Trust me, I've looked into it."

"Same." Harper nods her head, a knowing expression on her face. At our probing stares, she shrugs. "What? I wanted to write romance novels."

Mia snorts. "That explains the pirates."

Ignoring her, Sophie nudges me forward and pulls the curtain closed. "Try on that flowery one next. It's very feminine and flow-y."

Flow-y? I can do that.

After shedding the 'sex-me-now' dress, I do as she says, slipping the silky garment over my head, and loving the feel of it on my skin. The fabric hugs the curve of my waist and hips, then flares out mid-thigh. I turn back and forth, studying the way the tea-length skirt flows around my calves and how the ruched bodice does my girls justice without giving away the goods. The dress is still as sensual as the other one, but in a more subtle and sophisticated way. And it makes me feel sexy without putting me into the sex-worker category.

I can't suppress my grin as I shove open the curtain, its metal rings screeching over the bar as I step out.

Harper's eyes widen. "Oh, that's gorgeous on you."

Sophie nods. "Yep, we have a winner."

Frowning in her indecision, Mia tilts her head. "I still think the other dress would do a better job."

My nerves spike into the red again. "When am I even going to wear this? It's too dressy for work. And people wear shorts even to the nicest restaurants here."

Sophie waves me off. "We'll figure that out later. The goal today is to change some things that will help Wade decide he's tired of being in the friend zone and make a move."

"Right, like when I kissed him, and then *he* apologized for kissing me back. Yeah, a dress will work way better than that." Thick sarcasm drips from my voice.

Mia rolls her lips between her teeth, trying not to laugh.

Harper glances between them. "She has a point."

I splay my hand out toward her. "Thank you."

Sophie blows out a frustrated breath. "I have a plan…" She groans as she wags her hands. "But I didn't want to say anything until I figured out the details. I told my friend, Char, at the paper about the dating auction and about you and Wade. She's agreed to bid on him, but when he arrives to pick her up for their date, you'll be waiting for him in *that* dress."

"Huh." Lily crosses her arms. "As Payton would say, that's bloody brilliant."

Sophie makes a show of mock-bowing. "Why, thank you."

I'm still not convinced this will work. "What if your friend doesn't win the auction?"

She releases a long and noisy breath. "But what if she does? It's worth trying, don't you think? Like I said, I haven't worked out all the details, but I will. One way or another, you and Wade will wind up on that date together."

Harper nods in agreement.

My doubting self looks to Mia, hoping she'll have something to counter this plan that sounds straight out of a Hallmark movie.

She simply shrugs. "At this point, you have nothing to lose, babe. I think it's worth a shot."

Traitor.

Wade

"This is the most ridiculous plan I've ever heard of."

I thought we were going to play cards on the way to Atlanta when the fellas told me to sit at the table booth in the back of the team bus. Not make up some ridiculous plan to trick Bree into a date.

Mason holds his hands out. "Which part? My sister bidding on you at the auction, or you going on a date with your girl?"

"She's not my girl," I growl, more out of frustration that it's the truth than the idea of sideswiping her like this.

"Yet." They all say it at the same time. And the rumble of the bus's accelerating motor punctuates their point.

For a moment, I thought Bree might take a chance on me, but then she backpedaled us into the friend zone again. Or I did. Things got weird so fast, I'm not even sure anymore. And I know her—she doesn't like surprises especially after her parents dropped the bombshell on her about selling their ranch—her home.

While she was in college, I surprised her by showing up at her dorm. I was between games and in the area…close enough, anyway. Between studying for finals and working as a bartender at the local watering hole, she'd sounded worn out and down when we talked on the phone. I figured I could take her out for dinner, help her get away from it all for a few hours.

I'd expected a surprised reaction. Maybe even imagined her throwing herself into my arms because she realized she missed me more than just a friend. Silly, I know, but a guy can dream, right? Instead, she glared at me, asking what the hell I was doing there.

After she calmed down, she finally agreed to take a break from studying and grab a quick bite with me. Quick being the keyword. Afterward, she thanked me, of course, but man, I learned my lesson.

I glare at Mason. "What if your sister doesn't win, and I wind up going on a date with some random chick—or worse, a puck bunny—who I have no desire to spend an evening with?"

Elias's grin turns downright lascivious. "Would that be so bad?

"Yes! It would." I hold my hands out from my sides in exasperation.

His expression becomes sheepish. "Just thinking ahead. If things don't work out with Bree, maybe something good could happen with this other woman."

Mason pokes him hard in the chest. "That's my sister you're talking about, Brunner, and she's engaged."

Elias shoves his hand away. "I was talking about the other woman. Not your sister. Chill out, man."

Ethan scowls at Elias. "There is no other woman, doofus." Then he pins me with the same look of determination he had when he told us Mia was the one. "Trust me on this. It will work."

What other options do I have? Bree keeps avoiding being alone with me, and I'm desperate enough to risk her wrath over surprising her like this. I'm just not clear on how they intend to make the swap.

"How will you convince Bree to go on the date?"

"That was going to be my next question." Mathéo frowns.

Zayne tries to appear casual but fails. "I'll ask her out, but Wade will be the one who shows up for the date."

I don't like the sneaky expression on his face. Is he interested in Bree?

"You get anywhere near her, and I'll make sure you never pull another prank, let alone hold a hockey stick again, *Zanie*." I snarl out his nickname, so he has no doubt that I mean business.

He holds his hands up. "Just trying to help."

With a grunt, Luke drags him back a step by the collar. "Stay in your lane, bro. Besides, that would still mean Wade would have to go on a date with whoever wins him in the auction."

Zayne's expression shifts from confused to thoughtful, then settles into mild embarrassment. "Oh, yeah, I guess it would."

I lean my head on the seat. "Like I said, stupid idea."

Ethan shakes his. "No, it's perfect. Bree will have to be there to take pictures and video of the date for the fans."

Elias's eyes widen as he snaps his fingers. "But Mason's sister won't be there."

"Exactly," Ethan confirms, then looks at me. "And then you'll tell her."

I lean forward. "Tell her what? That she's my date?"

A sinking sensation fills my gut. I can already picture the rage on her face as she realizes her carefully planned PR event took a U-turn. She made it clear how much she loves her job and how important her reputation is.

I don't want to be that guy. The one who messes things up for her because he's too focused on what he wants instead of what's best for her. Like her douchy ex.

"That the plan was always *for her* to be your date. Women love that kind of thing." Ethan's excitement is almost contagious.

Almost.

"What thing?" Elias asks him.

Ethan rolls his eyes at him. "You know, finding out they were always the one."

"Oh yeah, they do." Elias takes on a goofy expression. And he kind of looks like the Disney character Goofy, too.

I shake off the image and this nonsense. "You fellas are off your rockers. This won't work."

But then Luke surprises all of us. "I think it will. And you're an idiot if you don't try."

Chapter Twenty-Nine

BREE

Planning the Fire & Ice event kept me extremely busy and blissfully out of my head. Rebecca told Harper to act as my dedicated assistant until the extravaganza was over. More often than not, Harper and I wind up eating takeout at the arena while we work through dinner. Then we go home and crash, only to do it all over again the next day.

So far, this crazy scenario has kept me distracted, except when I'm lying in bed at night. That's when he invades my thoughts. Not the Wade who's my best friend, but the Wade who kissed me back as if I were…his.

I keep reliving the moment he took control, the feel of his lips against mine, tender yet passionate, capturing a part of me—of my heart—I didn't even realize was waiting to be claimed. And I can't stop remembering how natural it felt to be in his arms, as if I belonged there all along.

Like it was just a matter of time…

But the moment I try to picture us as more than best friends, I backpedal—afraid this is all just a reaction to realizing how Wade *might've* felt about me for years.

I've lost count of how many times I've shaken off this line of thinking because I wind up spiraling down into a place where nothing makes sense. It's like the harder I try to zero in on what I'm feeling for Wade, the more everything slips out of focus, blurred and hazy.

How do I know if these growing feelings for him are real, or simply a reaction to what my new friends insist is true—that Wade *loves* me? We've always been close, the best of friends. Could they be mistaking that friendship for something more than what it is?

With the Fire & Ice event looming closer, I've had to turn down Wade's invitations to 'hang out'—whatever that means for us right now. Even though we haven't exactly had a lot of time together lately, our brief interactions at work feel…different as if something's building between us.

That's the problem. I don't know how to define us, or what's happening between us. Sure, I'm attracted to Wade. I mean, most women are. The man is a total smoke-show, no argument there.

The other downside of being this busy? No real time to spend with him, so I can figure out if we could actually be 'a we.' Until this event is over, I can't risk losing my focus. Rebecca and Zach have entrusted me with most of the details, and I don't want to let them down. Everything needs to go perfectly.

I refocus on the spreadsheet on my computer screen, checking the application count for the All Goalies Game. Zach had the idea of not just one game but four, with four teams battling for a trophy he's having specially designed for the event.

The first day will feature two games, followed by the Date a Hockey Player auction in the evening. Then on Sunday, the two winning teams will play for the trophy. We also have events planned during both days for families to take part in and clinics for the local hockey youth wanting to up their skills. The married players, who for obvious reasons aren't participating in the auction, will run those.

Considering the big weekend is less than a week away, and my to-do list keeps growing, I don't see how I'll settle the looming question about my feelings for Wade anytime soon. And maybe that's for the best. I don't want to get swept up in some imaginary fairy tale romance and lose my best friend, who probably thinks I'm avoiding him again.

I let out a long sigh. Maybe I am…avoiding him. Apparently, I'm the worst friend on the planet, too, because I should know better than anyone how he feels about the decision to sell their ranch, yet I haven't pushed him to open up and talk about it.

Maybe because it still hits a raw place for me, too.

When I called Piper to check on her and Ellie, to see how they're handling it, she sounded heartbroken but resigned. I understand the logic—Nana doesn't want the grandchildren she raised like her own to give up their dreams. She knows firsthand what that kind of sacrifice means, and now she has a chance to live a little herself.

That woman has always inspired me to reach for my dreams, too. Although, I wonder if I settled for an easier path. Don't get me wrong, I love the PR work I do, but sometimes I want to create something bigger, larger than life. The creative freedom Rebecca has given me has been wonderful, and I've loved planning these events for the Sun Kings, but there's still a part of me that longs for something of my own.

Like the dream I had for my family's ranch, to create a place where people could celebrate life-changing events like weddings and family reunions, or just spend a day experiencing new things like apple picking in an orchard, candle making in the barn, and horse or carriage rides through cozy paths lit with twinkle lights.

I remember sharing all of this with my parents only to get turned down, and I hadn't even gotten to the best part —a holiday wonderland that included a mini Christmas village with local vendors, snow machines, and plenty of goodies like hot cocoa and spiced apple cider, as well as vendor booths filled with handmade and unique gifts perfect for shopping for loved ones.

What if I'd pushed harder, stood my ground, and made my parents see it would have worked? That *I* could have made it work?

A knock at my office door draws my attention upward. Wade stands in the doorframe, staring at me. A sparkle dances in his eyes, making them appear more green than hazel, and his tilted smile makes my breath catch. He's wearing a pair of dark denim jeans, belted, with a white cotton T-shirt tucked loosely in the front. The short sleeves hug his defined biceps, and he has one hand nestled into the top of his front pocket, drawing my eyes to the tattoo trailing over the corded muscles of his forearm.

Since when do I notice things like this about Wade? And has he always looked at me like that? Heat courses through me, and a longing that makes my heart squeeze so tight in my chest, I can't breathe.

He holds up a bag, making his muscles flex, and my lungs constrict further. "I brought dinner."

"How'd you know I was here?" I can't help the smile spreading on my lips as I point to the chair in front of my desk. I'm just happy to see him, that's all. Plus, I skipped lunch, so I'm starving.

"I stopped at your place first, but Harper said you were still here."

He waits for me to clear space on my cluttered desk, then takes out several containers of Chinese food and lines them up in front of me. The tangy aroma of orange chicken makes my stomach growl and my mouth water. He knows that's my favorite—because he's my best friend, and of course, he would, right?

I open the container and inhale with a sigh. "I told Harper to go home and get some rest. We've been burning the candle at both ends, getting ready for the Fire & Ice event."

He glances at me as he sets a paper bag holding egg rolls on the desk. "So…you're really not avoiding me?"

A pang of guilt clenches my heart as I squirm in my seat. "No, not at all."

He raises a brow at me.

"Really."

Both brows lift this time.

I sigh. "Okay, maybe a little."

He nods thoughtfully. "Because of the kiss?"

"Because *I* kissed *you*," I rush to clarify. "Yet you're the one who apologized when I should have. I'm sorry."

He doesn't say anything, but judging by the tic in his jaw, I know I hit a nerve.

And that tells me everything I need to know. I crossed a boundary and should have said so sooner. "Wade, I don't want things to be weird between us."

His gaze softens as he studies me. "I don't want that either."

"Then, are we good? Because I really miss my best friend." Even as I say the words, something settles in me. As much as the Puck Babes would argue with me, this is the right path. My head is still a mess from Chase. If I were to get involved with Wade like that, how would I know it's real and not just me getting caught up in some fictionalized romance that exists only in my mind? Or worse, a rebound?

Guess I'll be taking that dress back to the store.

"Sure." Disappointment clouds his face. He grabs a pair of chopsticks and jabs them into the container of pork lo mein.

"Thank you," I whisper. He has to see this is best for both of us, at least for now. I need to figure out what my heart really wants.

His expression remains tight as he stares at his food, poking the noodles but not eating. I can't help but wonder if he's thinking about his nana and the ranch. I've been so busy with the event, I didn't make time to check on him. Or maybe I was afraid to.

I finish chewing a juicy bite of chicken. "I spoke to Piper yesterday."

His gaze shoots up and connects with mine. "Yeah?"

Is that hope I see in his eyes? Does he think I have news or a solution to their impossible predicament? "She sounds resigned."

His pained expression sends an ache through me, making me wish I hadn't brought it up. He clears his throat and sets his container on the desk, pushing it away, untouched.

I can tell he wants to say something, so I nibble on an egg roll, giving him time to speak what's on his mind. That's the least I can do for him, for my best friend.

"I don't know what to do." He scrubs a hand over his mouth as if to wipe away an unspoken thought.

"Maybe you don't have to do anything."

Something hard flares in his eyes. "I can't just let this happen."

"Have you and your sisters discussed any options?"

He shakes his head. "Not really. Some. Nothing helpful."

His words tumble out, making him sound more like a lost little boy than the formidable goalie filling the chair in front of my desk.

The urge to hug him overwhelms me, but I fight it off. We don't need a repeat of that accidental kiss—what I'm choosing to call it—when we're both feeling so vulnerable.

I take a deep breath and muster the courage to say something he might not like or want to hear. "Would it be the worst thing?"

His gaze locks onto mine like a vice I can't escape. "What do you mean?"

A wave of sympathy overcomes me for any player who faces him on the ice. The man can be outright intimidating if he wants to be. But I'm not about to back down yet.

"You have a life here. Piper is killing it, playing for the PWHL, and Ellie wants to live and work in LA. Maybe Nana is right about wanting all of you to step into a new chapter in your lives." As soon as the words leave my mouth, I regret them because the rising color in Wade's face almost matches the orange chicken.

Maybe he isn't ready to hear this yet. I can't bring myself to tell him I called Nana to talk to her myself. I figured I could be a voice of reason, for Wade's sake. But after hearing her out, I could only support her. She's not just doing this for herself; she's doing it for all of them.

A muscle in his jaw pulses. His eyes dart back and forth,

as if he's barely keeping control. "It's been in our family for three generations."

The gruff pain in his voice tells me more than his words. But his expression reveals how conflicted he is. Does he want to keep the ranch out of some misguided sense of duty?

"I know, but you've never expressed an interest in running the place. And you're one of the best goalies in the ECHL. Do you really want to give that up?" I know I'm pushing him into uncomfortable territory here, but isn't that what best friends do for each other?

He pushes up from his chair. "I'm tired. I think I'll head home."

"But you haven't eaten anything?" I blink up at him, bewildered by his sudden desire to leave.

"I'm sure Harper can help you with the leftovers." He attempts a tight smile. "I'll talk to you later."

And then he's gone. As is my appetite. I dump the rest of my egg roll into the container of orange chicken and plop it on the counter. Guess I should have let him talk more before suggesting he let go of his family home. I should have been more sensitive and less practical, especially considering I went through the same thing. Granted, my parents bought the ranch after I was born, so we didn't have a generational claim, but still, that was our home. And no place has felt like it since.

Sighing to an empty office, I pack up the containers and load them back into the bag Wade brought. Might as well take it home and eat with Harper while we finalize plans for the event and accommodations for the visiting goalies and their gear.

Before I close my laptop, I update the spreadsheet and check the latest additions for any names I might recognize from other teams. When I near the end of the list, the air in my lungs freezes, sending chills through my body.

Chase Langston.

How is that possible? He plays defense. Did he not read the rules?

I scan the columns populated with his specifics until I reach the additional notes in the last one. My chest grows tight as a very real panic rushes through me.

Recently switched positions to goalie.

He includes his goalie coach's name and contact information to confirm, as well.

No, no, no… This can't be happening. Chase can't come here. I push away from my desk in a near panic. Everything in me wants to pack up Old Blue and hightail it out of town like I did last time, but how can I bail on the people I love working and hanging out with? This is the best job I've ever had. And I finally have a group of friends who I can trust to have my back. I've made a life for myself here —a good one.

Leave it to Chase to make a mess of things, just like he did in Texas. Will I ever be free of him?

I highlight the row, then hover my finger over the delete button. Can I do this? Make it go away? Zach shares the spreadsheet, but he probably hasn't seen the latest update. Aside from the fact that it would be wrong, I'd have to notify Chase that his application was turned down, or else he'll still show up, knowing him.

No matter what I do, I can't get rid of this creep.

The burn behind my eyes builds until my vision swims with tears. To make matters worse, another thought hits me hard. What will Wade do when he finds out? Should I tell him now so he has time to adjust to the idea, or wait until the day of the event and hope his teammates can keep him from going off the deep end?

If he and Chase wind up on the ice at the same time, which they will, I'm afraid of what Wade will do. He reacted so severely when he found out Chase was my ex. I can't let Wade risk his career like that, not over me.

I grab my phone and open the chat for the Puck Babes.

Bree: SOS! Houston, we have a problem!

Chapter Thirty

BREE

"What does Houston have to do with this?" Mia's skeptical expression holds a glimmer of humor.

I shrug. "I'm a Texas gal, so it seemed appropriate."

"Not for long. We're going to make a Sarabella beach gal out of you yet," Sophie quips.

When I sent out my text for help, I didn't expect to arrive at my apartment and find the whole gang there already. Sophie, Mia, and Lily literally dropped everything to come over, and they don't even know the details yet. These women take this stuff seriously, and witnessing it heals something deep inside me. I feel like they've claimed me and that maybe, just maybe, I've found a place to call home again.

Yes, I had—have—great parents. They were there for me whenever I needed them growing up. But since they divorced and sold the ranch, it's like they started a whole new chapter of their lives that doesn't include me.

I get it, though. I'm an adult, responsible for my own choices and decisions, but sometimes, a girl really needs her peeps. I haven't known Mia, Sophie, Lily, and Harper that long, but in some ways, I feel like I've known them forever.

And they're my posse. They have my back. And boy howdy, do I need that right now.

We're squeezed around the small coffee table, sitting on the floor in the living room of Harper's and my apartment. Mia sets five small glasses on the glass top and opens the bottle of wine she brought with her—red this time. It seems that Mia chooses her wine according to the seriousness of the situation. When she asked how bad it was, I said *really* bad, which, according to Mia, required a meaty red aged in bourbon barrels—her words.

I can't think of a worse-case scenario more treacherous than what's headed my way. Chase never does anything without having multiple motives. I've no doubt his change of position is as much about Wade as it is about his long-running desire to be a goaltender.

As Mia pours, I fill them in on the details of the latest Chase Files, earning gasps from all of them when I show them the spreadsheet on my phone.

Sophie growls, sounding like her fiancé, Luke. "He hinted at some kind of exciting change in his hockey career, but he wouldn't tell me the details when I interviewed him."

Harper chews on her thumbnail. "Can't you just delete it and claim there was a technical glitch?"

"I thought about it, but then I'd have to notify Chase that his application wasn't accepted, and knowing him, he wouldn't believe me and still show up. Besides, I've sacrificed enough of myself for that slime ball. I refuse to compromise my values, too." Hot tears burn behind my eyes as bitter regret sours my stomach.

"Nor should you!" Sophie rushes over and hugs me

from behind as Mia and Harper each hold one of my hands.

"How could I have been so stupid? And now I'll never get rid of him." Months of bottled-up fear, worry, and stress stream down my cheeks as the dam breaks.

Lily looks so angry, I swear I can see steam rising from her head like some cartoon character. Her expression stern, she leans across the coffee table. "I know people. Want me to put a hit on him?"

Just when I think she might be serious, one side of her mouth ticks up. We all burst out laughing, and it feels good. So good.

I take the tissues Harper so thoughtfully went into the bathroom to fetch for me and blow my nose like the blubbering fool I am. "Is it awful that I kind of wish you were serious?"

Lily lifts a single brow, her eyes penetrating. "I could still have someone rough him up for you."

She cracks a smile, but a tiny shiver runs through me. Who is this woman?

Sophie tugs her hand free. "Or, we take him down with words."

Mia nods. "I've read the first draft. It's epic."

"But I thought the article wasn't planned to be published for another month?"

Sophie taps her chin in thought. "That's for print, but not the digital edition. I might be able to pull some strings and see if they can do an early feature." She picks up her phone and taps out a message. "Can't hurt to try. I'll ask the editor if they can run it like an exposé."

Her words are like a lifeline of hope. "Before the event?"

No way would Chase still come to the All Goalies game in the midst of that embarrassment.

She holds her hands up. "I don't know. Maybe."

Sophie glances at her phone and frantically waves us over. "Oh, he's already replying!"

We all scoot around to watch those magical three dots pulse and turn into a reply. At seeing his affirmation that he could pull some strings, we all cheer as if we just watched one of our guys score a goal.

One of our guys…is Wade my guy? He's kind of been my person for years, but nothing more. Not really. Yet today in my office, how he looked so disappointed when I asked if we could go back to how things were before I kissed him, I think part of me wanted him to say no.

But things are better this way, really —for both of us.

Just as we return to our places around the coffee table, Sophie's phone pings again. "But the best he can do is the weekend of the event."

I feel a fresh wave of tears piling up behind my eyes. "There has to be some way to keep Chase from coming."

They all exchange glances, appearing as much at a loss as I feel. I need a miracle at this point.

Mia pushes up on her knees, lifting a finger up like a politician making a point. "At the very least, we'll make sure people know the truth. Bree, if you had a link to the article, could you put it somewhere on the event page on the website for people to find?"

I nod like a banshee. "Yes! We're doing bio features on each of the players. I could include the link there as a feature interview along with his stats. And it will be in the fans' newsletter, as well."

Lily nods her approval. "I think we have a plan, ladies. Operation Take Chase Down."

Mia snorts. "You are so official."

Without saying a word to confirm or deny, Lily gives her an evil grin before taking a sip of her wine.

But there's still one more thing to figure out. "How do I tell Wade?"

Mia's eyes widen at this. "I didn't think of that. What if you don't tell him?"

Sophie tilts her head. "How did this rivalry between them start?"

I take a deep breath. "They were actually friends when they played junior league. When it became obvious that Wade was meant to be a goalie, Chase tried to be one, too. But he couldn't cut it."

Lily groans. "And now he is. He'll rub it in Wade's face."

I nod. "Without a doubt. And knowing Chase, he'll try to demean Wade or instigate something to get him suspended."

"What if you didn't tell him?" Mia stares at me over the rim of her glass.

"If he knows, he can prepare for it." Elbows on the table, I cover my face with my hands. "He's going to hate me when I tell him."

Sophie pulls one of my hands down. "Why would he hate you?"

I drop both hands into my lap. "Because it's all my fault. If I'd seen Chase for what he was, none of this would be happening."

"No, that's not on you." Lily's fierce tone and expression take us all by surprise. "You did nothing wrong, Bree. He's a liar, a cheat, and the worst example of how a man should treat a woman. He didn't appreciate you, nor did he deserve you."

Tears fill my eyes, but I can still see the agreement on

Sophie, Mia, and Harper's faces. "Thank you. Maybe one day I'll believe it."

Harper grabs my hand. "You know the saying, fake it until you make it?"

I'm not sure where she's going with this, but I nod as I grab for another tissue.

"Sometimes we have to pretend it's true until it is." She gives us each an awkward glance at our silence. "When I was working for my father, he pretty much told me every day that I was his biggest disappointment in life. But then Rebecca took over and told me the opposite, that I was talented and capable. Did I believe her at first? No, but I decided I would pretend I did until it became my truth."

"And now?" Lily's voice holds an element of wonder, as if she's seeking something similar. Maybe we all are.

Harper's lips spread into a slow smile. "Now I believe it. No, I know it."

I'm not the only one in tears now. Mia tries to say something but winds up throwing her arms around Harper, which sets off a chain reaction in the rest of us until we're one big blubbering pile.

After a few minutes of this, we abandoned the floor for the couch and an overstuffed chair that Harper and I found at a yard sale. Our faces are blotchy from tears and rimmed with runny mascara. Harper makes another trip to the bathroom to fetch more tissues, returning with two boxes, just in case.

Sophie swipes under her eyes, catching most of the inky black smear. "And here I thought we'd be solving world hunger tonight."

This garners additional giggles from the rest of us, but the thought of telling Wade still feels like a boulder sitting on my chest.

"I have to tell him." I exhale with a loud sigh.

Sophie nods. "I agree. What if you tell Rebecca and Zach, too?"

"No, I can't do that." My words sound panicked, even to me.

Donning her school teacher's voice, Mia turns to face me on the couch. "Let's think this through for a moment. What's the worst thing that could happen if you told them about Chase and what he really is?"

"They fire me." I hiccup, then push my wine glass away —no more wine for me.

"Not likely," Harper chimes in. "I thought for sure after she fired my father, I'd be next. But Rebecca told me my actions spoke for me, not my father's."

Sophie taps my hand. "Rebecca knows better than anyone what it's like to be mistreated by misogynistic men in this industry. She and Zach could be your greatest allies."

I take a deep breath. They're right, but that means I'd have to show them that awful picture. But what other choice do I have?

Mia squeezes my hand. "If we could do it for you, we would."

"I know." I give her a watery smile. "I'll let them know I need to talk to them about an issue with the event and that it's urgent."

Sophie sits forward. "Here's a thought. What if you asked Wade to come with you to the meeting? That way you don't have to do this twice."

"Wouldn't that be weird to include him?" I try to picture myself telling them all the sordid details and imagine their reactions.

Lily shakes her head. "Considering the history between

Wade and Chase, not at all. Makes perfect sense, actually. They'll probably help temper Wade's reaction, too."

"Okay, I'll put on my big-girl pants and handle it." I blow my nose with a noisy snort.

But I'm dreading it already. Wade didn't react well at all when he first found out my ex was Chase Langston. I still can't completely shake his expression when he confronted me about it—like I'd disappointed him somehow.

I know that's not me in that picture, but that doesn't really make it less embarrassing. Telling Rebecca and Zach won't be easy, but I'm more concerned about Wade's reaction.

Lily's probably right about Rebecca and Zach's presence helping Wade not go completely off the rails. But my biggest fear lies in what's to come, when the article comes out. What will people think of me?

More importantly, what will Wade think?

Chapter Thirty-One

WADE

I shouldn't have walked out on Bree like that last night. My plan had been to take her dinner and ask if she was getting back together with Chase. If that's what she wanted, I'd find a way to be okay with it, even though the thought of him touching her drives me out of my mind. Like full-on anger that makes me want to tie the dude to the pipes and shoot pucks at him until he begs for mercy. Better yet, begs Bree to forgive him for treating her so poorly.

But when she asked if I was willing to give up hockey to keep the ranch, I couldn't give her an answer, which pissed me off.

Do I want to keep playing? Hell, yeah. Being a goaltender was always my dream. But I also don't want to give up our family home, the place I'd imagined landing after hockey.

Bree thinks I'm not interested in taking over the ranch, but the truth is, I am. I just never shared that with her because I always pictured us both there one day, running it together as business partners…and more, if I had my way.

Like I've said before, a guy can dream, and I've had lots of time over the years to indulge my fantasies.

I know I can't be in two places at once, but I also know I can't ask Nana to give up on her chance to live the life she's always wanted. I just thought I'd have more time. More time to play hockey, more time to make plans, and more time to show Bree how I truly feel about her. Now it feels like there's a ticking time bomb on all of it.

Elias and Ethan's voices precede them before they walk into the locker room.

"No way, man. You're on your own." Ethan tosses over his shoulder as he walks in.

"But you said you'd be my wingman." Elias tails him like a dog hungry for his attention.

The image makes me chuckle, which feels good, actually. After tossing and turning all night, I gave up trying to sleep at four in the morning. I went for a jog, then got to the arena for an early skate before practice—all that to clear my head.

"That was before I got married, dude."

"Which makes you an even better wingman now. As soon as the ladies find out you're married, all eyes will be on me." Elias wags his brows.

"Sounds more like you'll be his decoy," Mason titters behind his hand to Zayne, who snorts in agreement.

Ethan points, wagging his finger between Mason and Zayne. "Just take one of those jokers with you." When he notices I'm here, he does a double-take, then glares at me. "Why are you sweaty already?"

"Just getting a head start," I growl, keeping my head down.

"Liar," Luke grumbles as he saunters in. He sits down on the bench in front of his stall and pulls off his shoes.

Mathéo walks in. "What's the drama today, pinheads?"

Elias smacks him in the gut. "Nice to see you, too, pinhead."

Mathéo smirks. "That's the best you can do?"

"Didn't want you to feel left out," Elias shoots back.

"Burn!" Zayne cackles.

Patience thinner than the ice in springtime, I jump to my feet. "Enough already!"

All eyes land on me, most the size of the pucks we smack around the rink. I'm usually the calm one who keeps the peace in this place, not the one who blows his top.

I'm mostly geared up except for my glove, blocker, and mask. I gather them and my stick. "I'll see you out there."

As I brush by them, Bree's voice stops me in my tracks.

"Everyone decent?" She steps into the doorway, a hand shielding her eyes. She's in those wide-leg jeans with the fancy buttons along the pockets and that bright blue top that makes her eyes pop—at least, it would if I could see them. What I *can* see is the strip of skin at her midriff, exposed by her raised arm.

The kiss we shared floods back in a rush of heat as I remember the feel of her there as I held her.

"Define decent." Zayne snickers from behind me.

I swivel my head, intending to put him in his place, but Mason elbows him in the side and says with a snarl, "Cut it, man."

He and Zayne have been a constant stream of pranks and snark up until recently. But Mason has shut him down more often than not lately and shown more maturity toward the team overall.

"All clear, Bree," Luke barks.

Standing five feet in front of me, Bree lowers her hand. "Wade. Just the person I was looking for."

I'm sure she's here on business, but her words still bring a rush of warmth to my chest.

I tip the brim of a nonexistent Stetson. "At your service, ma'am."

She gestures to my gear. "Leave those for now. I need you to come with me."

Her smile falters. That's when I notice the nervousness in her eyes. Something's up.

"Sure thing." I stow my stick, glove, and catcher in my stall before following her out of the locker room to the elevator. "What's going on, Bree? Why are you taking me upstairs?"

When the doors slide open, she steps inside, then turns around. "There's something I need to speak to you, Rebecca, and Zach about."

I swallow down the sudden lump in my throat—I can only think of one thing that would make her want to talk to all three of us at once. Is she quitting her job to go back to Texas so she can be with *him*?

The thought freezes me in place. Getting on that elevator feels like admitting defeat, as if I'm taking the first step in letting her go. And I don't know if I can do that. Not again…

The doors start to close, but Bree catches them with her hand. "Please, Wade. It's important."

Her imploring blue eyes glitter with fear, which knocks every cell in my body into protective mode. She's afraid.

Seeing her like this shifts something in me. I push aside my feelings and hustle to her side, silently cursing all this goalie padding for making it damn near impossible to pull her close. So I do the next best thing—I hook my index finger around her dangling hand and close the loop with my thumb, like I'm lassoing a moment I'm not ready to let go of.

Because what if it's the last one I get with her?

"Whatever you need, Bree-bear." As much as I want to know what has her so scared, I don't want her to doubt that I'm here for her, no matter what.

She blows out a breath as if to steady herself. "Promise me you won't lose your cool, Wade."

I swivel my head to stare at her. "What's going on?"

She keeps her eyes on the elevator doors. "Just promise me."

That's enough confirmation for me to know I'm right. She knows how I feel about Chase. I just can't believe she'd go back to the scumbag, especially after how he treated her. Bree's better than that. Langston must have some kind of hold over her. If that's the case, then I have a new mission in life—find out what this guy has done to her and make sure he never sets eyes on Bree again.

But until then, I'll keep my word and do whatever she needs. "Fine. I promise."

"Good." The elevator doors open, and she launches out like an opponent making a breakaway with the puck. Except Bree isn't the enemy—Chase is.

With my skates adding a few inches to my height, I duck my head to walk into Rebecca's office. She and Zach are sitting on the small sofa, laptops open. Rebecca sets hers aside as Zach closes his and slips it onto the coffee table.

Rebecca gestures to one chair for Bree, then frowns at the other. "Sorry, Wade, we didn't think you'd be in your gear already."

"I got here early. No worries. I can stand."

Arms crossed, Bree holds her tablet against her chest. "I'd rather stand, too."

She glances at me before facing Rebecca and Zach again. "We might have a problem with one of the goalie sign-ups."

Zach grabs his laptop again and opens it, consternation masking his features. "I was just checking the list, but I didn't see anything off."

"That's because you don't know the whole story. Chase Langston is the one I'm concerned about."

"Langston? But he's not a goaltender," I blurt out. Seems like a simple mistake, but that doesn't stop the heat riding up my neck, making my head break out in a sweat.

Bree dips her chin, then looks up at me. "He recently changed positions."

The perspiration running down my back feels like ice now. What game is this guy playing, for real?

Rebecca shifts her gaze between us before landing on Bree. "Take your time and tell us everything. Zach and I are here to help."

The obvious tension Bree's carrying seems to lessen with Rebecca's reassurance. Bree launches into some details about her relationship with Langston, how things changed over time, and what led her to quit and ultimately move here. I can tell she's trying to stay calm, but I know my Bree-bear. I can hear the underlying fear in her voice, so maybe I have it all wrong about her getting back together with him.

"But last month, he sent me this with a threat." She opens her tablet, then holds it out to Rebecca and Zach. "It's not me. Lily was able to confirm the photo was altered to look like me. And the player in the picture is Chase. I recognized the piece of a tattoo that was left below his arm."

Rebecca's face flushes with anger as she hands over the tablet. "This is unacceptable."

Zach gets to his feet and starts pacing. "We'll reject his application."

"And tell him what?" Bree glances at my outstretched hand, reluctant to give it to me. "Trust me, he'll twist your words to make it look like he's the one being slighted."

I reach for the tablet again. "Bree, show me."

Tears spring up in her eyes as she whispers, "Remember, you promised."

My first look at the picture sucks the air out of my lungs. Then the rage hits like the worst gut punch of my career. Now I understand why she made me promise to keep my cool, but it takes every bit of strength in my body not to throw the tablet across the room and storm out like a bull seeing red.

Because I want blood—Chase's, to be exact.

I bite the inside of my mouth until I taste my own, keeping my face schooled as much as possible, as I return it. I'm furious to say the least, but I'm also relieved that she's not getting back together with that vile excuse of a human being.

Bree won't even look at me as she takes the tablet. She rushes to swipe away the picture, her face contorted with disgust.

"I did something I think will help." Her voice shakes as she speaks. "I probably should have run it by you first, but at the time, I had no idea Chase would sign up for the event."

She launches into another story about Sophie interviewing Chase for an article that will actually be an exposé. "I'd planned to put the article link on the website along with his player stats. But if you feel that would compromise the event, I'll understand."

No longer pacing, Zach starts to say something, but then looks at Rebecca. "What do you think, boss?"

Rebecca rises to her feet and approaches Bree. "Put the link on the website, but also send it to me. I will make sure it gets into the right hands."

Bree nods. "The article won't be live until the weekend of the event, which is less than a week away. I don't know what else to do. I'm so sorry."

Rebecca pulls her into a hug, which is what I should be doing. But instead, I'm trying to keep my anger in check behind a wall of padding.

"Don't be sorry, Bree. You didn't do anything wrong. And you shouldn't have to deal with this on your own. You're as much a part of this team as the players, and we have each other's backs." Rebecca leans back to look her in the face. "I wish you'd come to us sooner so we could have helped you, but I'm so glad to hear you have such an amazing group of friends who have been there for you."

Rebecca gives me a pointed look as she pulls Bree into another hug, almost like a reprimand. She must see how I'm holding back. Call me chagrined. As much as I want to renew my commitment to see Langston suffer and pay for what he's done, Bree needs her best friend more.

I acknowledge Rebecca's unspoken command with a nod. "We've got your back, Bree. All of us. I'll talk to the team so they know what's going on."

Zach raises his brows. "Make it crystal clear that they can't instigate anything. Langston will go down for this, but we have to ensure the Sun Kings' reputation doesn't get tarnished by some misguided heroics that come off more like vigilantism. Clear?"

I nod again. "I'll make it clear."

After more reassurances from Rebecca and Zach, I follow Bree to the elevator. When she goes to push the button for the first floor, I grab her hand and pull her into an awkward hug, again cursing the gear that protects me but creates a barrier between us.

Clinging to me, she sobs against my jersey. "I should have never come to Florida."

The anger over what that scumbag has put her through eats at me from within like acid. Sophie's article will likely get Langston suspended or, even better, expelled from the league, but in my mind, that's not enough punishment for what he's done to her.

"Moving here was the best thing you could have done, Bree-bear." I run a hand over her hair, then drop a kiss at her hairline, inhaling her sweet floral scent. That familiar ache hits me harder than ever, mixed with a ferocity to protect her at all costs.

Who am I kidding? What made me think I could ever get over her? I've spent more of my life in love with this woman than not, and I'll spend the rest of my days loving her, even if it has to be from afar.

A hum of pleasure escapes her lips, as if my touch surprises and comforts her all at once. She turns her head to stare up at me, eyes full of doubts and questions roiling like a storm.

"I'm such an idiot." Something deeper flashes behind her gorgeous blue irises, but slips away before I can identify it.

"No, you're not. Don't let that jerk make you feel responsible for his depravity."

She lifts herself onto her toes, wrapping her hands

behind my neck to pull me down into a hug. "Thank you for keeping your promise."

A slight tremble runs through her as I tighten my hold, as if my strength could wash away all the fear and trepidation she's feeling. If she only knew how much it's taking not to turn into a raging beast on a rampage, out for vengeance. In all honesty, the only thing helping me stay calm at this point is her proximity.

I close my eyes at the sensation of her warmth against me. Her sweet scent fills my nostrils again. My lips rest against the side of her neck, and the temptation to kiss that soft patch of skin just below her ear almost overwhelms me.

No matter how much I hate Langston, I have to hold it together. For her.

But once this all blows over, all bets are off.

Chapter Thirty-Two

BREE

Since there weren't any away games before the Fire & Ice event, Wade has camped out in my office every day after practice while Harper and I finalize plans. After the second day, I gave up trying to reassure him that I'm fine. That he doesn't have to babysit me. I'm not as fragile as he seems to think I am.

But secretly, I love that he's here. He makes me feel safe, protected. Like he always has, but it feels different this time. I can't quite figure out why yet—I just know I'm grateful that he's here.

Sometimes he tells me about the latest prank Zayne pulled during practice or pulls up silly cat videos that make me laugh. Other times, he simply sits in the chair near my desk, quietly scrolling on his phone. His presence has both comforted and strengthened me, but it's also caused a rush of new yet familiar feelings for him.

During the year I dated—and I use that term loosely now—Chase, I missed Wade. A lot. I assumed I missed the stability and grounding he always brought into my life. But now I'm wondering if it could have been more, like a longing for him in a deeper sense.

Yet no matter how much I try to tell myself these feelings aren't real or that they're just a product of circumstances, they won't go away. If anything, they're clarifying, making me realize that I do care about Wade—much more than I realized.

Nervous energy spikes through me at the thought, leading me to glance at him standing nearby like my own personal bodyguard. We're set up in the lobby of Sunfire Arena, checking in the goalies as they arrive, and showing them where to stow their gear in the locker room and the conference room, which we converted into another pseudo dressing area for the players.

As if he can read my mind, Wade moves close enough for me to feel his body heat before he rests his hand on my shoulder. His warm presence wraps around me like an embrace, making my eyes flutter shut. Without even thinking about it, I press my cheek against his fingers. When I realize what I'm doing, I snap my head up to look at him.

He draws his brows together, his gaze carrying a mix of curiosity and caring. "We've got you covered."

My stomach flutters at the protective tone in his voice, and the temptation to kiss him without a care for who might see almost overwhelms me. Perhaps a reaction to how moved I am by how everyone has rallied around me? Or maybe not…

Lily created an elaborate plan, using available security staff and players, to act as my protection detail—her words. Sophie's been my eyes and ears, keeping me up to date on any developments since the link to her article went live, and making coffee and latte runs. And Mia's standing guard at the entrance with a picture of Chase on her phone so she can text us when he arrives. I'd rather know when he's on his way than be surprised.

The whole thing feels like a sting operation designed to not only protect me from ever being alone in Chase's presence but also to make sure he doesn't try to pull any stunts during the weekend, especially after he's exposed for what he's done. That's the fallout I'm dreading.

But it's Wade's presence that keeps me from hightailing it out of here. My best friend, my rock. That man has stood by me through every crisis in my life, and what did I do to repay him? I dated his rival and ghosted him for a year.

Yet he still stands by me, no matter what. Never wavering, still caring. Every time he looks at me, I see it in his eyes, in his face.

How did I miss seeing that before?

After a while, I fall into a comfortable rhythm, registering the goaltenders as they arrive, assigning one of the Sun Kings players to show them where to stow their gear, and give them a brief tour of the facilities. Harper hands them the information packets we prepared and provides a quick rundown of the schedule for the weekend.

My phone pings at the same time as Harper's and Wade's. We glance at each other, knowing it's Mia sounding the alert. Wade shifts from his spot behind me to stand next to me. The back of his hand brushes my arm, letting me know he's here, ready to leap into action if needed.

A wave of goose bumps erupts down my arm. When I glance up, his grin tilts, drawing my attention to his mouth, reminding me of how his lips felt on mine. A small shiver runs through me, contrasting the heat I feel in my cheeks.

The last thing I want, though, is for him to act rashly and endanger his career. When the guys fight on the ice, there's an expectation and an unspoken set of rules that once it's done, it's over—left on the ice.

But any altercation outside of the rink could attract the wrong attention, leaving us with no control over the narrative. I know Wade understands this, but I also know how angry he is. He hasn't said anything, but I've always been able to read this aspect of him, and the fury I see brewing there worries me.

I recognize Chase's gait before I see his face. Then Amber's smug expression as she hangs from his arm registers in my rattled brain. I should have known she'd come with him. She wouldn't want to miss her chance to gloat over her prize goalie. Her face says it all.

"Aubrey Sutton," Chase speaks my name with a drawl that sounds more like a sneer coming from lips I once thought kissed only me. His focus shifts to Wade. "And her sidekick, I see."

Wade's shoulders pull back. The side of his clenched jaw ticks as he says, "Langston."

Chase's smirk widens. "Not sure if you heard, but I'm a goalie now."

"I heard." Wade's eyes glint like steel, harder than the ice coating the rink.

"You should congratulate him, then." Amber's whiny voice wheedles something in me.

Anger? Yes. But mostly pity. She's bought into Chase's twisted press and believes it. One day, she'll wake up and realize the man she thinks loves her is using her just like he did me. That he would use her body in that picture to ruin my reputation is more than proof of that.

I make a tick mark next to his name. "You're checked in. Our captain, Luke Jameson, will show you where to stow your gear and give you a quick tour."

Originally, I'd suggested Ethan have the honors, but Luke insisted on being the one to put a little intimidation into the situation.

Chase shakes his head. "I'd rather have my old friend Wade do the honors. I think you can make that work. Right, Bree?"

The skin on the back of my neck crawls with disgust. The idiot still thinks he can manipulate me. Wade's hand on my shoulder increases in pressure, reminding me he's here. My resolve not to let Chase get under my skin returns even stronger, but before I can reply, multiple footsteps come from behind. When I turn in my seat, half of the team stands behind us like an impenetrable wall. Luke steps out in front of them, arms crossed and a scowl on his face.

When I turn back around, I note the doubt flashing in Chase's eyes, and smile for the first time today. Let him have a taste of the intimidation he loves to wield himself.

Wade takes a step forward and grinds out, "You remember Jammer, Chase? He and the rest of the team will show you where to go."

His words finish with an unspoken threat that implies the locker room isn't where he really wants Chase, and sends a shiver of guilty pleasure through me at seeing Chase get a taste of his own medicine.

"The rest of the team?" Amber squeaks out, her eyes skipping to each of the hulking players waiting to move into action.

Chase's jaw twitches this time. He doesn't say a word, though.

Harper practically tosses the info packet at him, which

he catches with a grunt. Until finally, he walks away, tugging Amber down the concourse.

I hold my breath until I lose sight of them, led by Luke and flanked by Zayne, Mason, Ethan, Elias, and Mathéo. The Big Guns, as Wade calls them.

Tears of relief flood my eyes. Uncaring who might see, I stand up and throw my arms around Wade's neck, pulling him down. "Thank you for being here."

He presses me tighter against him as he kisses my temple. "I wouldn't be any place else."

Shivers run over my shoulders and follow his hand rubbing down my back. The clean, spicy scent of his jersey fills my nose. When I look up at him, his hands cup my face, and his thumbs sweep away the residual tears on my cheeks.

And now I see it—Wade cares for me more than I ever realized.

A wave of shame hits me so hard I can't look at him. I don't deserve the compassion and love I see there.

I don't deserve *him*.

Tonight's the cocktail party, kicking off the Fire & Ice event. I thought about wearing the dress I bought, since I decided to keep it, but now I'm thinking I want to use it for its original purpose.

If Wade cares for me as much as I suspect, maybe he'll give me another chance. I have to try, or else this elephant-sized question mark will come between us and our friendship. At the very least, I need to know he'll still be my best friend even if he doesn't want anything more from me.

After a sweep of the arena lobby, I locate Mia and Sophie standing together and sharing a soft pretzel.

Rebecca and Zach hired the vendors to stay open to keep the whole game day atmosphere throughout the weekend.

With Harper in tow, I stop in front of them. "Where's Lily?"

"Right here."

With a startled jump, I whirl around to find her standing behind me. How did she sneak up on me like that? "Good, you're all here."

They all stare at me expectantly. Except for Harper, who I think already suspects what I'm going to say.

I take a deep breath and spew my thoughts before I lose my courage. "I know I said I didn't want to go through with the auction idea, but I changed my mind."

Mia pumps her fist. "Yes!"

Sophie grins. On my left, Harper giggles, and Lily does her usual perimeter sweep with her eyes, but she's smiling as she does it.

"So, can we pull this off? Can you see if your friend Char is still willing to help?"

With a coy shrug, Sophie blinks at me. "I never canceled our plans."

The others study me, clearly waiting to see my reaction.

My gaze skims over each of them. "You all knew?"

They all nod in unison, like a secret mastermind organism working behind the scenes to orchestrate my love life. And I love them for it.

Sophie's expression turns serious. "I am curious, though. What changed your mind?"

I glance toward Wade, surrounded by the usual guys who tend to follow him around. I wonder if he knows how people are naturally drawn to him, to his quiet strength and presence.

That's when I notice Harper is studying the group, too,

more like one of them in particular. Mason looks our way, smiles at Harper, but then turns away, as if to hide his expression. Harper's shoulders seem to wilt. As I continue to observe Wade, I make a mental note to ask her about it later.

He must sense I'm watching him because he swivels his head and glances my way. Our eyes lock and, again, I see what I've missed for far too long.

It's almost torture to look away. "I see it now."

"And?" Mia practically bounces on her toes, much like the second graders she teaches.

"I need—" I stop myself, because I don't want to explore these growing feelings I have for Wade as if it's required. "I *want* to find out if there's something between us."

"Oh, there is, girl. Big time. Now that you see it in him, you just need to let yourself feel it." Mia's knowing gaze offers unexpected reassurance. The last thing I want to do is hurt him. I've done enough of that already.

Lily clears her throat. "All right, then. Operation Date Wade is officially on."

Sophie shakes her head at her. "I think you miss being a bodyguard more than you let on."

A blush spreads over her cheeks as if she came from the cold air in an ice rink. She rests a hand on her abdomen. "Even if I'd stayed in that field, I would have had to retire."

We all gasp and squeal as we encircle her in hugs. And surprisingly, she lets us.

I lean back. "Payton knows, right?"

With the biggest smile I've seen on her yet, she nods. "We're telling his family at Christmas, but I wanted you guys to know now."

"Awww!" Sophie cries as we all go in for another hug.

Lily laughs before playfully shaking us off. "Enough already."

"I hear wedding bells." Harper chimes in.

Biting her lip, Lily digs into her pocket, then pushes a ring onto her finger. "We eloped last weekend."

We all gasp again.

Her smile turns cringy. "After the way the paparazzi hounded the family when his cousin disappeared, we didn't want to give them fodder to create some nonexistent scandal."

Mia crosses her arms and stomps her foot. "Why didn't you tell us?"

Lily's eyes widen. "I just did! Payton wanted me to wait until after the holidays, but I told him I couldn't keep this from my best friends."

We all go silent at her words. Mia and Sophie have known Lily much longer than I have. So has Harper, but even I know how reserved she is when it comes to expressing emotions. So, for her to call us her besties is kind of a big deal.

Mia's outrage crumbles into a teary smile. "Congratulations!" Her face morphs into delight as she claps her hands in front of her. "I know! We can put together a reception for you and Payton."

"After Christmas." Lily tilts her head toward me. "First, let's get these two figured out."

As much as I appreciate her dedication to my cause, I'm still clinging a little to what she said about us being her best friends. These women have become that for me, too. I study each of their faces, filled with gratitude again. Even in the midst of whatever trouble Chase may bring this weekend, I know I'm safe, secure, and supported.

"Okay. Operation Date Wade is on." I don a cheerful

tone, belying the rush of anxiety hitting me at the thought of dating my best friend. Tingles spread through me only to be squashed by a sudden wave of crippling doubt.

What if, after the dust settles and clarity rushes in, Wade decides I'm damaged goods and not what he wants after all?

Chapter Thirty-Three

WADE

Fans fill almost every seat in the Sunfire Arena. The place buzzes with energy, excitement, and expectation. Our new mascot, Stingin' Ray, continues to be a hit with the crowd, especially the kids. Bree had the idea to create kid-sized versions of his sunglasses, which, of course, have sold like hot cakes, especially when the parents find out all the proceeds go to cancer research for children.

Wearing the special team jerseys Bree had had made for the All Goalies Game, netminders from all over the country skate around the rink, resembling a bunch of hulking lumberjacks on skates more than hockey players. It's a sight that's hard to look away from, actually.

The announcer introduces each of the teams to the spectators, giving a brief explanation of how the games will work today and tomorrow. Zach kept the rules simple, creating four teams with ten goalies on each one—no goalies in the crease.

Each team will play five-on-five for ten minutes, then swap in the second line for ten minutes more. That's way longer than normal players stay on the ice. But in all this gear, goalies can't really sprint as fast, so we can last a little longer. Even so, it's a stretch.

The two games planned for today will consist of three twenty-minute periods, like normal hockey, but with five-minute breaks in between instead of eighteen. The two winning teams will compete in a playoff tomorrow for a trophy Bree describes as epic. She won't tell me anything other than a big reveal is planned before tomorrow's big playoff.

But all of that is just background noise because the only thing I can focus on right now is Langston, who looks more like a grade schooler swallowed up in his hockey gear. He's a good five inches shorter than I am, and doesn't seem completely comfortable in his gear. Under normal circumstances, I'd laugh, but nothing about that scumbag hits me funny at the moment.

My team—the Sting Rays—will play the Sharks first. Chase's team—the Sea Turtles, which gives me some satisfaction—will play the Seagulls. The two winning teams will face off tomorrow, so there's a good possibility that Chase and I won't play against each other.

Fists clench inside my blocker and my catcher, I skate around the rink for the warm-up, careful to keep my distance from him and thankful that at least he's not on my team. I'm sure Zach and Bree arranged the games to avoid any direct encounters between us, but part of me hopes the two teams winding up in the playoff will be mine and his.

I don't miss the cautious glances he lobs at me or the smug grin he wears as if he's the big man on campus. The rage I've managed to keep in check flares hotter than ever. I want nothing more than to wipe that smirk from his face permanently. Better yet, leave him toothless. I don't think he'd be smiling much then.

But I won't. I can't do that to Bree. I know how much the success of this event means to her, so I'll behave at least until the weekend is over. After that, no promises. Sometimes, a man has to do what a man has to do. I'm not sure what that is yet, but I'll know when I see it, consequences be damned.

I take a seat with the rest of my team on the bench. Luke, who volunteered to act as one of our coaches, leans over my shoulder. "Is that him?"

Following his line of sight to where Langston leaves the rink to head down the tunnel, I rough out. "Yeah."

"Thinking reckless thoughts?"

I dart my eyes to his, staring at him through my grill as if to say, 'duh.'

"I see." He ducks his chin. "You know you're not alone in this, right?"

I tip my head toward the ice. "I am out there."

His lips purse as he thumps the thick padding on my shoulder. "Don't do anything stupid. Sophie's article will expose him for the scum of the earth that he is. This may be the last time he sets a skate on the ice."

I gnash my teeth together. "Let's hope."

He nods. "Good, just make sure it's not yours."

My team, the Sting Rays, beat the Sharks by one point. Unfortunately, Chase's team, the Sea Turtles, wound up faster on the ice than I expected and beat the Seagulls by three. That means we'll probably have to play against each other tomorrow, unless our line rotations don't happen to overlap.

Right now, I'm dressed in my game day suit instead of my gear, waiting for the Date a Hockey Player Auction to start. The rest of the guys roped into this madness congregate around the room, chatting or scrolling on their phones. A few look as nervous as I feel. I run my hand down my right thigh, attempting to calm my bouncing knee. I haven't seen Bree in hours, and I'm worried about her.

I check my phone again, but she still hasn't answered my last text asking if she's okay.

Is she safe? Has Chase tried to intimidate her? I know my guys are keeping a careful watch, but that's not the same as me being there.

Just as I'm about to use a need for the restroom as an excuse to leave and find her, she waltzes in, tablet clutched in her left arm and a bright smile on her gorgeous face. Her blonde hair is swept up into a high ponytail, and she's wearing her usual professional attire of wide-legged pants and a shimmering purple top that makes her eyes pop.

"Okay, we're about to start. Is everyone ready?"

A few mumbled yeses break the silence; most just nod.

"Guys, this is for a great charity. Most of the winners will be fans who want to take you to lunch with their kids."

"I'd rather have an actual date." Zayne lets out a rough laugh, trying to hide his own case of nerves.

Since Luke's not here to give his captain's speech, I rise to the call. "She's right. So get your game face on and be your best."

Bree shoots me a grateful look. For a long moment, we just stare at each other, but I don't miss the way her eyes drop and scan down, as if she's checking out my suit. When her gaze returns to mine, I lift a brow as if to ask if she approves.

She saunters over, smiling. "Looking good, Pierce."

My gaze drifts down her, slow and unhurried, before I drop my voice. "Not so bad yourself, Sutton."

Her perfect lips part in surprise, and her pupils blow out. The confirmation that I can affect her that way is heady.

She drags her eyes down to her tablet. "Time to go. Zayne, you're up first, so follow me."

Bree tosses a last look my way before she turns to leave. After that, I only see her when she peeks in to call up the next guy. Until it's my turn.

"Wade, you're up." Mischief sparkles in her eyes.

I'd kind of hoped I'd see some irritation instead. Something that would tell me she doesn't like the idea of me going out with an unknown woman. But she did say most of the auction winners would probably wind up as simple lunches with a family.

Still, I've seen the few regulars who come to all the local games and linger afterward. A few of those puck bunnies might want to jump in on the fun.

I step onto the small stage set up in the main lobby area. A large group of people fills the space—larger than I expected, actually. They clap when Bree introduces me, then start chiming in as Zach orchestrates the bidding.

A few early bidders die off, leaving only two vying for a date with me. I recognize Mason's sister from the picture he showed me, but the other woman I don't. She's a pretty redhead with a pleasant smile, but she's nothing compared to Bree.

Judging by the semi-panicked look on Mason's sister's face, she maxed out the budget the fellas gave her, which leaves me at the mercy of Red, who's about to become my date for the evening. I leave the stage, frustrated that I'll spend this evening with a stranger instead of protecting Bree.

I glare at Mason when I join him, where the rest of the guys stand behind the stage. "What happened?"

He holds his hands up. "Luna asked what our limit was, so I tossed a number out. I never figured it would go that high." He elbows me in the side. "You dog."

I shove him off. "Unlike you, I'm not looking forward to this."

He raises his brows. "Let's swap. A middle-aged mom and her twelve-year-old son won me."

The idea is tempting. I could offer them an entire day with me if we could reschedule. That way, I can stay near Bree the rest of the day. "Yeah, that could—"

"No swapping!" Bree's voice chimes out behind me.

I whip around.

Her expression is borderline feral. "Mason, don't you dare skimp on your time with the Bendersons. That boy is a huge fan, and he begged his mom for this for his birthday."

Mason appears genuinely taken aback. "Sure thing, Bree. I'll make it a birthday the kid will never forget."

"Good. Thank you." She hands me a piece of paper with an address on it. "She'll be ready for you in one hour."

I hold the slip like a foreign object, searching the crowd for the redhead who won me for the evening. "I thought she'd be ready to go now."

Bree shakes her head. "She wanted to change into something special for your date."

Her face remains unreadable, so I can't tell how she feels about this at all. I guess I'd hoped to see at least some irritation on her part, but maybe I'm just being a fool again.

A fool for a woman who can't seem to look at me as more than her best friend.

Resigned, I close my fingers over the paper. "I'll be there."

She turns to leave, but stops next to me, placing her hand on the lapel of my jacket, right over my heart. Her blue eyes sparkle with that mischief again, almost as if she's teasing me. "And maybe try to enjoy yourself, okay?"

What game is she playing? My gaze dips to her mouth, searching for that cute freckle I love, but it's tucked between her teeth. For once, I'm thankful for the thick fabric of my coat. Otherwise, she'd notice how hard my heart is pounding beneath her hand.

But two can play…maybe seeing me with someone else will make her rethink how she views me.

I lean closer to her, almost touching her delicate ear with my lips. "Count on it."

Chapter Thirty-Four

WADE

By the time I reach the address Bree handed me, my bravado has almost dissolved. Once I park, I pick up the slip of paper from the cup holder and check that I have this woman's name in my head.

Charlene Winston, who likes to be called Char.

I study that detail, written in Bree's familiar handwriting. She's the one I'd rather be spending the evening with, even if it means sitting in front of the TV eating one of those pizzas she likes.

Might as well get this over with. I told Bree I would enjoy myself—more out of an attempt to tease her back, but for the sake of this woman who had so generously donated her money to help sick kids with cancer, I put on my game face, ready to show her a pleasant evening.

I just hope she's not the handsy type. That I won't tolerate. I lift my hand to knock, then turn and stare off into the distance, thinking of Bree, of course.

The door whips open. A rush of sweet honeysuckle

teases my nose, painfully reminding me I won't see her tonight. I turn to face my date and freeze.

Bree stands in the doorway, her cornflower blue eyes more vivid than ever. My gaze coasts down her body like I did earlier, taking in every curve accentuated by a dress that appears made for her. My perusal stops at the folds of fabric dancing around her legs before shooting back up to her face.

"Bree, what are you doing here?"

She lets out a soft giggle. "I'm your date."

I look past her, searching the simple entrance to the small apartment for what, I don't know. "What about Charlene?"

The redhead I remember from the auction comes into view and makes a fake coughing sound. "I'm sick. So sorry. I hope you don't mind if Bree takes my place." She hands Bree a clutch and whispers, "Get going before I change *my* mind." Then she coughs again and winks at me.

Bree steps out, closing the door behind her. When she walks past me, headed for my truck, I grab her wrist and tug her back harder than I mean to. She tumbles into me, grabbing my shoulders with a gasp.

I hold her hips to steady her, ready to apologize, but she's so close now, and I'm not sorry at all. "What's going on, Bree?"

Her gaze drops to my lips for a brief moment. "Char's sick, so you get me instead."

Silly woman. She still doesn't realize what she does to me, and for the first time, I'm ready to lay it all out for her. No more holding back.

"You could never be '*instead*' for me, Bree-bear. More like the only one."

She gasps. Her eyes search my face as if she wants to believe me. And I intend to make sure she does by the end of this evening.

"Are you sure? Even after…" She looks down as if she's…ashamed.

I lift her chin with my finger, forcing her to look at me because I want her to know her worth and see everything I've held back for so long. "After what, Bree?"

Her eyes turn glassy, and for a moment, I hesitate in pushing her to be honest, but something deep inside says she needs this.

"Tell me." I keep my tone firm, yet soft so she knows she's safe with me.

"After dating Chase, after ghosting you—"

"We already dealt with that, Bree-bear. It's in the past. We're here, right now."

She nods, but I still see the doubt clouding her gorgeous eyes.

"Tell me what you're really afraid of?" I draw her against me.

Hands on my lapels, she swallows, then presses her forehead against my chin. I want her to look at me, but if it's easier for her to say it this way, then I'll let her hide for now.

"That you won't still want me anymore," she whispers.

"Look at me, please." I wait until her eyes meet mine. "I've always wanted you. I've known you were the girl for me since I was ten years old. Nothing can ever change that."

She tries to turn away, but I catch her chin and gently tug her back to face me. "I can see you're struggling to believe me, so let me say it a different way. Aubrey Marie Sutton, I love you. I'm *in* love with you and have been for years. What can I do to convince you that nothing will ever change that?"

Her eyes are so wide now, I'm worried she'll bolt like a scared rabbit. But then she lifts onto her toes as she wraps her hands behind my neck, pulling my lips to hers in a crushing kiss. I weave my fingers into her soft hair, tilting her head so I can kiss her. Really kiss her.

No holding back this time.

As I move my mouth over hers, she opens hers, inviting me to explore, which I do. She responds in a like manner, as eager to know me this way as I've wanted to know her. The ache I've felt longer than I can remember seems to grow and swallow us both, almost as if we're trying to make up for all the lost years.

"You know, I could leave and let you two have my place for the evening." Char's voice breaks in, making us smile against each other's lips.

Suddenly shy, Bree ducks her chin as she lowers herself to the ground.

I plant a gentle kiss on her hairline, inhaling her sweet scent again. "Thanks, but we have plans."

Then I grab Bree's hand and lead her to my truck, and for the life of me, I can't stop smiling.

Knowing we had much to discuss, I drove to the Turtle Tide first to grab takeout so we could find a quiet place on the beach to eat and talk.

Puffy clouds highlighted in bright yellow and orange hover above the darkening ocean that glimmers with the setting sun. Our food mostly gone now, we're perched on top of a picnic table nestled under some tall pines with our feet on the bench as a soft breeze wafts through her hair, lifting the loose tendrils framing her face in a delicate dance.

She pulled most of her hair into a large clip to keep it from blowing into her mouth as she ate, which exposed her neck. I haven't been able to stop touching her in some way all evening, as if I need to make sure she's really here and this isn't a dream. Soft touches to her hand, her face, and her neck, where my thumb sweeps a path over the sensitive skin there.

Bree leans into my touch while slipping a french fry into her mouth, smiling at me as she chews. I can't stop watching that freckle move on her lower lip until I finally lean in and kiss her right there—something I've always wanted to do. She tastes sweet and salty all at once.

As I lean back, I move my hand so I can brush my thumb over the spot on her lip. "I love that freckle."

She laughs. "I've always hated it."

"Why?"

Her eyes widen with incredulity as she points to it. "Because it's right there, in the way of everything."

"It's not in my way." I kiss it again, teasing her lips with mine.

She kisses me back, then, with a sigh, nestles into me as I wrap my arm around her.

We watch the fading sunset, quiet and content. I still can't believe we're here, together like this. I'd imagined it so many times, but in my wildest dreams? Never as good as this.

"How did you talk Charlene into letting you have her date with me?"

She tilts her face up. "I paid her."

I pull my head back. "Seriously?"

She bursts out laughing. "No, you goof. That was the plan all along."

"What?"

"It was Sophie's idea. Char is a friend of hers at the paper. Mia, Lily, and Harper were in on it, too." She leans forward.

I think if I were a rooster, I'd be strutting in the barnyard right about now. Instead, I scrape a hand over my mouth to hide my grin.

"I almost backed out." She glances over her shoulder in a way that I can only see her eyes. She's so damn sexy when she does that.

"Why?"

She pushes back, sitting even with me. "I wasn't sure if what I was feeling was real."

Her confession gives me pause. I shift, turning to face her with a question I don't want to ask but have to. "Are they?"

She tilts her head. "Wade, I wouldn't be here if they weren't."

My turn to drop my chin. "Guess I needed to ask."

Her hand cups my cheek, drawing me to face her again. "I think I've always loved you, Wade. Just took me a while to realize I was *in love* with you."

Her words stun me into silence. She said she loves me, something I never expected to hear from her this soon.

I pull her onto my lap so I can hold her closer. "I've had way more time to figure out my feelings for you, Bree, so please don't feel like you have to say anything before you're ready."

She brushes her lips against mine. The kiss is sweet, yet

filled with so much promise. She pulls back until our eyes lock. "I meant every word."

Her voice is breathy, impassioned, and her face tells me without words what I've dreamed of for so long.

She's mine. And I'm hers.

Always have been, even when she didn't realize it.

Chapter Thirty-Five

BREE

I wring my hands, more nervous about today than any game Wade has ever played in his entire career. When Zach and I planned out the All Goalies Game, we accounted for as many possibilities and wild cards as we could so that Wade and Chase wouldn't have a run-in on the ice.

So far, so good. As long as everyone follows the plan, Wade's and Chase's lines shouldn't be out there at the same time.

Shouldn't be.

But I know Chase. And I know from some well-placed birdies—aka Lily and Mia—that Chase got wind of the article. One of the guys on his team came across it on the website, from what I understand, and wanted to know if it was all true.

Supposedly, Chase tried to blow it off with some long-winded story of how this was my doing. That I'd taken our breakup badly, and would do anything to win him back.

As if. Just the idea makes me want to hurl into his skates,

then stick them in the hot Florida sun so the smell bakes right in.

Leave it to Chase to come out smelling like a rose. So far, I'm not seeing any fallout from Sophie's exposé. But at least the truth is out there, and maybe, hopefully, some of the higher-ups will take notice at some point.

At the moment, I'm more concerned about Wade's state of mind regarding Chase if they do wind up playing at the same time.

I sense Wade's presence before I see him, and spin around. Wade waddles out of the locker room in his full gear, making him appear larger than life.

He pulls me into his padding and kisses me before studying my face. "Hey, you okay?"

Less than a day has passed since our first official date, less than twelve hours since our last kiss, yet this all feels so…normal as if we've been together for years.

In a way, we have, but not like this. I'm not sure what to call us yet, other than we're together. We haven't labeled anything, and maybe that's for the best since it's all so new. But part of me wants to officially be called his girlfriend—not just his best friend who happens to be a girl—as if it's some kind of guarantee he won't change his mind.

"I'm fine. Really." I let out a nervous laugh.

His grin tilts as he stares, seeing right through me—through my brave facade like he always has. "Liar."

I exhale as much of this pent-up energy and worry as I can. "Promise me that if you wind up on the ice at the same time, you won't do something stupid."

"You mean like bash out all his teeth so he'll never smile again?"

"Yes, exactly that," I confess. The thought of him doing

that satisfies a need for vengeance, but also ignites a warm spark deep within me. Wade would fight to protect me… and fight *for* me because he thinks I'm worth it.

The realization leaves me heady.

"Losing teeth comes with the territory."

"Wade!" I swat him on the arm, which I doubt he can even feel with all his padding.

He sighs. "I promise."

I grab his head between my hands, forcing him to look at me. "I mean it. What we have is too important to let someone as small and petty as Chase Langston mess it up."

As if a curtain were pulled back, his eyes glitter with a spectrum of emotions, revealing his heart and…relief? "Glad to hear you say it, Bree-bear. He never deserved you. Never appreciated what he had."

This man has stood by me, loved me, and fought for me. I plan to fight just as hard for him. I brush my mouth against his, parting my lips to let him know I want him to kiss me deeply, to claim me, needing his reassurance that we're together in this now and nothing will pull us apart. Not ever again.

"Aww, how sweet." Amber's syrupy voice purrs, interrupting our moment. "Chase predicted you'd jump from his arms to Wade's. Actually, I think the word he used was *settle*. Guess that worked out better for me in the end, though, didn't it?"

For a moment, I'm tempted to grab Wade's blocker and smack Amber across the face with it, maybe knock some of her teeth loose like Wade implied wanting to do to Chase. Then, I feel overwhelming pity for her. One day, she'll experience a rude awakening as to who and what Chase is, just like I did. And if she doesn't, then they deserve each other. Better for two sociopaths to make each other miserable than two innocents caught in their webs of manipulation and cruelty.

I don a smile as fake as her voice. "Yes, Amber. You and Chase are perfect for each other."

Her smug expression falters. "Oh, well, thanks."

As much as I want to dropkick this woman back to Texas, I school my face and tone to reflect complete politeness because that's my job. "Was there something you needed?"

"Yeah. I almost forgot. Chase asked me to let you know he had to switch lines with one of the guys. Something about the guy having to leave because of some family issue, so Chase will be playing against Wade now. Okay?" She smiles with a wave, then trots off to who knows where.

My hands fist at my sides. I'm so tempted to march into the conference room assigned to Chase's team and tell him to take a flying leap, but in much harsher words.

Wade turns me toward him, then worms his fingers into my hands until they relax. "Everything will be fine. In a few hours, this will all be over."

Why does he sound so much calmer than I am? Or am I just not seeing what's boiling beneath the surface? "Promise me you won't instigate something with him."

He hesitates for a moment, eyes hard as steel, but then his gaze softens. "I promise. I won't instigate anything."

"Good." I let out a noisy breath.

He tips his head down the hallway. "Go do your thing. I'll see you after the game, right?"

I can't help but smile now. "Can't wait."

He pulls me in for another sweet yet lingering kiss. "More of that later."

Only when I know he's back in the locker room do I head for the rink in search of my gal pals. Trepidation still swirls in my stomach, so I keep reminding myself of Wade's words, that in a few hours, this will all be over, and we can move forward with our lives.

And a new relationship that's definitely more than friends.

"He actually promised he wouldn't instigate anything?" Sophie frowns as she asks what I'm sure Lily and Mia want to know, too. I already filled Harper in on our way to our seats to watch the game, and now she's braving the concession lines to grab us soft pretzels and sodas.

"After I made him," I explain.

Mia sits back in her seat and crosses her arms. "I can't imagine Ethan agreeing to that."

Sophie shoves her elbow into Mia, causing her arms to uncross. "Don't say something like that."

"I didn't mean it in a bad way." Mia semi-whines. "What I mean is, I don't think he could do it."

I'm not sure if that's actually what she meant or if she's trying to recover from her bluntness. But she's not far off. Part of me still has doubts about whether Wade can fully restrain himself. But he has to, or all we've done to dismantle Chase's attempt to use and manipulate me will get undone, and that jerk will wind up looking like the one who was victimized.

The thought of that makes my blood curdle.

Lily leans forward, peering past Mia toward me. "I have security stationed in the hallway outside the locker room and conference doors, and in the tunnel with specific orders to separate them if anything goes down."

I give her a watery smile. "Thank you."

She gives me a reassuring one and pats my hand.

After they sing the national anthem, the lights go down, and the music starts. Huge numbers counting down from ten fill the Jumbotron screens. Wade's team leaves the tunnel and skates onto the ice as a giant zero flashes and the emcee's announcement of the Sting Rays line-up blasts through the arena. It's dramatic and powerful, exactly what I wanted to draw the spectators into the excitement and energy of the game.

Next, the Sea Turtles skate out, warming up on the other end of the rink. The ribbon boards light up with the words *Sting Rays vs. Sea Turtles*, flashing and racing around the arena, and amping up the fans even more.

Then comes the puck drop, and the goalies go at it. I keep my focus on Wade, trying to gauge where his head's at. So far, he seems to be steering clear of Chase, who seems more interested in playing the game than causing trouble. But that's how he works, like a stealth attack you never see coming.

Lily leaves to do a security check, leaving me between Sophie and Mia, who each keep leaning into me as if they think they need to hold me up. But what they don't know is that I'm seething inside. I know Chase, and the only reason he would send Amber to tell me he'd made this change to help another player is to taunt me. To make sure I know he has something planned to try to hurt Wade. I'm sure of it.

The first period ends, giving me a five-minute break to recover and prepare for the next one. Thankfully, the second one plays out smoothly, except for a goalie losing a blade on his skates. After a short stoppage, they head into the second intermission without any more complications.

That leaves twenty minutes of playtime—ten with Wade and Chase sharing the ice.

Sophie pats my arm. "It's almost over."

I appreciate her attempt to reassure me, but I'm still on edge. "I know Chase is up to something."

"You think so?" Mia asks.

"I know so. Chase only does what serves him. I've no doubt he'll try to pull a stunt before the game ends."

Third period starts with Wade's team in the lead by one point. One of the players on Chase's team pulls off a Michigan, which seems like it would be impossible to manipulate the puck like that using a goalie stick and in all that gear, but he does it—picks up the puck with his stick from behind the net and scoops it into the top shelf as he rounds the crease.

The move is stunning and beautiful, but I wanted Wade's team to win so this would all be over. Now it's looking like a tie game.

The horn blasts, signaling the end of the third period. Instead of the usual shortened overtime period, Zach planned a shootout as the tiebreaker. Each team picks a goalie in net and three goalies to take shots against the opposing team. The one with the most points wins.

Wade gets picked to be in the crease for the Sting Rays. The Sea Turtles select a goalie from a team in North Carolina, which means Wade will have to face Chase one-on-one.

But there's a game—a win—at stake here. I can't imagine Chase blowing that in an attempt to take Wade out.

Wade and the other goalie both block the first two shots on goal, leaving the tie in place. If neither team scores in the last round, we go into sudden death.

The third goalie from the Sting Rays skates down the ice, working the puck in a slow glide, moving to the left side of the net as he gets ready to take his shot, but at the last second, stretches his stick to the right and pulls a deke, sending the puck over the line.

The fans cheer, chanting, "Sting Rays! Sting Rays! Sting Rays!"

Then Chase skates out, pausing at center ice as he gets ready to take his shot. The hair on my arms prickles. I glance at Sophie, then Mia. On the other side of the rink, Lily stands in the tunnel, ready to unleash her security team if needed. There's nothing more we can do other than hope Chase decides to keep things professional and honor the game.

He taps the puck with his stick as if he's testing the waters. Wade squats down, blocker and catcher in front of him, bouncing a few times to get ready.

Chase pushes off, stickhandling the puck, picking up some speed as he gets closer.

Wade skates forward, just past the edge of the crease, tracking Chase's every move.

About five feet from the net, Chase finally takes a shot, sending the puck into the air and heading for the gap above Wade's right shoulder, but he lifts his blocker and stick, knocking it away.

The crowd explodes into cheers, chanting the winning team's name as the rest of the Sting Rays flood back onto the ice to congratulate Wade and each other. Chase heads toward the tunnel to leave the rink, but then he doesn't.

I grab Sophie's hand. "Why isn't he leaving?"

She follows my line of sight with hers and squeezes my hand. "Don't worry. Lily and her team are there."

I know she's trying to reassure me, but I hear the uncertainty in her voice, and mine's twice as intense. I know Chase won't give up that easily. He has something planned. I just don't know what yet.

Wade's team heads toward the tunnel but stops when they see Chase hanging back. Wade drifts closer, gaze fixated on Chase while leaving a good distance between them. Chase removes his helmet and his catcher, tucking them under his left arm before holding his right hand out.

Sophie tugs my shirt sleeve. "Look, he's trying to make peace with Wade. Maybe the article had an impact after all."

My stomach hollows out, then fills with dread. I shake my head. "No, he's luring Wade in."

I jump up from my seat and race down the steps until I'm at the boards, pressing my hands against the glass. Wade has to see me. He searched for me in the stands enough times during the game to know where I am.

Wade tugs off his helmet and catcher and drifts closer to Chase. The excitement of the crowd has simmered to a soft rumble as everyone watches what's playing out on the ice.

Chase's mouth moves, but I can't hear or figure out what he said. Is he actually offering an olive branch? Or is he trying to stoke the fire I know blazes deep inside Wade?

I pound the glass, yelling Wade's name, although I'm sure he won't hear me over the growing chants of the crowd.

But then he turns his head, locking eyes with me. Everything in me tightens with a need to reach him, to tell him not to cross that line, that he doesn't have to prove anything to me. I don't want vengeance or justice for what Chase did to me. I just want Wade.

I want us.

He lifts one side of his mouth in that tilted smile I love. It's the one that's somewhat self-disparaging while coming across cocky as hell. I pound my hand on the plexiglass, desperate for him not to do what I suspect he's about to do.

He skates toward Chase, slow and deliberate, until he's a mere two feet away.

Chase thrusts his hand out again, but Wade stands there like a wall, strong and unmoving. And without a word, he shakes his head.

Something shifts in Chase's stance. His hand drops, and his shoulders go back. After a pause that feels more like a decade, he tosses his stick, blocker, and catcher to the ice and throws a punch at Wade.

His head spins toward me, a spray of blood and saliva flying from his mouth. He holds his jaw as he straightens, glancing briefly at me before turning his full focus on Chase.

And his rage, which propels him at Chase in a slew of fast punches.

They turn into a tangle of flailing arms, targeted fist punches, and jerseys pulled at odd angles. Until finally they both wind up down on the ice.

The referees skate in at this point to separate them. Wade backs off immediately, but Chase still lies prone on the ice.

And unmoving. One of the refs signals the medical team with an urgent shake of his arm. The chants of the crowd die off as spectators realize the fighting they'd so gleefully cheered on had turned into something more serious.

Wade shoves a hand through his hair as he watches the medics help Chase up, and then he turns to face me. His lip is already swelling, and his eyes glitter with a hardness that makes me shudder.

I don't know what Chase said to Wade, but I'm guessing it was awful based on how angry he looks.

A war of emotions slams into me. Fear over what this could potentially mean for Wade and his career. Anger at him for risking everything like that after he promised me he wouldn't. And finally, a devastating need to get to him, to hold him and make sure he's all right.

The rest of Wade's team rallies around him until the ref leads Wade off the ice and down the tunnel.

And I'm racing up the steps, desperate to get to him.

Chapter Thirty-Six

WADE

I wince as the medic dabs the split in my lip with a swab. The disinfectant burns, making me hiss through my teeth.

"You need stitches," he says as he probes the swollen skin and presses his gloved finger against my incisor. "The tooth is slightly loose, so don't bite or chew on this side for a week. Might want to have your dentist check it."

I nod, noting his skilled hands as he prepares the needle and thread to repair my lip. I'll probably have a scar, but it was totally worth it. I knew Chase would start something—I not only expected it but craved the opportunity to make him regret he ever hurt Bree.

The things he said about her—it will take every ounce of strength to wash them from my head. I'll make damn sure she never knows the vile words that scumbag had the nerve to say about her.

Her voice reaches me before I see her. She plows into the room, her blonde hair flying around her flushed face, making her appear even more beautiful than ever. But it's the feral look in her eyes that stops and makes me take notice.

She's worried about me. Sure, she's shown concern when I've gotten hurt in the past, but not like this. As if I'm her world and she's terrified she might have lost me.

I attempt a half smile, enjoying the show. "Hey, Bree-bear."

Putting her fists on her hips, she lets out a huff. "Don't you dare try to sweet-talk me, Wade Anthony Pierce. You promised!"

Her blue eyes glitter like the lights hitting the ice. If I didn't have a busted lip, I'd yank her against me and kiss her until she couldn't remember her own name. I find this protective side of her rather sexy. But I probably should explain that I did, in fact, keep my promise.

"I promised not to instigate something. *Not* to finish it." I inflect a sharp tone, so she understands it's a closed discussion. She's suffered enough at the hands of that jerk. I won't let him hurt her ever again.

"Semantics." She crosses her arms.

She's adorable as she tries to hold her resolve, but the rising fear in her eyes makes a strong appearance as she relents and takes a step closer. "Why wasn't he moving?"

I shake my head. "Dunno. I didn't think I hit him that hard."

"It was about me, wasn't it?"

The medic begins stitching my lip, giving me a reprieve from answering her question.

Annoyance crosses her features at the timing. Maybe if this takes long enough, she'll let it go. The sooner we put all this behind us, the sooner we can move on with our lives. Together. Because all I want right now is to be with Bree, in whatever way she'll have me.

Once he finishes, the medic hands me an ice pack.

Bree takes it from me and holds it up to my lip, making me hiss. "What did he say to you?"

I let the cold permeate my busted lip for a few seconds, then I tug her wrist away so I can talk. "I'm not sharing any of it because I refuse to let that asshat have any more power over you. Do you understand?"

Her eyes go wide, filling with tears.

And now I'm the asshat. I cup her face with my other hand. "I'm sorry. I didn't mean to sound so harsh."

"No, it's okay." She shakes her head. "I can't believe you did that. For me."

I pull her closer, wishing I could kiss her, but settling for resting my forehead against hers. "I'd do anything for you, Bree."

A voice clearing her throat pulls us apart. Bree jumps back, her cheeks flushed with embarrassment, which intensifies my desire to kiss her. I don't even care who would see us.

Rebecca glances between us. "Sorry to interrupt a private moment, but I thought I'd come and give you an update on Langston."

Bree waves a hand in front of her. "I'm sorry. I should be handling the PR mess."

Rebecca stops her from leaving. "Yes, but that can wait a few minutes more. Once the article link was live, I shared it with a few key people on the Board of Governors, along with the evidence Lily provided. And based upon the brief reply I received from the Chairman, I suspect an investigation will soon follow."

"Thank you." Bree lets out a sob through her smile. "Thank you for believing me."

Rebecca seems almost startled. "Of course, we believed

you. What that man did was reprehensible. There was no way we could just sit idly by and let him get away with it."

She looks over at me next. "However, I also suspect this will result in a suspension for you. I'll do my best to explain the extenuating circumstances and make it clear that he instigated the fight, but beyond that, it's out of my hands."

I nod. "I understand."

Rebecca smiles. "You know, there could be a bright side to this. If you are suspended, you can visit your family early for Christmas."

"That's a great idea." Especially if I can take Bree with me.

"I thought so, too." She turns to leave.

"Rebecca." I wait for her to turn around again. "I'm sorry for letting the team down."

Her gaze darts from me to Bree before settling back on me. "You haven't let anyone down."

After she leaves, Bree and I stare at each other. She starts to laugh, but then slaps a hand over her mouth, which makes me chuckle.

But not for long. I wince in pain. "Ahh."

"Sorry." Bree lunges forward with the ice pack, touching it gently to my mouth.

Since I can't kiss her, I do the next best thing and drink her in as she attempts to play nurse. Her blue eyes look like gemstones in the bright lights of the room, and that freckle on her lip keeps playing peek-a-boo with me every time she tugs her lip between her teeth as she concentrates on keeping the ice pack on my injury without pressing too hard.

I trace a finger down her cheek. "Come with me."

She blinks at me. "Where?"

"To the ranch. For Christmas. Nana said you weren't sure you could make it. Was it because of Langston?"

She drops her gaze. "Originally, yes."

I tip her chin up, forcing her to look at me, which I seem to have to do a lot of late. But I will make it my life's mission to ensure this amazing woman knows how priceless she is. "You don't have to worry about him anymore. It's over."

Something wars in her eyes, but then it flits away. Is she having doubts about us?

A small smile spreads across her kissable lips. "I'll see if I can take a few days off and leave early, too."

"Good." My relief is palpable. I need her there with me to face what comes next. Possibly say goodbye to the only place I've ever called home. My sisters and I are in this weird tug of war, each of us offering to walk away from our careers to run the ranch, only to be shot down by the other two. Not that Nana would let any of us do that. Knowing her, she'd secretly sell the place first.

The next words practically rip me apart. "This may be our last Christmas there."

Bree's eyes connect with mine in a deep exchange of understanding. Her fingers touch the uninjured side of my face. "I believe everything is going to work out better than you think."

Holding my hand over hers, I press my cheek into her palm. She smells of sweet honeysuckle, like the stuff that grows wild on the fences back home.

That's when it hits me. Bree Sutton *is* my home. Not a piece of property. Sure, my family has owned the ranch for generations, but maybe that timeline is supposed to come to an end.

The thought isn't as painful this time, and I think I can

move on as long as I have her. "I'll send Nana a text to let her know you're coming."

She tilts her head in an adorable yet coy manner that heats everything in me. "How about we surprise her?"

"Are you nervous about telling them we're together?"

"Maybe a little?" Her eyes search mine.

I'm half tempted to tell her I want it all—a marriage, a family, a life. The things I'd dreamed of having with her but had lost hope that they could ever come true. Yet here we are.

But I've had years to fall for this woman, while she's only discovering who I am to her now. I'll give her all the time she needs to figure it out as long as it leads her back to me.

I slide off the table, towering over Bree in my skates. It's killing me to not kiss her and show her she has nothing to worry about. "Bree, they've known for years how I feel about you."

"They have?" Her expression shifts from surprise to mortification. "Do they know I ghosted you for almost a year?"

"Over a year." I stride toward the locker room, ready for a shower, food, and some alone time with my girl.

"Again, semantics. What if they think I'm horrible?" She cringes.

"Trust me. They could never think that. They adore you. Always have. Always will."

Bree blinks teary eyes at me. "I adore them, too."

I tilt my head toward the door. "I'm going to get cleaned up. I suggest you don't follow me unless you want to see a bunch of goalies in various states of undress."

She taps a finger to her cheek as if in thought. "Tempting, but no."

I scowl at her, regretting it the minute I feel the pain shoot through my lip. "Hey, now. I'm the only one you look at from now on."

"That works both ways, you know." She pretends to pout.

Unable to resist touching her one more time, I hold her face and press our foreheads and noses together. "There has never been, nor will ever be, any other woman for me, Bree-bear. You're it."

She places a gentle kiss on the uninjured side of my mouth. "Same. I know that now."

No words have ever meant more to me. "It's about time."

Chapter Thirty-Seven

BREE

There's nothing like existing in wide open spaces. Most of the fall leaves have, well, fallen, exposing gangly trees hibernating for winter. A rare snow flurry came through last night, leaving a light dusting of white on the terrain. It's gorgeous and feels like an omen, telling me this is the right thing to do.

Wade insisted we drive back to Texas for the holidays since we had plenty of time, citing how road trips help him relax. I suspect it has more to do with him wanting me to himself for the two-day trip, before we arrive at the ranch where he'll have to share me with his family.

We talked about everything and anything. He insisted on holding my hand for most of our trip, as if I might disappear in a dream if he let go. I've never felt so loved and cherished by a man before—such a drastic contrast to how Chase treated me.

Rebecca turned out to be correct. They suspended Wade for the last three games before the holiday break since the altercation resulted in a player getting knocked out, even though it wasn't a regulation game. However, Chase Langston is officially no longer playing hockey.

Thanks to Rebecca putting the article in the right hands, Lily and her mysterious connections, and then Sophie's stellar interviewing skills, the news went viral in the ECHL world, which revealed more of Chase's shady activities.

The Texas Stars dropped him like a hot potato, and just before we left town, I heard Amber had as well. Guess she doesn't find former hockey players interesting enough.

Karma is real, people! The thought makes me laugh out loud.

"What's so funny?" Wade hands me a cup of coffee as he sits in the Adirondack chair next to me. The back porch —more like a deck—faces the lake situated between the house and a copse of trees. Every morning, a deer and her fawn approach to drink, so we've started having our coffee out here so we can watch them.

"Karma." I sigh, inhaling the aroma of chicory and cardamom while snuggling my down jacket closer around my neck.

He chuckles, letting me know he's tracking my thoughts without me even saying a word about the interesting turn of events since we left Sarabella. I absolutely love it when he does that.

"Yeah, well, you know what they say about her."

"Only if you're mean. Karma can be a force for good, too, you know?" I squeeze his hand, loving how he wants to touch me all the time, as if I'm his source of peace and strength, and he can't exist unless he's connected to me. And every time he tells me he loves me, his voice takes on a reverent kind of wonder, as if he's waited his entire life to speak those words to me, which I suppose, in a way, he has.

I just hope he's okay with my big surprise. I've spent weeks on the phone with Nana, hatching a plan we're both excited about. It's our big gift to Wade and his sisters, one we hope they'll love, too.

Piper and Ellie probably will. I'm almost certain of it. Seeing them again has been like the icing on an already delicious cake. My parents actually agreed to join us tomorrow on Christmas Day. They haven't spent the holiday together in several years, of course, but when I told them about Wade and me, they readily agreed to come. I think they'll love my idea, too.

It's Wade I'm most worried about. He's so selfless where I'm concerned. I know he only wants what's best for me. But this? This might be a difficult challenge, convincing him it's the right thing for all of us, including me.

Once we finish our coffee, Wade and I head back inside the house. He heads toward the living room to build a fire, so we can lounge and relax in the den where the Christmas tree stands.

I stop by Nana, who's slipping another tray of her famous chocolate chip cookies into the oven. She also has gingerbread and sugar cookie dough chilling in the fridge for more baking this afternoon.

"Everything ready?"

She closes the oven door and tosses her oven mitts on the counter. "I put the boxes under the tree."

Butterflies swarm in my stomach. It's the moment I've anticipated all week. I can't resist making a quiet squealing sound. "I just hope Wade gets on board."

Nana gives my chin an affectionate pinch. "Don't you worry about him, sweetness. He'll figure it out. He always does."

She plates several of the warm cookies and follows me

into the den. Wade and his sisters are already spread out on the sectional, exchanging more stories about recent events in their lives. I love how close he is with them.

When we drove in on the first day, Nana, Piper, and Ellie walked out on the porch to greet us. Wade opened my door, like the gentleman he is, and then pulled me into his arms and kissed me, surprising us all.

I thought his sisters were going to lose it, which they kind of did, holding each other's hands while they jumped up and down, squealing like baby pigs. Nana just stood there, smiling as if she'd known all along—I kind of suspect she did.

Wade pats the spot next to him, which I gladly oblige. He wraps his arm around my shoulders, tucking me against him as he presses his lips against my temple, inhaling and kissing me at the same time.

Ellie rolls her eyes. "Weren't you two just together on the porch?"

He smirks at her. "Yeah, so?"

"Get used to it, El." Piper nabs a cookie as Nana sets the plate down. "They're gonna be like this all the time."

Nana's special guy, Clint, who we've all fallen in love with already, presses a kiss to her cheek. "It's these Texas women. Hard to resist."

Watching Nana blush and wave him off fills me with all kinds of warm feelings and imaginings. I tilt my face toward Wade, trying to picture us at their age. Will we still feel like this about each other?

He meets my gaze, then kisses my nose. "We'll be even better."

This beautiful bear of a man…reading my mind again. I pinch his side before standing up. He grabs my hand in an attempt to pull me back down, but I manage to evade him.

Nana gives me a small nod—the go-ahead.

My breath is shaky as I take the three slim boxes from under the tree, handing one to Piper, Ellie, and then Wade.

He holds the bright green and red wrapped box in his hands. "Don't we usually wait until the evening?"

"Nana and I have something extra special for you this year, and we want you to open them now." I return to my spot next to him, leaving him plenty of room to unfold the documents.

The rustle of wrapping and tissue paper fills the room, accompanying the crackle of the fire. Studying all three of their faces as they unfold the plans we had drawn and absorb what they're holding is probably the most exhilarating and trepidating thing I've ever experienced.

Piper is the first one to gasp. She holds her hand to her mouth, darting her shocked gaze between Nana and me.

"No way." Ellie's voice drips with disbelief.

But it's Wade's reaction I'm anticipating the most. He keeps scanning the top page, which gives the complete picture of the transformation we're planning. I referenced my old binder with all the plans I had wanted to make for my parents' place when I had the idea of turning it into a venue for weddings, vacations, and weekend events, so all we had to do was put a plan together and hire an architect to bring my ideas to life.

Wade carefully folds the papers and places them on the table. He stares into the fireplace, making it difficult to read what he's thinking, but his silence feels heavy.

But I know what's going through his mind. That I'm sacrificing us for an old dream, and I'm pretty sure he's not saying it because he's afraid he'll wind up being the one to crush it this time.

He stands and leaves the room, heading toward the door leading to the back porch.

Nana gives me a small smile. "Maybe give him a few minutes to absorb it."

A long sigh seeps out of Ellie. "He can be so stubborn sometimes."

Piper gives me a knowing look. "There's more to it than that, El."

Clint makes a tutting sound. "Want me to talk to him? Help him see this is a good thing for all of you?"

As much as I appreciate his heart on this, I know I'm the only one who can help Wade see past the early hurdles of my idea. "Thanks, Clint, but I think he needs to hear it from me."

He nods as he reaches for Nana's hand. "It's not like we won't be here on occasion to help out. Just not in the beginning." He plants a kiss on her fingers. "We have some exploring of our own to do first."

Nana beams at him. I love seeing her so happy, and I want that too, for Wade and me.

I rise from the couch, running nervous hands down my thighs. "I'll go talk to him."

When I walk out onto the deck, Wade's leaning on the railing overlooking the lawn and the dock by the lake. I run my hand up his back, letting him know I'm here. His warmth strengthens me, as I hope my presence will for him.

"Wade, we can make this work. Once we have everything in place and things start moving, I can go back and forth. And you travel so much of the season as it is. I can come for visits and drive to nearby games. Then, in the summer, we can be together. Here."

He turns his head, staring at me over his shoulder. "Is this really what you want?"

"Yes. You know this was always my dream." I run my fingers along the side of his head, loving the feel of his auburn strands. He's let his beard and hair grow in more for the second half of the season, and it suits him.

He drops his gaze. "I know, I just thought you were happy in Sarabella. With me."

I push his shoulder back so he'll face me. "I was—am. But this is an answer that works for all of us. You won't have to give up the ranch."

His jaw pulses. "Bree, I care more about you than this ranch. And I thought you felt the same."

"I do. Of course I do." I try to hug him, but he steps back.

"But you're choosing something other than me again."

My heart lurches at his words, and at the rawness baring itself in his face. "What do you mean?"

He scrapes a hand over his mouth before letting out a resigned sigh. "When I found out you dated Chase, my first thought was, why didn't she pick me? I know that sounds crazy, but it's the truth."

My eyes burn. "Oh, Wade. I'm so, so sorry. If I'd known how you felt—"

"I know. That's on me." He holds my hands in his. "Just tell me that's not what's happening here. That you don't want this more than you want me."

I step into the circle of his arms. "Wade, I'm not doing this for me. I'm doing this for *us*. For our future. For the family we'll raise here. For our family gatherings—"

"Family? As in kids?" Wonder blankets his gaze, making me realize I haven't said THE most important words in all of this.

I link my fingers behind his neck, lifting to kiss him lightly on the lips, careful not to touch the area still healing.

"I love you, Wade. Being your best friend is great, but I want a lot more with you."

His lips slowly spread into a smile that makes my heart stutter. "I want all of that, too. I just didn't realize you'd thought that far. About us."

"It's you. How could I not?"

Heat ignites in his gaze, mixed with love. So much love. And I drown in it as he lowers his head, capturing my lips in a delicate yet soul-changing kiss that claims me as his in all the best ways. I don't know how I missed it all these years, the way this man loves me, making me feel cherished and wanted as if I'm the center of his world.

But I know now. I see it. I want it. I love it.

More importantly, I love *him*. With all my heart.

Epilogue

WADE

Six months later…

The truck rattles as I turn off the highway onto the long drive leading to the house. The old gate has a new wood and metal sign arching overhead with the words, Piercing Hearts Ranch.

When Bree proposed the name, I think I fell for her all over again. How she managed to keep our family name, yet make it sound like a mission statement for what this new venue is all about, completely blew me away.

And reaffirmed once again how right she was about all of it.

We coordinated the renovations and launch for the beginning of summer, so that I can be a part of it now that hockey season has ended. Opening is a week away, which gives me time to acclimate and, more importantly, a chance to spend some alone time with Bree before this place starts humming with visitors. Bree already has a family reunion booked in two weeks and a large wedding three weeks after that.

Her big surprise is already proving to be the best thing for us. Nana and Clint returned from a month-long European tour—their second one since Christmas—and are now on a river cruise down the Rhine. Piper's hockey career is taking off, and Ellie is coming home to help over the summer before she starts her sophomore year of college.

Everyone is doing what he or she loves.

But what Bree doesn't know is that I have a big surprise planned for her this time. A couple of them, actually. That's part of what has me on edge. I'd like to think I know how she'll react, that she'll be as excited about this as I am. But I may have to convince her it's what I want.

The tires make a dragging sound on the gravel as I come to a stop. When I step out of the truck, I'm hit with the familiar scents of earth, hay, and horses. The barn, freshly painted and renovated, spans to my left near a new, smaller corral that's for pony rides and a weekend animal farm that will be held once a month. Bree set up partnerships with other ranches in the area to "borrow" animals for those events.

Despite the changes, this place still feels like home. My home.

The sound of the porch door opening spins me around toward the house in time to see Bree launch herself down the steps, blonde hair flying behind her. She races toward me and jumps into my arms, wrapping herself around me like she did when she arrived so unexpectedly at the arena.

I wrap my arms around her, holding her close, eyes shut as I breathe in her familiar scent. Her warmth settles all the points of concern that cropped up during the drive.

"Bree-bear, I missed you." Between my amped-up

schedule through the playoffs and finals and Bree finishing the renovations and scheduling the venue's first events, we haven't seen each other in almost two months.

She nuzzles her face into the crook of my neck. "I missed you, too."

When she lifts her head, I do what I've been itching to do since I left Sarabella—I kiss her like a man starved of water.

I spin her around, pinning her against the truck door so I can hold her head and take this kiss to a whole new level. She lets out a soft moan that ignites the longing I've held in check for weeks.

"In case you forgot, this is a family-friendly place." A woman's voice I don't recognize brings me back to awareness.

Bree smiles against my lips. "That would be Georgia."

"*The* Georgia?" I let go of my hold on Bree so she can slide down.

She grins up at me. "The one and only."

Known locally for her bees and honey, Georgia Manning used to work for a PR company in New York before she retired early and landed in Creeks Bend. But bees didn't keep her busy enough, so when Bree reached out, wanting to work with Georgia and her honey, Georgia proposed a different kind of partnership.

Now she's Bree's partner, which couldn't have worked out better than any of us envisioned. Where Bree is the one who brings new and original ideas to the table, Georgia has the experience and skills to bring them to life.

Bree holds her hand out. "Georgia, this is Wade."

Dressed in boots, jeans, and a T-shirt, the middle-aged woman looks right at home here. Never would have imagined she spent most of her life in Manhattan.

"Pleased to finally meet you, Wade." She shakes my hand, smiling. Her keen observation glides over both of us. "I have some paperwork to handle. I'm sure Bree can give you the tour and show you what we've done so far."

My gaze automatically drifts to Bree, catching her blush as she tugs that freckled part of her lip between her teeth.

"I love that idea." I study her, waiting to see if she catches what I'm really implying, that I love her, everything about her, and especially being part of this next chapter of our lives. Together. But more importantly, I've missed her beyond belief and want to show her.

Her eyes glitter in the sun, telling me she did and more.

"Okay, I'm going inside before you two completely lose it for each other." Georgia's throaty laugh drifts back as she scales the steps, and the soft bang of the screen door tells us we're alone again.

I twine my fingers into Bree's. "You heard the woman. Give me a tour."

First, Bree drags me into the barn, dragging me up the stairs to the second level that used to be a wide open space for hay and storage. Now, a cozy sitting area fills the middle, flanked on three sides by doors leading to guest suites, each one sporting a sign on the door with a specific name.

Bree opens the door labeled 'Heart-Strings.' Bright light floods through the windows on either side of a four-poster bed covered by a fluffy beige comforter with a stripe of black musical notes dancing from one corner to the other. Music-themed pictures decorate the walls, and so many throw pillows. I still don't get the point of those things, but Bree reassures me they're an important part of the ambiance.

"There's a basic bathroom in this one. Some of the

other suites have soaking tubs in addition to a walk-in shower."

"Wow, sounds luxurious." I should take in the details of the room, but she's what I'm most interested to drink in.

Bree laughs. "Did you think we'd use hay bales for the beds and leave a bucket in the corner?"

I roll my eyes at her. "No, just didn't expect this level of comfort."

"We want people to come back. Amenities make all the difference."

She shuts the door and leads me to another suite on the back side of the barn with 'The Forever Suite' brandished across this door in a flourishing script.

I point to the sign. "Nice name."

Bree grins. "We wanted something better than just the honeymoon suite, which makes it more versatile, too."

She swings the door open to a lush room in soft rose and rich greens. A king-size bed sits on one side with a cozy sitting area in front of the fireplace.

"The fireplace is electric, but still generates heat. We didn't want to deal with adding a chimney to the barn or using gas."

The picture on the mantel draws me closer. I remember the picture from our family albums, the one of my parents on their wedding day. But this isn't a tiny aging photo in a scrapbook. It's a beautiful painting that sets the tone for the room.

I work to swallow down the lump in my throat. "Bree."

Her hand slips into mine as she comes alongside me, warm and comforting. "I wanted something about your family to define this room, so I commissioned an artist to paint the photo. I know your mom…left. But they seemed so happy on their wedding day. I hope you like it."

I study the brushstrokes capturing my parents' youthful faces, filled with the joy of the day as they stare into each other's eyes. The painting moves me in a deep and unexpected way as I imagine newlyweds celebrating the start of their marriage in this space. Granted, my parents' marriage didn't last, but I have to believe what they shared in the beginning was real.

Surprisingly, it's almost symbolic of the years I've spent loving Bree, hoping for a future, a lifetime with her. I want that with her, more now than ever. "I love it."

She presses her face against my chest, head tilted up to look at me as she clings to my arm. The love I see in her eyes steals all the air from my lungs, leaving me in this euphoric place of wonder and disbelief that this is real between us. Finally.

I didn't plan to do this now, but I couldn't have picked a more perfect moment. Time for surprise number one.

"Bree, I want to start building our life together. Now."

She moves to stand in front of me, her back to the painting. "We are. That's what this is all about."

"I know, but I'd like to make some aspects more official."

"Like what?" Her expression shifts to something hopeful. Does she suspect?

Might as well get the hard part out of the way so we can move on. "I made a decision."

"Wade..." Her beautiful face contorts with concern.

"I'm not renewing my contract with the Sun Kings." I thought the decision to leave hockey would be more difficult. In reality, leaving the daily camaraderie with the fellas is what I'll miss most, but now I have a new future ahead of me with the promise of a relationship of a lifetime.

"But you love hockey. You can't do that. The whole

point of my doing all this was so you didn't have to." She starts pacing back and forth.

I tug her to me. "And I'm grateful for that. You gave me time to finish this chapter in my life."

"With a Kelly Cup. The Sun Kings are becoming a force to be reckoned with. Are you sure you want to walk away from that now?"

"More sure than I've ever been about anything." I tilt my head from side to side. "Well, maybe there's one other thing I'm more sure of."

Her eyes widen as I reach into my pocket. I've carried the small velvet bag with the ring I picked out for weeks as a way to keep going until I saw her again.

As I slip the ring out, I go down on one knee.

Tears fill her beautiful blue eyes that match the wide-open skies above us, full of promise and things to come. And more—her love for me.

"Bree-bear, you're my best friend and the love of my life. Even when you didn't know it, I have loved you with every fiber of my being. If you'll have me, I promise I'll make sure you know every day just how precious you are to me. Will you marry me?"

Hand covering her mouth, she nods vigorously, lowering herself to her knees in front of me. "Yes, of course I will."

She lets out a watery laugh as I slip the faceted blue diamond, nearly the same shade as her eyes, onto her ring finger. Then she throws herself into my arms, knocking us both to the floor, her on top of me.

Her laughter fills me with the confirmation that this is all as it should be—every part. Even leaving hockey. I think the fellas had a harder time with it than I did, but seeing Mason rise to the challenge will make the transition easier.

I hold her face and kiss her deeply, communicating as

best as I can how much I love this woman. She's everything to me, which made my decision easy. Almost too easy when I think about it.

She pulls away, lifting her head, her eyes searching my face. Her hair falls around her face and mine, creating our own private little world. She brings her fingers to my temple, touching the moisture there. "What's wrong?"

I didn't even feel the tear slip from my eye, but I know it's from me. "I've imagined this for so long."

She makes an aching noise. "I hope it was worth the wait."

I brush her hair back, cupping the face that has the power to make or destroy me. "Worth every year, every month, every week, every hour, every minute, every second—"

She stops me with a kiss. "I think you ran out of time increments."

I shake my head, knowing that the best kind of time spans in front of us. "Not possible. Because now we have a lifetime."

More by Dineen Miller

vinci-books.com/bloomedmessy

A flower shop. A former bully. One year to find out if love is worth the mess.

When my aunt dies and leaves me her old flower shop, I have to run it for a year before I can move away and chase my dreams in New York. Then Kade Maverick turns up: the guy who bullied me in high school. He seems changed and is willing to help me fix up the store. But I'm going back to New York when my year is up, and he's just not a part of those plans. Right?

Turn the page for a free preview…

Bloomed to Be Messy: Chapter One

AMANDA

"Wait…can you read that part again?" Sitting in a lawyer's office on a Saturday afternoon is not what I call fun. And neither would my Aunt Paula. But here we are, just two weeks after her sudden departure from the living and one week after the funeral.

My aunt's lawyer, Mr. Tate, clears his throat as he shuffles papers on his desk. "You have to run the business for one year before you can sell or close it."

"From what date?" One needs to be clear on these things, right? Because, if I'm understanding things correctly, this is about to mess with my plans.

Big time.

He checks the document again. "The date of her death."

I bounce forward in my high-backed chair and slap down the top of the pages so I can see the proverbial fine print. "Well, look at that. Says from the day of her death."

"That's correct." In lawyer-y fashion, he shakes the papers back up. "Shall I continue?"

"Yes, please. Sorry." I give him a grin-like grimace and shrug.

As Mr. Tate continues to read the stipulations of the will, sunlight streams through the bay window to my right, warming the right side of my body. I turn to gaze out at the bustle of this small Florida beach town that moves with the ebb and flow of tourism.

Mango Lane runs the entirety of downtown Sarabella and is known for its quaint shops and bistros that are mostly comprised of converted houses originally built around the turn of the twentieth century. Along with a close-knit community, the business district here shares a special camaraderie that hasn't changed much in twenty years.

By the way, mangos are to Sarabella, Florida, as garlic is to Gilroy, California.

Big.

We even have a festival in the fall that boasts foods made out of mangos that you never imagined possible, like mango wine and savory mango fries made from green mangos. And the tourists make sure to arrive in time to attend this event that draws vendors, from all over the state of Florida and beyond, who sell their wares.

Being back here brings a flood of memories. Mostly good. Some not so much.

I left several years ago to pursue my own dreams, convinced my days of living under swaying palms and my mother's brow-raising reputation were over. Yet now I'm yanked back by Aunt Paula, whom I adored, but she always had a unique gift of meddling.

Yes, I'm calling it a gift. Otherwise, I'd stomp out of the lawyer's office, refusing to take over the flower business my aunt has so *graciously* willed to me—a ready-made business that has nothing to do with my dreams of being a communications and product designer in the Big Apple, something I'd imagined since being a high school senior in art club. Plus, New York had one of the best art schools in the country.

I *could* cite Mad Men as part of what cultivated my interest in the advertising world, but it only fueled it. In reality, Aunt Paula is to blame for that one because her father—whom I never had the pleasure to meet—was a real live Don Draper in his day. He even had the same first name!

Thus, I grew up listening to her stories about him and his life as an ad man in NYC that bordered on the scandalous at times. So in reality, she helped set the trajectory of my life, even though she would never have admitted it.

Not that I wanted to do something scandalous. I just wanted more. More adventure and excitement, to see more of this big wide world I lived in. And more distance from my mother's notoriety, which never seems to fade when you live in a place with people who have long memories and sometimes loose tongues.

And finally—the final decider—I wanted out of this beach town that hummed half of the year and slept the other.

Mr. Tate's throat clearing snaps me back to the present.

I give him a smile to reassure him I'm listening. Well, half listening. Most of what he's relaying now has to do with his law firm's involvement in the handling of the will, so I'll just go back to justifying my decision to get out of Dodge nine years ago and reminisce about how well things have worked out.

Well…mostly…

When I moved to New York to go to art college, I figured the Big Apple had room for one more designer. So did my former classmate and current roommate, Sasha, who's more of a fine artist. And since graduation, we've managed to scrape by (not starving, mind you) in a tiny two-bedroom walk-up. Not exactly ideal for creating art, let me tell you.

I'm still more of a production assistant at this point, and Sasha has to work on her paintings on the fire escape, which leaves a lot to be desired but makes cleanup very easy. As long as the downstairs neighbor doesn't happen to be outside at the moment. That's a story I relish telling at any and all opportunities.

But we've persevered, sustained mostly by the belief that our next break was just around the corner. Which one? We had no clue. We just kept turning those corners as they came. Early on, we lived mostly on ramen noodles, peanut butter and jelly sandwiches, and the fancy appetizers at the art shows I frequented with Sasha. Plus, the occasional event my boss needed me to help him schmooze old and new clients.

Over time, Sasha and I have upgraded our menu and splurge on an occasional night out on the town. Not exactly how I imagined my life would look at this point, but it is what it is, right?

"Ms. Wilde, do you have any other questions?" My aunt's lawyer blinks at me through his designer glasses as he neatens the stack of papers in front of him. He sits behind a broad desk with a stack of folders on one end, an overflowing inbox on the other, and a wall of books behind him that appears rather dusty on the upper shelves. Just like his head.

"Did I understand you correctly, her condo is mortgage free?"

He shuffles through a separate stack of papers on his

desk. "That's correct. Just the property taxes due at the end of the year, and the monthly HOA fee."

Mr. Tate clears his throat before giving exact figures with his official lawyer expression of authority. I had no idea how pricy living in this beach town had become, which has sprouted and expanded quite a bit in the last five years alone. Not so sleepy anymore, it seems. I do a quick calculation in my head. Less than what I pay for my half of the rent in New York but not by as much as you'd think.

He continues reading where he left off, but my mind has flitted to yet another thought.

"Any stipulations about selling *it*?" Even I can hear the edge of desperation trying to peek its way out in my voice. Maybe Aunt Paula's meddling—I mean generosity, of course—could be used to my advantage for once.

And the way Mr. Tate raises one brow tells me he knows exactly where I'm headed with this. "Once the transfer of ownership is complete, it's yours to do with as you wish. But if you don't mind a word of advice?"

"Yours or Aunt Paula's?"

"Mine."

I give him a nod.

"Sarabella has grown a lot in the years you've been away. Property is valued at an all-time high, but that has thrust rental prices through the roof as well. A one-bedroom apartment would cost you more than twice the HOA fees on your aunt's place."

Okay, closer to New York rates than I thought. "So, keep the condo?"

Now his other brow rises to create a uniform, fur-lined wrinkle in his brow. "You need a place to live, don't you?"

Boxed in again by my crafty aunt. She always did have an interesting sense of humor that tended to break the rules of decorum but in very subtle ways. To meet her was to be immediately enchanted by her Savannah-born and raised southern charm. The woman knew how to get people to do what she thought was best for them. All out of love, she would tell you. But despite that somewhat irritating trait (only because she was usually right), she was one of the strongest and noblest people I've ever met.

Mr. Tate clears his throat again.

Clearly, he's trained his guttural sounds and facial muscles from years of lawyering. (And yes, that's a word. I looked it up.)

"Any other questions?"

"No, just trying to figure out what my aunt is up to."

He gives me a knowing smile that tells me he knew Aunt Paula better than most. "Paula always had a mission."

"That's one way of saying it."

Mr. Tate either didn't hear my mumble or chooses to ignore me as he slides a set of keys across his desk. "These are to the store and her condo."

I hook the ring on my finger and count five keys. "That only accounts for two keys."

"Paula loved a good mystery, too."

I drop the keys into my bag as I stand and extend my hand. "Thank you, Mr. Tate. I'd like to say it's been a pleasure, but the verdict is still out on that." I smile and give him a short laugh so he'll know it's nothing personal. I know who's still pulling the strings in this scenario, even if she's watching from the heavens she so dearly loved.

After shaking my hand, Mr. Tate comes from behind his desk to walk me out. He's taller than I realized and towers a good ten inches above me. And I'm not short. Now I understand why he's seated in his family picture that sits on the shelf behind his desk. The camera would have been hard-pressed to fit his wife and kids without him looking like a giant.

"I'm here if you need anything. Paula was very special to my family, as well as the firm. Please don't hesitate to call if you need anything, Mandy."

"Amanda, please." What I don't say is that since my mother, born Josephine Wilde, hijacked my nickname to create her stage name, Mandy Wild, I preferred not to bring her up at all in this scenario. But knowing my aunt as I do—did—Mr. Tate is probably aware of our history to some degree.

He blinks and drops his gaze. "Of course. I forgot..." He clears his throat and his gray sideburns stand out against the blush darkening his cheeks. "Whatever you need, I'm happy to help...Amanda."

"Thank you, Mr. Tate. I'm sure I'll be in touch."

I leave the Law Offices of Tate and Tate, which makes me think of the expression 'tit for tat'—a phrase that aptly describes this scenario. My aunt's scheme could very well be her way of telling me moving to New York was a mistake, which at this point in my life, I could be persuaded to see it that way if she were still alive and having this conversation with me.

But she's not and now I'm a prisoner in her little scheme for the next year or more. The next task on my agenda is to let my roommate know that I'll be gone for a while. Maybe she can sublet my room.

And then?

Check out the flower shop I now own and am required to run successfully for an entire year.

As I walk up the steps and unlock the back door of the shop, I'm transported to the past and the fragrant memory of flowers and greenery. I spent most days after school helping Aunt Paula at the shop and always had a guaranteed job during the summer, which was a mixed bag of love and hate. As in, loved having money to spend at the movies or at the mall but hated being stuck at the shop, working while my friends hung out at the beach.

But as I open the door, the putrid stench of rotted flowers assaults me, making me gag. Seems things have been neglected much longer than anyone realized. And let me tell you, the smell of rotting greenery is like none other.

The culprit is a large garbage can of discarded flowers and clippings that clearly never made it to the dumpster before Aunt Paula's sudden departure. With my hand over my mouth and nose, I drag the can outside, walk a few steps away, and inhale the humid mid-morning air that carries a hint of the beach in its scent.

For a moment I'm tempted to lock the door and head in that direction—to the beach and deal with whatever else lurked in the flower shop of death tomorrow. But I've never been one to put off what I can get done today. Especially in light of the big picture. The sooner I get the place up and running again, the better my chances of making it through this next year so I can move on to my original plan. Maybe even with a financial cushion to give me more time to make NYC notice my creative talents.

I snicker out loud at my own thoughts. What does that tell you?

"Mandy?"

I whip around and see a face that brings a flood of childhood memories that includes building sand castles on the beach and hanging out at the movie theatre on Friday nights. All the wonderful memories of growing up in Sarabella.

"Zane!" A flood of warm affection launches me into his bear hug.

"How are you doing?" He steps back but hangs onto my hands, giving me that look that requires only the truth. "I wanted to stop by sooner, but I had to fly out for a conference in California right after the funeral."

Zane Albright is the quintessential surfer, who turned his childhood passion for the beach into a full-blown career. He worked as a lifeguard at Mango Key Beach straight out of high school. Not long after, he revamped the training program for the Sarabella County Lifeguards and now he's Director of Operations.

"A conference full of lifeguards? That sounds like way more fun than a funeral."

"Seriously, how are you?" Zane gives me his concerned, big brother look, which always made things seem better in high school. He's also the only one who completely supported my dream of moving to New York.

"I'm okay."

Overwhelmed by the concern I see in his eyes, I drop my chin, feeling the heavy weight of grief twisting around my neck like the string in my gym shorts caught in the dryer. I refuse to shed more tears over my aunt while I'm still wrangling the mess she's left me to clean up.

Maybe it's payback for all the years she wound up raising me while she waited for my mother—her little sister—to "hit it big" and come back to claim her daughter. "I still can't believe she's gone."

His voice rumbles up in a deep baritone. "I know."

I shield my eyes against the sun that's now peeking over Zane's sun-bleached head and blasting me with its brightness and heat. Sweat trickles down my back. Though nearing its end, summer is still very much present, as is the humidity.

"What are you doing here? Why aren't you at the beach?" I finish my words with a laugh.

"Mom figured you'd need some help. She called me when you left Mr. Tate's office."

Sally is the owner of The Pink Hibiscus, a super cute clothing boutique, and has been my Aunt Paula's best friend since they opened their shops around the same time. Supporting each other in their businesses translated into a close friendship in other areas of life, which meant Zane and I pretty much grew up together.

"How did she know when I left his office?" I know the answer to this question, but I still have to ask.

"She told him to call her when you left."

The small town grapevine was alive and well in Sarabella. I look over my shoulder at the can of putrid death oozing its noxious smell like an evil gas looking for a new victim. Who knows what else lies in store for me inside? Maybe giant cockroaches have invaded and set up shop. Or one of those ornery raccoons Aunt Paula always complained about raiding the dumpster behind her shop because she shared it with Peppery Pete's Wine and Cheese Shop.

Now there's a rank smell in the summer.

Zane glances at his watch. "I can spare a couple of hours before I go on duty. How about I help you figure things out?"

Gratitude nearly brings me to tears again. "Thanks. I can really use the help."

He winks at me before grabbing the garbage can and tipping it over into the dumpster. His face scrunches up as he turns his head away, revealing his pure disgust, which says a lot for a guy who's had to deal with red tide and rotting fish.

Therefore, I am vindicated that I nearly barfed my own putridity at my first encounter with what shall forever be referred to as 'The Can.' God only knows—Him and my Aunt Paula, that is—what else lies in wait for me in the place.

Somehow having Zane's help to navigate the unknown jungle inside boosts my lagging confidence that I might be able to handle what lies in store. In *that* store. I go back inside and scan the back room, which used to be a kitchen when the place was a residence. A plant cooler sits where a refrigerator used to go and a work counter and stool filled the place where a stove might have once stood.

At least that's what I imagined as a child when I helped my aunt. The cabinets needed some paint and small repairs—one seemed to be missing its door—and smears of green, yellow, and red stained the wood table. Evidence of who knows how many floral arrangements crafted over the thirty-plus years my aunt owned the shop.

The storefront itself is spacious and thankfully free of giant cockroaches and angry raccoons. Aunt Paula didn't have much set up display-wise, except for a rickety greeting card display near the counter, a bookshelf with various mugs and decorative pots displaying plant themes, and a table near the front door that touts several dead flower arrangements, an emaciated cactus, and a few orchids that still have blooms—the only things still living in the place.

Three glass-front coolers line the wall to the right, one unlit. The flowers and greenery in the buckets inside have either dried out or drooped over the sides. I can only imagine the stench waiting inside to greet me. Although the baby's breath seems to have persevered.

Does baby breath ever die or does it just dry out?

Zane comes alongside me, toting the can he just emptied. "How about I empty the coolers while you water what's still living over there?"

He must have seen the look of horror on my face as I stared at the contents. "Thanks. Not sure I can handle any more of that smell."

I open the front door to create a cross breeze, giving up the air conditioning for some hot but fresh air. Outside, I turn around to look at the sign above the door.

Bloomed to Be Wilde.

If you're thinking of the Steppenwolf song, you're on target. My aunt loved that song. So much so she modeled the name of the flower shop after the title, using the spelling of our last name, which aptly describes the women in my family, it seems. Aunt Paula said it was the family motto, which my mother seemed to have lived up to in spades.

And here I stand, the new owner of her legacy.

I glance upward and sigh. Aunt Paula had to be loving this.

Bloomed to Be Messy: Chapter Two

KADE

"What did you expect to find out?"

I'm sitting on the sofa in my mother's small but immaculate trailer, wishing I were back in my studio, torching metal. There's a certain satisfaction in controlled destruction. That probably sounds strange, but if you knew my past, you'd understand.

But now my future is about to get way more complicated.

By a four-year-old.

"I didn't know Shannon was struggling."

"Maybe you would if you bothered to check in more often with your family. After she lost her job, she had to move in with a friend. Things got overwhelming for her."

I run my hands through my hair and let out a long exhale. "I'm sorry. Business has picked up over the last year."

What I don't say is that my reputation in Sarabella has grown. An increase in custom home builders wanting original metal work detailing for homes has doubled my orders in the last six months alone, thanks to the popularity of a couple of DIY home shows on TV and social media.

But that won't matter to my mother. She only sees the man who left the confines of a toxic family that boasts a long line of motorcycle-riding 'bad boys.'

Cliché, I know, but we do exist.

However, I shifted gears five years ago in order to pursue a more creative and lucrative future. It's not that I don't love my family…I do, but I no longer share their perspective that life deals us what we get and we're stuck with it. Nor do I subscribe to the belief that men who are creative and artistic are somehow…unmanly.

Plus, watching a person die brings life-changing side effects. Don't ask me how I know.

Do I need therapy?

Maybe?

Probably.

Right now, all I know is I'm doing what I love and now I may have to redirect for a compact human being whose big green eyes and dimpled smile melt my every resistance.

"I'm so glad life worked out for you while the rest of us are stuck here in the muck."

Acknowledging her comment will only feed her pessimism. I learned not so long ago that you can't reason a person out of a place they didn't reason themselves into to begin with.

I also know she's still bitter. "What else did she say?"

My mother shrugs. "Just that she needed time to get back on her feet, which I was happy to give her. Elly is my granddaughter, and I want the very best for her."

We interrupt this guilt-laden dialogue to interject that this is my mother's way of reminding me of all she's done for me. She's the queen of passive-aggressive dialogue and part of the reason I had to get out of close proximity. The constant reminders of how much I've disappointed her became life-sucking.

"But then this happened," she gestures to the brace encasing her foot and ankle, "and there's no way I can keep up with a four-year-old."

I nod but say nothing because I'm trying to picture how to adjust my life to accommodate a child. Which isn't mine, by the way. Just want to be clear on that. Eliana is my niece. And the daughter of my brother Devon.

"Of course not." I rise from the couch. "Where is she now?"

"Preschool, or what we used to call daycare. My neighbor dropped her off for me. Figured it might be easier for us to figure this out without little pitchers around."

"Little pitchers?"

My mother waves me off. "An old expression. Means big ears, even though hers are small." A hoarse laugh rumbles in her chest.

"When does she get back?"

My mother looks up at me with an expression I've come to recognize as her loaded gun. "That's up to you, now isn't it? Her bag is packed on the bed, and they're expecting you by three."

Unbelievable. "You could have told me this before I drove out here."

"Why? And spoil the fun?"

"No, so I could have planned for a passenger. I rode my motorcycle." I notice her flinch as I check my watch. Maybe she cares more than she lets on. All I know is I have about an hour to get back to Sarabella, get my truck, and come back to pick up the squirt.

I push up to my feet, careful not to let my work boots bump against her coffee table.

A flash of regret moves behind her eyes so fast that I would have missed it had I not been looking for some sort of recognition. But it's gone before it can do anything to soften the hardness that's settled permanently around her mouth. "Then I guess you better figure something out quick."

And now I've clamped my jaw so tight I can only nod. I grab Eliana's bag from a makeshift cot in the corner of the tiny bedroom.

At the front door, I pause. Despite the chasm between us, she's still my mother, and I'm a duty-bound son. "Do you need anything? Help with anything around here? I can come by this weekend."

She waves me off. "No, I've got great neighbors and people who love me nearby."

Guilt trip received. I exhale, drop my chin, and count to ten. "Bye, Mom."

My mother just stares at me. She doesn't move. Doesn't say a word.

I'm guessing she's disappointed again that I didn't allow her to manipulate me, but as I said, I can't reason someone out of a place they've chosen to be in.

I close the door and stride to where my motorcycle sits. After lashing down Eliana's small bag, I hop on, pulling my helmet over my head, and then crank the motor.

The ride home will give me some time to think and plan, as will the ride back.

Because I don't have a clue about how to take care of a four-year-old.

In a split second, Eliana recognizes me and comes running. "Uncle Kade!"

Her little pink backpack bounces behind her as she runs toward me. I scoop her up with a grunt, realizing she's grown nearly half a foot since I last saw her. And in preschool, no less.

"Hey, squirt."

Her little arms hang onto my shoulders as she stares into my eyes. "You smell funny."

"Yep. I was working."

"Why are you picking me up today?"

My gut clenches because I see Devon staring back at me through green eyes that are an exact duplicate of his, even down to the freckle in the right one. I have one too, but in the opposite eye. Mom said we got our green eyes from our father, who left town around the time Devon was born. Which left me to become the man of the house.

"Because Grandma sent me to take you on an adventure."

Her little mouth forms a circle to match her rounded eyes. "Do I get to ride on your motorbike?"

She couldn't get the hang of the word "cycle" when she was younger because of a lisp she's mostly outgrown. Bike became her default and stuck.

"No, not yet. You're still a squirt."

She wiggles to let me know she wants to get down. When her feet hit the floor, she stands straight with her shoulders back and her chin up. She lifts her heels off the floor to look taller. "But look how big I am now."

I squat down and hold her hands. "Yes, you are, but this adventure is bigger than my motorbike."

She frowns, but her eyes are round with wonder. "Bigger than a motorbike?"

I can picture her father's proud smile right now at his daughter's awe of motorcycles. But my mother would kill me if I let Eliana anywhere near one. Shannon, too, for that matter.

"Way bigger. You get to come stay with me for a while. And you can see my metal shop."

"What's a metal shop?"

"A place where I make things out of metal with a blowtorch."

"What's a blowtorch?" Torch sounds more like *torsh* with her residual lisp peeking out.

"I'll have to show you. So, what do you think?"

She lowers her chin. "Did I do something wrong?"

I can almost hear the "r" in wrong this time. She really has grown a lot since I last saw her. As much as I don't want to admit it, my mother was right. I've been too busy and away too much.

I hug Eliana. "No, squirt, not at all. Why would you ask that?"

"Because Mommy said she needed a break and now Grandma does, too."

I smooth a rogue, pale brown wisp behind her ear. Even her hair has grown, judging by the Rapunzel braid she now sports. Braiding hair—another thing I'm going to have to learn.

"Grandma broke her foot, which means she can't run around and play very well right now."

"So she called you?"

"Yeah, is that okay?" I almost hold my breath because if she says 'no,' I've no idea what to do next.

The corners of her mouth lift slightly as she nods, looking at me again with Devon's eyes. "Yeah, as long as you promise I can sit on your motorbike."

I stand and tousle her bangs. "I'll think about it."

Eliana crosses her arms and pouts. "All right."

As I take her hand, the teacher walks over, holding out a slip of paper. "Mr. Maverick, can you sign this so we have it on record that you picked Eliana up?"

Nodding, I take the slip of paper and pen.

"Will Eliana be coming back?"

That's a good question. One I don't have an answer to, though. "Uh, I'm not sure, to be honest."

She gives me a sympathetic smile that makes me think she's more aware of what's been going on with Shannon than I am. "No problem. I'll just mark down on her file that she'll be away for a while."

"Thanks, I appreciate it."

She points toward an odd-looking chair near the doorway. "Don't forget her booster seat."

I scrawl my name on the blank line and hand the paper and pen back to her.

A simple slip of paper, yet somehow I feel like I've signed up for something way bigger than I can handle.

Bloomed to Be Messy: Chapter Three

AMANDA

For the last two weeks, my days have been filled with cleaning the shop, painting cabinets and walls that haven't seen a new layer of paint in at least ten years (the initials of my first crush plus mine are still on the bathroom wall), and scrubbing a squeaky floor that I discovered used to be white when I moved a small display cabinet that I remember from when I was a kid.

And my nights? Well, party girl that I am—snort—those I spend binge-watching YouTube videos showcasing the latest trends in floral arrangements and researching the best marketing strategies for small business owners.

The sooner I can open for business, the better because the meager reserves my aunt left to me for running the place are dwindling fast and my paltry savings have gone toward food and the utilities for my new condo.

Yes, I'm now a condo owner—free and clear. My one relief in this crazy scenario. And one of the keys on that ring turned out to be for a storage area in the building's basement. I found a few pieces of small furniture and about a dozen boxes I've yet to explore. Add that to my unending to-do list.

But today's challenge is—

DUN, DUN, DUUUUUUN…

The cash register.

I'm impressed that Aunt Paula upgraded her system to something this sophisticated sometime during the last year, in which I didn't make it back for a visit. When I tried to figure out this thing yesterday, the machine locked me out. Today I found the owner's manual online and am reading the small print on my phone as I push buttons. So far, the only success I've had is unlocking the cash drawer only because I tried one of the other keys on that mysterious key ring.

That leaves one key to figure out.

As I study the cash register manual, I hear a tapping on the glass, which brings my attention to the front door. Sally is standing there, holding a drink tray with two cups and a small sack bearing The Last Bean logo. I've made *that* place my daily reward for cleaning up *this* one.

The grumbling in my stomach launches me forward. As I unlock the door, the distinct aroma of banana bread—my favorite—fills my nose. Which means she had it warmed up. Saliva has now filled my mouth so full, I'm afraid to say anything lest I drool all over my aunt's best friend in the world.

Aunt Paula may have raised me like a mother, but Sally was like the favorite aunt that played backup. Oh, the irony…

"Anything I can do to help? I brought supplies." Sally holds up the drink tray.

I push the door open wider and wave her in. "Any idea how to operate that thing?" I point to the sleek black beast sitting on the counter as I grab the sack holding my banana bread.

"As a matter of fact, I do. I have the exact same one."

"Seriously?" Banana bread crumbs spray out of my mouth as I say this.

She wags her finger. "Say don't spray, please."

"Sorry." I cover my mouth as I mumble my apology and nab one of the coffees. Once I know my mouth is clear, I dare to speak again. "How did you wind up with the same cash register?"

"Both of us needed new ones, so your aunt negotiated a deal with the vendor."

Of course she did. Aunt Paula knew how to wield her southern charm better than anyone I knew. I once watched her not only charm her way out of a speeding ticket, but then convince the police officer that we needed an escort to the hospital in order to deliver a bouquet to a patient in critical condition.

I have more stories like that one, too. Maybe I should write a memoir about her. I think I'll add that idea to my bucket list.

Sally stands in front of the cash register, her fingers tapping the screen that's illuminating her face with a soft glow. A little tune rings out and she smiles. "There. I entered you into the system with the password, born to be wild with an 'e' and no spaces."

Of course she did. That makes total sense, too.

I crumple the empty sack and mourn the end of my baked goods fix for the day. "Thank you for the banana bread. That's my favorite."

Sally glances at me as she picks up her coffee. "I know. I remember."

A sudden rush of emotion pushes tears into the corners

of my eyes. The banana bread threatens to make a reappearance as well.

It's been years since I saw my mother. She didn't show up when I graduated from high school or college, so it didn't surprise me when she didn't show up for her sister's funeral. Her occasional notes or Christmas cards always mention her busy schedule. When they arrive, that is. Come to think of it, I don't think I've seen one of those in a couple of years either.

I don't know where my mother is these days, only that she lives somewhere in Hollywood and is living her dream of being an actress. Like me, when she turned eighteen, she left Sarabella in pursuit of her dream to be a movie star.

Three years later, she came back broke and pregnant.

Being the good sister that she was, Aunt Paula took her in and tried to help her figure out life as a single mother. That lasted all of three years. After which my mother fled back to Hollywood with the promise to come back for me once she hit her fame and glory.

Which she finally did around the time I entered my teenage years. By then, it just made no sense to uproot a teenager and take her to LA. That's what she told Aunt Paula on one of her sporadic visits. Plus, her life of 'glamour' didn't allow her much time to keep up with a teenager in her formative years.

Fine. She could have her life of fame. By then I had a good idea of what I wanted to do with my life and that didn't include her either.

So what did I do as soon as I graduated from high school? Left Sarabella as fast as I could to go after a dream that now seems hazy at best. Funny how many times I've wondered if this was what my mother went through in those early years of pursuing her dream.

Sally's expression turns somber as she looks at me, then over my shoulder at the sparse shop. "Paula planned to do a total makeover on the shop next year."

I hear the sadness in Sally's voice and realize I'm not the only one who lost someone close. Sally was more like a sister to Aunt Paula than my mother was. And Sally's husband, Jacob, owns the local nursery and was Aunt Paula's main supplier since she opened the flower shop.

Sally, Jacob, and Zane are the closest thing I have to a family now. They're all I have in the world. Except for my roommate and best friend, Sasha, but she's more like a porcupine when it comes to relationships. She'll tell you she loves you, but it might prick a little.

I swipe away the thought with a rogue tear. Jacob is supposed to deliver my first order today. Once I get a feel for all of that, I can figure out what else the place needs to step business up a notch.

Or two.

Because a lot has to happen in a year…

Sally gives me a sympathetic smile. "This will get easier. I promise."

I nod and take a deep, shuddering breath. "I know. Just didn't expect to see the shop in this condition."

She blinks away the moisture that's trying to collect in her eyes, too. "I know. Paula didn't expect things to go the way they did either. None of us did."

I actually laugh, because I can imagine my aunt arguing with death that she had too much to do and needed to get back to her shop. "I can only imagine."

As I sip my mocha, Sally walks me through the system like a pro. And at each step, she backtracks and has me repeat what she showed me so that I can remember the order of functions.

Just as she finishes the last run-through about entering inventory, she scans the rest of the store and frowns. "You have so much open space. Have you thought about expanding the business to more than just plants and flowers?"

I've done little more than eat and sleep the last two weeks, but her suggestion sparks something to life in me. Could this place be more than floral arrangements, flowers, and plants?

"No, actually. I've been on overload, trying to figure out what to order and what to do with it." I finish with a pathetic laugh that borders on sounding like a sob.

Sally leans her hip against the counter. "And I can tell you are oh-so-thrilled by it, too."

"Am I that obvious?" I huddle tighter behind my coffee cup to no avail. Nothing can hide the discouragement that's lodged in my throat right now.

If the store fails, I walk away with nothing. Except for the condo. But at this rate, I may have to take a loan just to make it through the year. I'd rather not wind up in debt.

"You're an artist. You'll figure something out."

"More of a communications and product designer really."

Sally holds me by the forearms. "Then figure out how to communicate with your customers in unique ways. Use that talent of yours to expand this business into something you love. Put your skills to work and create new revenue streams with things you design. You won't succeed if you're not doing something you love. Not really."

She's right. More right than I thought possible. My vision blurs as tears build in my eyes again and drop down my cheeks as she pulls me into a hug. And it feels so good. I can't remember the last time someone hugged me.

Like I said, Sasha isn't the affectionate type.

But Aunt Paula always was, and she knew how to make me feel loved better than anyone I know. I regret not coming back for Christmas last year. Or for Easter or the Fourth of July. Then she got sick and things went sideways fast before I could even get back in time to say goodbye…

I'd give anything for one of her hugs right now.

Sally leans back. "Grab some paper and a pen and let's brainstorm some ideas. We're going to figure out how to make this business a huge success."

About the Author

Dineen Miller is an Amazon best-selling and award-winning author who loves to write closed door romantic comedy, where witty banter, sizzling chemistry, and unforgettable characters leave readers smiling long after the last page.

She's a dog-mom to two furry rescues that answer to wiggle butt and snuggle boy, and she's married to a punny guy, who thinks she's unique.

Acknowledgments

A very special thanks to Jane Litherland for reading the early manuscript and sharing her encouraging insights. You are the unexpected gift that showed up for this story, my friend.

As always, great appreciation for my editors, Judy DeVries and Alice Shepherd, their diligence in making my words better. It always makes me happy to hear your heart for my stories.

Continued thanks to Sophie Britton and the team at Vinci Books, LTD, for all that you do to bring my books to the world. I'm so excited to see what 2026 holds for our partnership. Thank you!

And finally, to my wonderful readers, who make this writing gig one of the best adventures of my life! I couldn't do this without you, my friends. Your messages, shares, and continued support are the best gifts ever.

May you live authentically, love fully, and laugh often.

And watch hockey!

~Dineen

www.ingramcontent.com/pod-product-compliance
Lightning Source LLC
La Vergne TN
LVHW040921110826
845155LV00041B/716

* 9 7 8 1 0 3 6 7 1 6 4 2 4 *